Dance Without Music

PETER CHEYNEY

Dance Without Music
Peter Cheyney
First published by William Collins,
London, England in 1947.
This production Copyright © 2023
Cover design by Mats Ingelborn
with photo by Nejron Photo, Shutterstock
ISBN paper: 978-91-89225-94-7
ISBN e-book: 978-91-89225-95-4
Published by Yabot AB, Stockholm, Sweden, 2023

A FOREWORD

BEING a private detective is a strange sort of business. A business which sometimes attracts odd types. I do not necessarily mean bad types. It has always seemed to me that the primary attraction to the profession is a desire for adventure; to live a life apart from the day-to-day routine of normal affairs—an irregular, sometimes boring, and occasionally exciting life.

Often, experienced and responsible police officers—sometimes of high seniority—become private detectives on retirement from the police and detective forces. Even they—after a lifetime spent in dealing with crime, mayhem and skullduggery in general; in meeting the weird types that abound in the half-world and underworld—still feel the fascination for the game that bring with each "case" the lure of fresh adventure or the matching of wits against a sequence of peculiar events or people.

There are, generally speaking, four types of private investigators; and although these types may occasionally overlap, it is interesting to consider them. They are: The retired police officer who starts his own agency; the Specialist Investigator retained by an Insurance Company for "insurance" investigations; the man who has gone into the game because he likes it and either runs his own office or works as a "staff-man" in an Agency; and lastly—because I think he is the most interesting "type"—the "free-lance" investigator who works for any Agency or organisation that cares to employ him he likes the job and the money is good enough.

Quite obviously, the "free-lance" has to be good at his job. He must be. If he isn't he won't eat. He is dependent on work being put in his way by other organisations, or because of a personal recommendation from a satisfied professional client. He is usually retained in a case because it presents features or difficulties at which he is known to be expert. He must be trustworthy because he is not a "staff-man" who can be sacked if he makes a mistake. In other words, he lives on being known and recommended as a good, trustworthy man who is fitted to work on his own; cautious—yet a man who, in spite of his caution, will, if the job requires it, "take a chance." Because, believe it or not, every private investigator, at some time in his career, has to take a chance. Especially in England where—unlike the U.S.A.—he is not recognised in any way by the official police forces, and where official records and information are not (or not supposed to be!) at his disposal.

The work that comes to the "free-lance" is varied. Often it is an extremely confidential—essentially secret—investigation which the head of an established agency prefers to be handled outside the office for one of a dozen reasons. Sometimes the work is concerned with cases that end in the Divorce Court. These cases are often more interesting than appears on the surface. Sometimes a divorce investigation presents the most thrilling, subtle features. Often the actual evidence—sordid as it may seem—given at the hearing of a divorce case, presents only one very small aspect of a picture that, very often, began with love; went on to indifference, distrust and infidelity; finished with hatred—and worse than hatred.

It must be obvious that the private detective, is subject to many temptations. Sometimes he falls. Private detectives are human like people in other professions. They may be good, bad or indifferent. But if they have failings, it must be remembered that they also have virtues. They serve their purpose; otherwise they would not exist.

And if they seldom add up to the picture of the invariably moral, forthright, brilliant and virtuous private detective presented in the usual "detective" novel; if they are human enough not to possess all—or any—of these qualities, still they are often adequate to "steer" their clients through some of the difficult mazes of life and eventually to write "Closed" on a folder in which are written the notes of some secret story which, if published, might possibly redound to their credit.

This is the story of Leonora Ivory, of Alexis and Esmeralda Ricaud, of John Epiton Pell and a few other people who came into it, said their little piece and walked—or were pushed-out again.

It is also a part of my life because I handled the Ivory business from the start and I have tried to tell the story without any frills.

Cheyney has written it pretty well as I told it to him. He has found it necessary to alter names, switch dates and localities and time angles.

But, fundamentally, the story differs little from the one that I told him after our first (and now historic!) meeting at Trubshaw's place—The Lamb Inn—on the Eastbourne-Hastings road in 1946.

Caryl Wylde O'Hara.
Steynehurst,
Near Wych Cross,
Sussex.
February 1947

Peter Cheyney

CHAPTER ONE

MONDAY — IVORY
1

THE street looked like a river that led nowhere. Just like that. The lamps were dimly reflected on its flat, wet surface.

The houses and warehouses at the side, the pavements, were in the darkness. You couldn't see them. All you could see was that the flat surface of the curving street with the reflection of the lamps and an occasional shadow made the street look as if it were flowing like a river.

I stopped on the corner to light a cigarette. I'd looked at the goddamned street so often—at so many different times of the night or day—that I knew every inch of it. And I didn't like it. I thought that as streets go it was second-rate and everything in it was like that—including the office. That office was second-rate all right. So was I. I was worse than second-rate. At the moment I was fourpence a gross C.O.D. and please return the empties.

One of these days, I thought, I was going to get out of this dump and go somewhere where there were green fields and cows with no intelligence grazing in them. And sunsets. And no hooch. Where women were women and the men didn't worry about the fact too much.

Somebody—Montaigne or some brain like that—
said that adversity is the time for philosophy. Like hell
it is. Philosophy being the process of adapting a new
frame of mind to an extremely dull set of circumstances.
Which sounds to me like sympathising with a gumboil.
It doesn't do much good but it doesn't make it any
worse. You only think it does.

Here and there down the street were the rear lights
on parked cars. Like fireflies on the river. I passed a new
Armstrong-Siddeley. It looked sleek and out of place.
When I opened the downstairs door the smell of dust
came out and hit me. I was used to it but tonight it
seemed worse than ever. I began to climb. I went up
slowly, making up my mind. Which is something I can
usually do very quickly. I could either take Pell's money,
close up the office and get out for a little fresh air, or I
could stay put and see what happened. I thought that
if anything was going to happen it wouldn't happen
immediately—or would it? How did I know?

It seemed to me that the matter should be decided
with whisky. There was a half-bottle in the office. Which
was about the only good thing in the set-up.

I walked along the passage on the second floor. I
passed all the bum little offices where odd types fronted
at being agents for something or other and often looked
harassed to hell in the process. At the end was my own
door. And there was a light inside.

That was funny. But perhaps it wasn't. Perhaps Pell
had already sent round the pay-roll. It could be. But
I doubted it. I'd never known Pell to be in a hurry to

                    Peter Cheyney

pay—not even when the money was so well-earned as this was.

Still... you never knew.

I opened the door and went into the outer office. The door of the inner room was half-open and the light was on, I took a quick sniff at the air and smelt perfume—good perfume.

I pushed open the door and went in. I stopped just inside and had a good look. This, I thought, is the end of a perfect day.

She was seated in the one big leather armchair in front of my desk. She was relaxed and her arms lay along the sides of the chair. She looked at me coolly as if I was some new sort of animal. Not unpleasantly, but with a detached—a rather vague—interest.

I looked at her for quite a while. She wore a dull pink dress with a full length coat of the same colour over it. The pockets and collar of the coat were powder blue velvet. The coat was cut in at the waist and showed off a figure that was very inviting. Her hat was of dull pink felt with a blue ribbon to match the velvet. Underneath, her chestnut brown hair gleamed with bronze tints. Her stockings were sheer and expensive and she wore blue glacé court shoes. Her gloves and bag lay on my desk. She wore two or three gold rings and one very good diamond clip-brooch.

I felt in my pocket for the packet of cigarettes. I took one out and lighted it. I was still looking at her. Her face was long and heart-shaped. She had fine eyes and a straight nose, a mouth with a short upper lip, and one of those complexions that take about four generations of beauty treatment to acquire. And she wasn't worrying a lot about anything.

I said: "Good evening." I went behind my desk; took off my overcoat and hat; hung them on the hat stand behind the chair and sat down. I switched on the desk lamp, got the half-bottle out of the lower drawer, drew the cork and took a long swig. It made me shudder a little. I remembered I hadn't eaten for quite a while. I put the bottle back in the drawer.

She seemed faintly amused. She said: "You are Mr. O'Hara, aren't you?"

I nodded.

"When did you arrive?" I asked.

"About ten-thirty. Mr. Pell said he thought you would return after drinking hours. He said he thought you'd be doing a little drinking this evening."

"Did he tell you why?"

She nodded. A small movement of the head. Whenever she made a movement you wanted her to repeat it. She was worth watching—if you know what I mean. "He said you'd spent most of today in the Divorce Court, and that he thought Counsel had been rather unkind to you."

I grinned. "An understatement," I said. "Counsel for the other side tore me in pieces." I shrugged my shoulders. "One of the risks of my profession."

She moved a little. "He wasn't very kind, was he? He said that you were unscrupulous; cheap; a hired raker of dungheaps. He said that it was appalling that evidence

                                        Peter Cheyney

such as yours should be necessary or possible; that you must be lost to all sense of decency to have undertaken to give the evidence you did give."

I said: "You must have been reading the evening papers. The fact remains that my evidence clinched the case." She nodded. "It was not suggested that you were an unsuccessful raker of dungheaps," she said slowly. She was nearly smiling.

I got out the bottle and took another swig. "And you've been sitting here waiting to tell me this?" I asked. I was wondering.

She shook her head. "You were working for the Pell Agency, I believe. I went to see Mr. Pell to-day to ask him to handle some business for me. He didn't like it at all. He told me about the case you gave evidence in. He said he'd never handle another case like that after the beating-up you got this afternoon."

I drew on my cigarette. "I like that. I handle the case. I get the beating-up and Pell snivels. Is that all?"

"No," she said. "When I told him what I wanted done he said that he wouldn't have any part in it. He said that after today he was through with anything of that sort. He said they'd employed you and that you'd secured your evidence by the most unethical methods—judged by the lowest standards. He said that in no circumstances would Pell ever employ you again. He said that after to-day he doubted if any Investigation Agency would employ you."

"Very nice of him," I said. I grinned again. "Pell never had an over-developed sense of gratitude."

I decided to finish off the whisky. Then I thought I wouldn't. I was interested.

I sat there, drawing on my cigarette and looking at her. She was quite unperturbed. She seemed not to mind being looked at. She was relaxed—reposeful. She knew her own mind—that one. She was the sort of person who knew what she wanted and went straight for it. She was so goddam certain of herself that she could afford to be cool about it and not worry about other people's reactions. And she was very easy to look at. I went on looking.

After a minute she said: "Well... aren't you going to say anything, Mr. O'Hara?" She picked up her handbag. "And do you mind if I smoke?"

"Go right ahead," I said. I put my hand in my pocket for my lighter, but she beat me to it with a small gold Ronson. She lit the cigarette—one of those fat expensive Egyptian ones, inhaled, and sat looking at the office wall. After a while she repeated; "Well?"

I asked: "Well... what? I'm supposed to react, am I? I'm supposed to listen to that piece you just gave me about Pell not using me any more and doubting if any Investigation Agency—no matter how cheap or near-the-knuckle—would ever use me after to-day's business in Court? Well... I'm not reacting. Maybe I'm supposed to say that the K.G. who led for the respondent was talking through his wig; that I was merely doing my duty; that somebody has to rake over dungheaps in not-so-nice divorce cases?"

She blew a smoke ring. When she did it she pursed up her mouth and that was definitely something to look at. It showed you just how her mouth would look if she was kissing you. I thought that if she ever got as far as Hollywood, and somebody like Pandor Berman ever got a look at that smoke-ring blowing thing, he would sign her up for keeps. Not that her type ever had to go to Hollywood.

I fished out a fresh cigarette.

"Maybe," I went on, "I'm supposed to say that Pell is a louse. Such a louse that he passed the buck to me in this business so that he could keep out of it, collect a lot of dough from a rich client, and still keep his nose clean. Maybe I'm supposed to say all that. Well... I'm not saying it."

She raised her eyebrows and took a quick look at me. She had clear blue eyes that were quiet and unhurried.

She said: "Exactly what are you saying then?" I grinned at her. "What the hell has that to do with you?" I asked.

She laughed. I liked hearing her laugh. It was a low rippling sort of business, and it was an amused laugh. She really meant it.

"Of course, you're perfectly right," she said. "I haven't even explained my presence here. I wanted to hear you talk."

"Well, you're hearing me talk. And I'm not even charging a cover fee. What would you like next? Shall I recite or go into my song and dance act?"

She got up. For a moment I though she was going. Just for a few seconds I began to be a little disappointed. But it was all right. After she'd got up, she turned the chair round so that it was facing me. Then she sat down again and crossed her legs. Her legs and ankles matched the rest of the outfit. Everything was definitely very good.

She stubbed out the cigarette in the ashtray. She said: "Let's imagine——just for the sake of argument—that I have some sort of right to be here; that you don't mind talking to me; that you know who I am; that..."

I laughed. "I'd rather imagine that you were paying me money. I like that better."

"Very well." She gave another of those little laughs. "Imagine that. And go on talking. You finished on the note that you were not saying any of the things that I expected you to say—about Mr. Pell. And about the things he said of you."

"Right," I said. "That was the note. I'm not saying any of the expected things, because if I did they wouldn't be true. I knew all about that case when Pell asked me if I would undertake to get the evidence. I knew about it first of all because of what he told me, and also because I'm a very good investigator, and I had a pretty good idea as to how the thing was going to shape. Getting evidence in defended divorce suits when the parties would pay money to see each other laid out on a morgue slab is never a business for people with sensitive nervous systems. The evidence is never particularly nice, and the methods used to get it are usually extremely unethical, to say the least of it. You understand that?"

She nodded. She said she understood.

"I also guessed that Pell would throw me to the lions afterwards," I continued. "I knew he'd have to. But his people would win their case and why the hell should he worry about me? All Pell could do would be to wash his hands of me and say that the whole thing was just too shocking; that if he'd known what sort of business it was in the first place he would never have touched it with a barge pole—and all the rest of it. I knew all that before I started."

She nodded again. "Then please tell me," she asked, "why you did it?"

"Don't be silly," I said. I got up and came round the desk. I stood away from the side of the desk and looked down at her. From that angle she looked good enough to eat except that she had some sort of aura round her that reminded you of Iceland. "Don't be silly," I repeated. "Why do you think I did it? I knew there was gold in them thar hills. One hundred down; twenty a day for expenses; and a thousand pounds on the successful completion of the suit; that is the decree nisi. Well... they've got their decree nisi and I can use the thousand pounds."

She moved a little. "You think it was worth it?"

I shrugged. "I never think about what's worth what. I'm not like that. I weighed it up and concluded that what was coming to me was worth the thousand pounds."

"And you've received the money?"

"Not yet," I answered. "I'll get that tomorrow."

She said: "I don't think so."

I drew on my cigarette. I asked: "Just what is this?"

"Mr. Pell talked to me," she said. "He was very frank about all this. He wasn't feeling at all pleased about it. I think he talked to me much more freely than is usual because he appeared to want to stop me doing something that I wanted to do; something which he thought would be very foolish. He..."

"Let's take all that for granted," I said. "Why don't I get paid?"

"He seems to think that the loser of the case today—the respondent—isn't at all happy about it." She smiled—a soft little smile. "Not at all happy. You can understand that. It seems that the respondent has been threatening all sorts of things ever since this afternoon. One of the things he says is that half of your evidence, supported as it seemed by independent testimony, was false; and the independent testimony secured by bribery—from you. Mr. Pell says he's going to wait to see what happens; that there may be an intervention in the case, and that he's not going to pay you until he knows. That isn't so good for you, is it?"

"No," I agreed. "That isn't so good. It was nice of you to come here to tell me about it. I like that. It's very friendly."

There was a silence—one of those silences that you could cut with a knife. I went back and sat down in the chair.

I asked: "Where do we go from there?"

She opened her bag; took out another cigarette. She lighted it. She said: "You're not awfully curious, are you?" When she said that she looked at me and smiled gently.

I said: "I gave up being curious years ago. People are only curious when something in life surprises them. Nothing surprises me."

She said: "No?" She raised her eyebrows.

I went on: "When you've been a private investigator for as long as I have, take it from me that when something surprises you, you fly a blue flag and fire a twenty-one gun salute."

She didn't say anything.

"I'm not even surprised," I said—I was grinning at her—"that Pell, who is supposed to be one of the cleverest private investigators in this country, should sit down and discuss somebody else's business with you at length, in order to stop you doing something which you wanted to do. And I've never known Pell to be so confiding. Something must have happened to him. The only thing that would make Pell confiding or altruistic would be money."

She said: "You're quite right. I was prepared to pay him quite a lot of money for advice."

"Nice work," I said. "Having got the money he gave you some sweet and negative advice. When in doubt, don't do it. That sounds like Pell. I hope you got your money's worth."

"So I take it," I continued, "that ever since then you've been having quite a struggle with yourself. You go to Pell, pay him a large fee and ask him what you're to do. You open your heart to him."

I stubbed out the cigarette. I was sick of smoking cigarettes.

"And a woman like you doesn't do a thing like that unless she's in a spot. So I take it you're in a spot. Pell warned you off whatever you wanted to do. But you tried to talk him into it. I imagine that he still wasn't playing, but he had a nice fat fee on the desk in front of him and he thought he'd give you some value for your money, so he told you about the last case he'd handled. He told you about me. He told you what a son of a bitch I was; what Counsel had said about me and people like me generally. Pell held this up to you as a grim warning." I grinned at her.

She smiled again. She settled herself back comfortably in the armchair. She fascinated me. Every time she moved I watched her. Every movement, no matter how small, was imbued with an unstudied, almost perfect, grace. I thought as a woman she could cause plenty of trouble. Maybe she had.

She said: "You're a very discerning person, Mr. O'Hara. Your instinct seems sound."

"Instinct my eye," I said. "The facts are sticking out like Brighton Pier. People like you don't hang about in a dingy office like this at this time of night, waiting for the proprietor to return from a spot of drinking, just for the pleasure of telling him that he is a discerning

                                    Peter Cheyney

person. Why don't you cut out the frills and get it off your chest? I've an idea that whatever it is, it's very tough."

She asked: "Why do you think that?"

"It has to be," I said, "You wouldn't have been giving me all this Pell stuff—what he said and what he didn't say—unless you were preparing me for something even worse than this afternoon's experiences."

She got up. She got up quite suddenly and quickly. She stood on the other side of the desk, the cigarette held between her slim white fingers, looking at me seriously.

She said: "I expect you're very disappointed about the Pell money."

"It's very nice of you to be concerned," I told her. "I take it you're referring to the thousand pounds that Pell told you he wasn't going to pay me?"

She said slowly: "Yes... that's what I meant."

I said: "Listen... do I look like the sort of man who's not going to be paid? Pell made a deal with me. I've carried out my part of the bargain. I'm going to see he carries out his."

She asked quickly: "You think you can make him pay?"

"I haven't thought about it at all yet," I answered, "but I'll back myself to find some means of making Pell cough up that money. And now, if you don't mind, I'm rather tired of discussing Pell. In any event, it has nothing to do with you."

"It has quite a lot to do with me," she answered. She hesitated; then: "You see, I shall be glad to give you the thousand pounds that Mr. Pell isn't going to pay. And you can take it from me he won't. I know when a man means what he says. He's scared. He has the idea that if there's an intervention about the divorce case he might be affected. After all he was the person who hired you. He thinks if he gives you the thousand pounds, the fee is large enough for somebody to suggest that there may have been bribery."

I shrugged my shoulders. "So you're going to make it up to me? That's very nice of you. Why?"

She said: "Of course there are conditions."

I laughed at her. I said: "Sit down. Sit down and relax. I like to look at you sitting down."

She sat down.

"So there are going to be conditions?" I went on. "Extraordinary! You're not just going to give me a thousand pounds because you like my personality."

She said softly: "You're being fearfully whimsical, aren't you, Mr. O'Hara? Of course I'm not going to give you the thousand pounds for nothing. But I'm prepared to pay a thousand pounds because I don't want you to be annoyed with Mr. Pell, and also because I'm rather grateful to him in a way. If I hadn't gone to his office this afternoon I should never even have heard about you."

"And you're glad you did?" I queried.

She nodded. She smiled again and showed me a perfect set of teeth.

She said: "I'm very glad I did. What I've heard about you tells me that you're the person I'm looking for."

I started a new cigarette. "Let me hear the worst."

She paused for a moment; then: "Is there anybody you're particularly fond of, Mr. O'Hara—really fond of?"

I shook my head. I said: "I can't remember anybody. There are one or two people I've liked. I don't know anybody I'd go to bat for in a really big way." I smiled at her. "I think about people superficially," I said. "It's easier."

She moved in her chair. "You sound to me like a man who's been disappointed about something—possibly a woman."

"What man hasn't?" I asked.

"Precisely—but you particularly," she said. "You sound rather cynical."

I didn't say anything.

She went on: "I asked if you'd been very fond of someone because if you had been you'd understand the way I feel."

"And how do you feel?" I asked.

She shrugged her shoulders. "I'm very unhappy—very miserable. Not about myself personally... I've nothing to be unhappy or miserable about. But I'm terribly unhappy about a friend—a woman friend. She's younger than I am. She was a very sweet girl."

I said: "And what do I do about that?"

She was silent for a few moments. She seemed to be trying to make up her mind about something. I had time to look at her and concentrate on the business. I came to the conclusion that she was an extraordinary type. You just didn't see people like her in those go-ahead days. She was unique. She had beauty and style and breeding and practically everything that goes with those things, Also she was clever. She had brains. She had to have brains to have pulled a fast one on Pell. And I was certain that she had pulled a fast one on Pell. I wasn't so pleased about that.

Eventually she said: "It's rather a long story, but it's better that you hear it from the start. Then you'll know how to handle it. You'll be able to tell me if my idea is right. Would you like to listen?"

I nodded. I said: "Go ahead."

She began to talk in a quiet voice. She looked at her hands, folded in her lap, whilst she was talking. I had the impression that it annoyed her a little to have to talk.

She said: "When the war began I thought I was in love with an officer in an Infantry Regiment. He was a little younger than I was and I know now—now that I've had lots of time to think about it—that I didn't really love him. I suppose I liked him a lot and felt a little maternal about him. Can you understand that, Mr. O'Hara?"

"Why not?" I said. "That's easy enough."

She went on: "He wanted to marry me before he went to Burma, but I wouldn't do this. I said that when he came back would be time enough. He was sorry about that but he agreed. He was an awfully nice person."

She stopped talking and I could see her long fingers clasping and unclasping. She was feeling nervous about something.

"He was captured by the Japanese and he had a terrible time in a prison camp," she said slowly. "Eventually he died. I expect you can imagine that life had been pretty grim for him before the end."

"I can imagine that," I said.

"When I heard about his death I was terribly upset. I felt that in any event I ought to have married him. I was angry with myself and unhappy about everything. I thought that the best I could do would be to travel and not think about things. I was rather ill and my doctor thought it might help if I went away. I went to America and I took my friend Esmeralda with me."

I asked: "Does she come into this?"

She nodded.

"What is Esmeralda like?" I asked.

"She's younger—five years younger than I am." she said. "She used to take a rather superficial view of life. She was carefree and happy and inclined to be romantic. I was very fond of her. I still am."

I told her to go on.

"After I'd been in America for a few months I met a man—Alexis Ricaud. I'd just begun to get over my previous unhappiness, but I was still restless and unsettled. And Ricaud seemed charming and friendly and strong. He seemed to be very much in love with me and to be rather a nice person. I married him in

America and found out that I'd made a mistake a little too late."

"What sort of mistake?" I asked her.

"I found out about Ricaud," she said. "I need not go into details, but a few months after we were married I discovered, by an add accident that he wasn't at all a nice person. I discovered that he lived mainly by blackmailing women; that his charming exterior concealed an extremely nasty and sadistic nature; that his record was an unpleasant one; that he had married me merely for my money."

"And you did something about that?" I asked.

She nodded. "I had straight talk with him. I told him that I knew about him. I told him that I intended to divorce him immediately."

"And he didn't like that?" I asked.

"He didn't like it, but he couldn't do anything about it. I told him that if he tried to put any obstacle in the way of the divorce I should go to the police..."

"His record was as bad as that?" I queried.

She said: "Yes... it was very bad. He agreed to the divorce and admitted that everything I had said was true. Knowing him I ought to have suspected that his prompt acquiescence in my wishes meant that some scheme was already in his mind. But I didn't suspect. I told him that I was leaving the United States immediately and returning to England; that I had instructed a New York attorney to bring suit for divorce against him; that I should take steps to free myself from him as soon as possible.

"I returned to England. Esmeralda returned with me, I had no suspicion at this time that Ricaud had already been making love to her; that she was fascinated by him; that she believed everything he said."

"Has Esmeralda any money?" I asked.

She nodded, "She was quite well off." She shrugged her shoulders. "But not now."

"Go on with the story," I said.

"In due course my divorce came through. Then, almost immediately, I learned that Ricaud had come to England; that he was engaged to be married to Esmeralda. I was horrified. I wrote to her and told her what I knew. I entreated her not to go through with the marriage until she had talked to me."

"But she didn't believe you," I said. "They never do."

"You're quite right... she didn't believe me. On the contrary she wrote and told me that I had concocted the story about Ricaud because I was sorry that I had divorced him; that I was jealous of her. She refused to see me. Soon after, she married Ricaud."

"And now she knows that you were telling the truth," I said.

She nodded her head. "She knows now," she said softly. "Now that it's too late. Mr. O'Hara, she's in an awful state. Ricaud has had most of her money. She has very little left. She discovered quite soon after her marriage to him that what I had said about him was only too true. But she was absolutely and completely in his power. Once or twice she wrote to me and told me that she was going to divorce him. Then, for some unknown reason, she would change her mind. She left him, came to me and told me stories of his conduct and cruelty, and then returned to him. I realised that he had some strong hold over her. Something that was greater than her own will-power, her self-respect, every good thing about her—something so beastly that one can't imagine it...."

I said: "Dope?"

"Yes," she said slowly. "He started her on drugs, and now I believe she's a complete addict. She makes half-hearted attempts to get away from him, but always fails. She won't let any of her relations or friends help her. She's absolutely and completely in his power."

She stopped talking. There was quiet in the office. I could hear the clock on the mantelpiece ticking. It was a cheap clock with a hell of a tick. In the silence it sounded like an infernal machine.

"Is that all?" I asked.

She said miserably: "Isn't it enough?"

I asked: "Enough for what?"

She put her hands on the edge of the desk. I could see that her fingers were trembling.

She said quickly: "Isn't it enough, Mr. O'Hara? Isn't it enough for you to do something about?"

I stubbed out my cigarette. "What do I do about it?" I asked her.

She said: "Listen to me, Mr. O'Hara. I'm afraid. I'm awfully afraid for Esmeralda. I think she's reached the end of her tether; that she isn't quite responsible for what she's doing. Something must be done and done quickly."

"What's in your mind?" I asked. I was almost interested.

"I can't prove that she's getting drugs from Ricaud," she said. "But I'm certain of it. So is her doctor. And Ricaud is afraid of the law. I'm certain it would help if you went to see him. If you told him that you were acting for Esmeralda's relations; that you had discovered that she was getting drugs from him; that unless he agreed to leave the country immediately and to leave her entirely alone so that she could be properly looked after and cured, you would go to the police. But I want you to do that immediately, Mr. O'Hara. At once. There isn't any time to be lost."

I lit a cigarette. I said: "It doesn't seem worth a thousand pounds to me. It's too easy."

"It might not be so easy," she said. "He's clever and unscrupulous. And he has some peculiar friends. If you threatened him there might be some after-effects."

I grinned at her. "I see. You mean that I might have to look after myself for a bit?"

"Yes," she said. "That's what I meant."

I asked: "By the way, who are you?"

She smiled. "You're the oddest man, Mr. O'Hara. I think your attitude is quite enchanting. You arrive here and give yourself a drink and sit down and very kindly listen to what I have to say; then suddenly you decide that you'd like to know who I am."

` "Is that odd?" I asked her. "It really hasn't mattered until now."

She looked at me. Her eyelashes were long black and very well-mascaraed. So well done that you could hardly see the make-up.

"Of course you're perfectly right," she said. "It hasn't mattered until now. And now when it does matter you want to know." She smiled again, suddenly. "You become curious only when it's really necessary. You must be very bored with life to be like that."

"All right," I said. "Let's take it that I'm very bored with life. And now the name...?"

"My name is Ivory," she said quietly. "Mrs. Leonora Ivory. That was my maiden name. I re-took it when I received my divorce from Ricaud."

"It's a nice name," I said. I wrote it down on a pad. "Can I have the address?"

She said: "I'm staying at the Culloden Hotel at the moment."

I wrote that down too. I asked: "Have you got the thousand pounds?"

She smiled again. "Yes. I knew you'd help." She opened her handbag. She brought out a fat packet of notes and laid it on the desk.

I smiled back at her. "It's a pretty sight," I said. "A packet of new notes like that. If I were an artist that would be my idea of still life."

She said: "Perhaps it's a pity that you aren't an artist."

I said: "I shall have to try to be artistic about Mr. Ricaud, shan't I?" I put the notes in the desk drawer. "Where does he live?"'

"He has a house not far from Maidenhead—a house called 'Crossways.' It's on the outskirts of the place. He's usually to be found there."

I asked her: "Does he live there alone?"

She said: "I think so. He's not there very much in the day, I believe, but usually at night. Some women come in and look after the place in the day. I think he's usually alone at night." She hesitated. "Unless he has someone with him...."

"A woman?" I queried.

"Usually a woman," she answered.

"Right," I said. "Thank you very much, Mrs. Ivory."

I got up; threw away the cigarette.

She asked: "What are you going to do?"

I smiled back at her. "I'm not going to do anything."

She rose quickly. She stood looking at me across the desk. Her eyes were suddenly very cold. She said: "Do you mean that?"

"Why not?" I asked. "What I lose on the swings I make up on the roundabouts. I've got the thousand pounds. The money that you say Pell isn't going to pay me."

She said coldly: "You think that you are safe in doing this? You think you can afford to behave like this?"

"I'm damned certain I can," I said. "Do you think anybody is going to believe you if you tell them that, after seeing Pell this evening; after hearing what he had to say about me; after knowing what Counsel said about me in Court this afternoon; do you mean to tell me that anybody is going to believe that you put a thousand pounds in that nice handbag of yours; came round, sat alone in my office and waited for me to come back? Do you think anybody is going to believe any part of this story?"

She said: "Mr. O'Hara, the notes I gave you were five-pound notes. The bank will have the numbers."

"No, Mrs. Ivory." I grinned at her. "Banks used to keep the numbers of five-pound notes, but they don't today. They haven't for the last two years."

There was silence; then: "So it seems there isn't anything more to be said." She sounded very unhappy.

I came round the desk. I said: "That's how it seems to me."

I was going to move the door to open it. When I got near her, I stopped. She was looking at me and her eyes were filled with tears. She looked like a dog that's been beaten. I don't know what perfume she was wearing, but it was unobtrusively devastating. I stopped and stood looking at her. I liked the view.

She said in a low voice: "I was rather scared when I came here tonight to wait for you—scared of what you'd be like; what you'd say. I'm not used to this sort of thing. I grant you I came here because I thought you weren't a very scrupulous person. I wanted someone who wasn't very scrupulous, because the thing I was going to ask wasn't a particularly nice thing. When I'd talked to you for a little while, in spite of myself, I got a vague impression that you might not be quite so black as you were painted."

I said: "And now you know you were wrong?"

"I'm still wondering if I'm wrong," she answered. "I can't quite believe that you'd do a thing like this."

"I'm doing it," I said. "You can't believe it because you don't like believing it."

She did an odd thing. She took a step towards me and put her hand on my arm. The whiteness of her long, slim fingers seemed strange against the dark background of my sleeve. She said in a low voice: "Mr. O'Hara... please... oh please..."

I said: "No soap...! Thanks for a pleasant evening. I'm sorry you'll have to go down the stairs, but we haven't a lift."

She flushed. Then she hung her head. She moved to the desk and picked up her handbag and gloves. Then she walked out of the office. The tears in her eyes weren't imitation. They were very good.

I heard her high heels tapping down the corridor.

I sat down in the revolving chair, opened the desk drawer and took another swig at the whisky bottle. By now it was only a third full. Then I walked out of the office and down to the end of the corridor. I opened the window and looked out. Below me lay the street, the lamps still gleaming on its wet surface.

After a minute she came out of the downstairs doors. She walked along to the Armstrong-Siddeley; unlocked it; got inside. She made a "U" turn and drove off.

I went back to the office and sat down. I began to think about Mrs. Ivory. She was a person you could spend a lot of time thinking about.

But at that moment I wasn't very fond of her. At the back of my head was the idea that she had been trying to frame me somehow; trying to push me into something... .

Not that her story hadn't sounded O.K. It was plausible enough, but it was the Pell thing that I didn't like.

I knew Pell. He was old in sin and tricky as hell. But he wouldn't take me unless he was very badly tempted. He knew goddam well that I knew the solicitors in the case; that I knew that they knew that I'd pulled the chestnuts out of the fire for their client and not Pell. Pell had that thousand pounds for me, and if Mrs. Ivory hadn't turned up he would have paid it. He always paid promptly when he had to. And this time he had to and knew it. Until she came along.

She'd gone to him and told him some story, and Pell had told her that I'd probably handle the business for her if I was interested, and if I was sufficiently hard up. He would have told her that I was like that. He would have told her that I never handled cases unless I was interested—for some reason or other—and unless I wanted money. My guess was that he'd told her that I didn't want money just now because he owed me a thousand pounds.

And then she'd got to work on Pell. She'd made it worth while for Pell to say he wouldn't pay me because

                                    Peter Cheyney

he thought that there might be an intervention. This way she thought she was making a certainty of me. She knew I'd have to take the case because I needed the money. It suited Pell because he thought that with luck he'd be able to hang on to the thousand for a bit, and that I shouldn't worry him because I'd have her money and think maybe that more would be coming. She'd talked Pell into it, paid him well, and he'd supplied her with the story, my address and a description of what he considered to be my somewhat peculiar characteristics.

Mrs. Ivory, I thought, had had what was coming to her. But I didn't like it. Not a lot. She was too beautiful to try to pull fast ones on O'Hara.

That's what I thought. I thought it and then I finished the whisky.

2

THE chime of the church clock, striking the half-hour, sounded as if it was cracked. Maybe it was cracked. When it had finished striking I listened to the clock on the mantel-piece ticking.

I decided that I wouldn't think about Mrs. Ivory any more. I took her money out of the drawer and put it into my inside breast pocket. Then I put on my hat, switched off the lights, closed up the office and went away. Out in the long dark corridor I could see the moonlight flooding through the window at the far end. It was like walking out of night into broad daylight.

My footsteps echoed down the wooden, carpetless stairs. I closed the outer door, locked it, and walked down the street.

It took me ten minutes brisk walking to get to Joe Melander's place—The Desert Room. Joe was waiting at the bottom of the long flight of stone steps that led down to his Bottle Party. He looked like he always looked—plump, well-fed, and freshly shaved, with just a spot too much talc powder and a hair-dressing that was over-scented.

He said: "Good-evening, Mr. O'Hara. Glad to see you. Always glad to see you." He grinned at me. "I see Mr. Lamberley, K.C., was a little harsh about you this afternoon, These barristers..." Joe shrugged his shoulders. "It's very hard on you private eyes," he went on. "Come and have a little drink with me out of my bottle?"

I left my hat and coat with the girl in the entrance lobby and went in with him. We sat down at a table in the far corner. The waiter—who looked as if he'd got sleeping sickness—brought a bottle of whisky, a siphon and some glasses.

I said: "A private detective is entitled to be shot at in a divorce case. If the suit's defended. The other side always try to discount his evidence. When it's a bad case like this one was, a Private dick is lucky to get out with a whole skin."

"Yeah," said Joe. He poured out two big slugs of whisky. He smiled a little.

                                    Peter Cheyney

"They must have paid you a lot of money. That man was very very unkind to you." He squirted in the soda water.

"You're unreasonable," I said. "Why should a Divorce Court pleader be kind to a detective? It wouldn't be human."

Joe said: "You've certainly got a sense of humour."

I looked round the big room. I thought that the idea of calling it The Desert Room was subtle. But then Joe Melander was like that. The walls were painted to look like an oasis in the desert, with palms, camels and things. Looking at the clientele you could be certain that the only interest it took in camels was a professional one. Anything that could go for eight days without any sort of drink would really mean something to these boys and girls.

They were an extremely tatty crowd. Especially the women. The men had plenty of money acquired by all sorts of strange methods that come after a war. The women were thinking up ways and means of getting some of it. You could see them doing it. I think some of the girls were having a hard time. But then anything would seem hard after the Americans had gone home.

"I thought you didn't handle divorce cases, Mr. O'Hara?" Joe refilled the glasses; then he grinned; shrugged his shoulders. "Sorry about that," he said. "Me—I'm always too curious."

"It's all right, Joe." I said. "I don't usually handle that sort of thing. But things aren't too good these days and the money was very attractive."

I began to feel restless. It was a sudden sort of feeling. I didn't know why.

Joe said: "You look tired to me. You look like you need a holiday."

I nodded. "It's an idea. If anybody comes here asking where I am, you can say I've gone on a holiday."

"You expecting somebody to ask?" His expression was what they call old-fashioned.

"Maybe," I said. "You never know." I got up. "Can I use your telephone?"

He nodded. "If anybody wants to know where you are, you've gone on a vacation. And you didn't leave an address."

"That's right," I said.

He gave me the key of his office and I walked across the dance floor, up the little flight of stairs; let myself in to the office; switched on the light. I closed the door and put the catch on the lock.

I looked up the number of the Culloden Hotel and dialled it. I asked the night clerk to put me through to Mrs. Ivory.

He said there wasn't any Mrs. Ivory staying in the hotel; that there was no pending reservation in that name; that they didn't know anything about Mrs. Ivory.

That surprised me a little. But not much.

I relaxed in Joe's big office chair. I began to think about the picture I'd seen of the hotel in Torquay; with the palms and the long vista of the sea and the sunshine. An attractive picture. I thought that Torquay would suit me very well for a few weeks. The idea of sitting in a

Peter Cheyney

deck-chair, listening to music and watching the sea, seemed good and—at the moment—desirable.

I thought that Torquay was the place.

I wondered what it would be like to sit in a deck-chair and listen to music, and watch the sea, and talk to Mrs. Ivory. That, I thought, would be something.

As ideas go it was good and it went.

I picked up the telephone and called Pell's flat. While I was waiting for the buzz I looked at my wrist-watch. It was nearly twelve o'clock. Pell would be getting his beauty sleep.

He came on the line. He sounded a little short.

I said: "Pell? This is O'Hara. I'm coming round to see you."

He yawned. "I'm in bed. I'm tired and I've got an office to see people in. What's the matter with tomorrow morning?"

"Nothing as far as I know," I told him. "Except that I'm going to see you tonight—in about ten minutes."

He asked: "Are you going to try to make a lot of trouble?"

"How do I know?" I said. "I'm not a mind reader."

I hung up. I went out of the office, down the stairs and back to Joe's table. I gave him the key.

I said: "Good-night, Joe. Thanks for the phone call."

He put the key in his pocket. "So you fixed it, Mr. O'Hara. Are you off tonight?"

I nodded. "I'm going to Torquay. It ought to be a nice night for driving. I saw a picture once of an hotel there. I liked it."

"Torquay is a nice place," he said. "I hope you have a good time."

It took me twelve minutes to walk round to Pell's place. The apartment block was in darkness except for a light in the front hallway. I went up in the lift, switched on the passage lights, walked along to the flat and rang the bell. A man in a black alpaca coat opened the door. He was a short, thin character, with a twitch in one eye. He looked pallid, careworn and fed-up.

I said: "I'm Mr. O'Hara. Mr. Pell is expecting me."

He stood to one side and, after he had shut the door, I followed him down the long passage. The flat was airy and well-furnished. Some of the pieces were very good.

He opened a door at the end and I went in. Pell was sitting at a desk, facing me, on the other side of the room. He was wearing a finely-checked black and white dressing-gown and a scarf. He was smoking a green cigar and there was a whisky glass on the desk.

Pell was plump in the face and bald. He had a peculiar skin that looked grey in some lights. His mouth went down at the corners. His lips were thin but looked better when he smiled. He had fat white hands and wore a valuable ruby ring, which he said some Indian Princess had given him, on one fat little finger. Pell was successful and clever and tricky and grasping.

I looked at the other man in the room. This was a very big one. He was sitting in an armchair on the right of Pell's desk. The armchair was big but seemed too small for him. He seemed about six feet two or three in height, and as wide as a house. He had a face like a rock and an underslung lower lip. His clothes were too smart. He was smoking a cigar and looked very happy about something. I didn't like him much.

Pell smiled at me. I closed the door behind me and walked over to the desk.

He said: "Hallo, O'Hara. What's the trouble?"

"There isn't any," I said. I got out a cigarette and lighted it. "I want to talk to you. I thought it was important. And it's private." I looked at the man in the chair.

Pell waved his hand. "Don't worry about Lennet. He's an old friend."

"I'm not worrying about him. I'm just saying I don't think he's necessary. I want to talk to you."

Pell shrugged his shoulders. "Look, O'Hara. The way things are I thought it better if Lennet was here. That's fairly reasonable, isn't it? He's not doing any harm and maybe it's a good thing to have him here. For everybody's sake."

"No," I said. "He has to go."

The man in the chair laughed. It sounded like the tide coming in. Out of the corner of my eye I could see him measuring me; assessing my six feet of thinness and lack of muscle.

"Don't be silly, O'Hara," said Pell. He meant his voice to be soothing.

I said to the man in the chair: "Go away, Stupid. Go and get some sleep. Your type needs a lot of sleep."

He put the cigar on the edge of the desk. He pushed himself up with hands that were like meat plates. When he was up, he looked very intimidating.

He came over to me. He said: "What did you say, Clever?"

I let him get close. As his hands went up I flashed a shin-clip with my left foot; side-stepped and pushed with his weight as he went back to avoid the foot-blow. At the second that he was off-balance I put two quick fingertip blows on the neck muscle; then, as he turned away from the pain of the neck blows, I gave him the side-of-the-hand blow downwards on the kidney. He gasped; hesitated; tried to stand away. I went with him and let him have two fast simple judo blows with a hard hand—a direct neck and muscle blow on the Adam's apple.

He made a noise like a wheezy bagpipe. He went backwards into the chair.

I stood watching him. I said to Pell, over my shoulder: "That's judo. It's nice, isn't it?"

Pell drank some whisky. He nodded. He seemed impressed.

"Get up, Fat," I said to the man. "I didn't mean to hurt you. Get up, shake hands and go home. You're safer in bed."

He got up. He held his hand out and I took it. When I saw his left arm move I put the neck lock on. The neck lock done from the handclasp.

He gasped. It didn't sound at all nice. He stood there, his head and neck held rigid, staring straight in front of him.

I said to Pell: "It's pretty, isn't it? He's paralysed. He can't move. When I take this lock off he'll still be suffering from shock for a minute or two, and during that time he's mine."

I took off the lock and let go his hand. He stood quite still, moving his neck and head warily. I gave him a backhand smack across the face to help him a little. His lip began to bleed. Some colour began to come back into his face.

"Get your cigar and get out of here," I said. "Be quick, because I'm getting tired of you."

He looked at Pell uncomfortably. Pell nodded. The man picked up the cigar with fingers that were a little shaky. He went out. I heard the front door shut.

"That's very nice stuff," said Pell amiably. "Where'd you get that, O'Hara?"

I told him.

"You've been around," he said. He got up; went to the sideboard; mixed a glass of whisky and soda; brought it back to me. I sat down in the chair. He went to his seat behind the desk. He relit his cigar; drew on it with pleasure. He exhaled the tobacco smoke slowly. He seemed to be enjoying himself.

He grinned at me. "You're a tough egg, O'Hara. What's troubling you?"

"Nothing," I said. "Nothing much."

I lighted a fresh cigarette. "Tonight," I went on, "when I went back to my office, some crazy woman was there. A Mrs. Ivory. A very striking piece of femininity. Maybe you know her?"

He nodded. "So she went round to your place after all. What did she want?"

"I don't know," I answered. "I didn't ask her. I didn't get so far. She bored me. She told me that she'd been to see you and that you'd given her a long piece about not doing something she wanted to do. You warned her off whatever it was she wanted to do. She told me that you held me up as an example of what happened to people who did things they shouldn't. That you quoted Counsel's attack on me this afternoon in Court as a further example. She told me that you said you expected an intervention in the divorce case; that you weren't going to pay me until you knew there wasn't going to be an intervention."

Pell said: "She must be nuts."

"That's what I thought," I said. "I told you she was crazy. If she'd had any sense, she'd have known that the judge wouldn't have granted the decree nisi unless he believed my evidence, no matter what Counsel for the other side said. Any child of two ought to know that Counsel always goes bald-headed for the detective who supplies the evidence in a defended action for divorce, especially when the respondent has brought a cross-suit—as this one did. Any child ought to know that."

Peter Cheyney

Pell chewed on his cigar. "Women are very funny," he said. "Obviously she didn't know what she was talking about. I didn't tell her anything like that."

"I'm prepared to believe that," I said. "By the way, what did you tell her?"

He stubbed out the cigar butt. He finished the glass of whisky. Then he said: "She came here this afternoon with a long spiel about something or other. I wasn't particularly interested. I told her that the Pell Agency never handled a case unless the client was personally recommended by someone we know; that I was sorry but I couldn't handle her business. You see?"

I nodded.

He went on: "She went on talking and I thought she might make a scene. She was good and worked up about something or other. I wanted to get rid of her. So I told her about you."

"What did you tell her?" I asked.

"I told her that you'd just handled a job for me that required a lot of tact, ingenuity and guts. I said you'd done a great job and that even if Counsel had attacked you in Court the judge had believed your evidence and granted the decree nisi to our client. I told her that if she liked to go round and see you and tell you about it, there was a chance that you might handle it. I told her that she couldn't be in better hands."

"That was nice of you, Pell," I said. "Maybe I ought to have talked to her and heard what she had to say."

He shrugged his shoulders. "You never know—there might have been something in it." He got out another cigar. "Is that all you wanted?"

"No," I said. "I want a thousand pounds."

He raised his eyebrows. "You're in a hell of a hurry, O'Hara. Come in to the office tomorrow and we'll fix it."

"No." I told him, "the money was due to me when the decree nisi was granted. That was this afternoon. I'll have it now."

Pell said: "Supposing I haven't got it?"

"You'll have to get it," I said. "I want it now."

He grinned at me. "You like a joke, don't you? It's all right. I've got the money here for you. I thought you'd be coming round for it. And you earned it all right. My people are tickled silly about today. The lawyers were on to me this afternoon. They said you'd done a terrific job."

He opened a drawer in the desk. He took out a quarto envelope and passed it over to me. I opened it and counted the notes inside. It was all there. I put the envelope in my pocket. I got up.

Pell said: "You can send me a receipt tomorrow." He yawned. "Perhaps it would have been a good thing if you'd listened to what the Ivory woman had to say," he went on. "Maybe there would have been something in it for you."

I picked up my hat. I said: "Why did you have to have that bruiser around here when I came, Pell?"

Peter Cheyney

He laughed. "Oh, him.... He's an old friend of mine—Lennet. He thinks he's good. He thought you were taking a rise out of him. I was very glad when you put him in his place. When I said that it would be a good thing to have him here I was just pulling your leg."

"Of course," I said. We stood smiling at each other. Then I said good-night and went out.

Outside, the streets were cool. I began to walk slowly towards Mack's place near Leicester Square.

I liked the walk. I began to think about the picture of that lunch in Torquay and the sea and the sunshine. I liked thinking about these things.

After a bit I thought about Pell. Pell was very clever and very tricky. He knew his way about. I wondered why the hell he had pulled all that stuff on me about the woman Mrs. Ivory. I wondered if he thought I believed any of it.

But he'd been goddam clever about Mrs. Ivory. Now I begun to get an idea about the way he'd played it. She'd paid him good money—probably a lot——to promise that he wasn't going to give me the thousand. She'd come round to me believing that; thinking that I'd work for her because I was broke.

But Pell was ready to pay me if I got tough about it. He thought I was going to be tough so he paid. That way he saved the amount she'd paid him that afternoon. Everyone, it seemed, was fairly happy—except Mrs. Ivory.

Mrs. Ivory paid everyone and didn't get anything much—except a brush-off. Which is what inevitably happens to beautiful ladies who try to be very clever.

And Pell believed the stuff I had told him about not knowing what she came to see me about. He knew nothing about my having had the thousand from her. If he had, he would never have parted with his money.

That meant she hadn't seen him since she left my office. She hadn't attempted to see him. She'd gone off somewhere. But not to the Culloden Hotel. I wondered why she'd given me that address. Maybe she'd meant to go there if I'd agreed to do what she wanted. Maybe if I'd said yes she'd have gone to the Culloden and made a reservation. She knew the place was half-empty anyhow and that getting a room there would be easy.

But why hadn't she made the reservation first?

There might be an answer to that one. Supposing I'd really done what she wanted me to do; supposing I'd said yes and taken the thousand and gone off and started in? Would she have gone to the Culloden then P?

I thought not. Definitely not. It was a certainty that nobody had seen her come to my office. She'd carefully left the car right down the street. If I'd taken her money and agreed to try to fix Ricaud, she was going off and she was going to say that she'd never seen me in her life. If I tried to find her at the Culloden I should draw a blank. She wouldn't be there and they wouldn't know anything about her.

I thought Mrs. Ivory was nearly good. She had brains.

3

MACK was sitting in the little glass office in the corner of the all-night garage. He had a thin face and big luminous brown eyes and sandy hair. I'd known him for a long time. He liked running an all-night garage because he didn't like people a lot. I think he'd had a lot of trouble in his life and in a place like that you didn't have to talk much. People who came in just wanted petrol or oil or something. They paid and went away.

He was reading The Evening News. He grinned when he saw me. He said: "Hallo, Mr. O'Hara. I see you've been in the wars again."

I looked at the newspaper. "Oh... that...! Yes, if you like to call that a war." I gave him a cigarette. I asked him if he had a car for sale.

He asked: "Is it for you?"

I nodded.

He said: "I've got the very thing for you, Mr. O'Hara. I'll guarantee it. The owner brought it in two days ago. He's going abroad. It's a 16 Rover—a sports coupé— only done nine thousand miles. I've been over it and it's in perfect condition."

I asked: "Can I drive it away?"

He nodded. "It's licensed and insured till the end of the year. I've got the log book. If you like to pay for it, all it needs is some petrol and oil. It costs seven hundred and fifty pounds, and it's a bargain."

I took the packet with the Pell money inside it out of my pocket and counted out the notes.

I said: "Give me a receipt, Mack... and fill the car up."

He asked: "Are you going far?"

"To Torquay," I said. "I haven't had a holiday for a long time."

He said: "That ought to be good." He went to the back of the garage and drove the car up to the pump. It looked in good condition. And the tyres were good. He began to fill the tank.

I asked: "How do you go to Devonshire, Mack?"

He said: "That's easy. From here to Chiswick High Street and the Great West Road, branch off for Staines and Virginia Water, and then it's near straight as damn. You'll be all right. They've got 'A.A.' signs up now. There's only one thing you want to remember... when you curve off from the Great West Road you come to a fork. The left hand side goes to Staines. That's what you want. Don't take the right hand fork; otherwise you'll end up in Berkshire."

I said: "All right."

I watched him fill the car with oil.

He asked: "Shall I send the receipt round to the office, Mr. O'Hara?"

I said: "No... I won't be there for a bit. Send it to the Malinson Hotel, and put on the envelope 'To await arrival.' I expect I'll be going there when I come back."

He said "O.K."

I got into the car; started the engine; drove off. The car sounded good to me. I liked having it. Altogether it seemed as if it had been a pretty good evening—except for Mrs. Ivory. I thought that the situation about Mrs. Ivory wasn't really very satisfactory. But that was just one of those things. Life is like that. Mainly because I had nothing else to think about, and you've got to think about something when you're driving a car at nearly one o'clock in the morning—I began to think about some of the things she'd said.

I found myself getting a little angry about her. I found myself thinking about Mrs. Ivory and trying to remember what her perfume was like. I found myself wondering about Esmeralda, and trying to work out what might—or might not—have happened if I'd taken the job and gone down and seen Alexis Ricaud and played it off the cuff and watched results.

It might have been interesting....

Except for the phoney address she'd given me. And perhaps there were some strings to the job. Perhaps if I'd done what she wanted I should have walked into something. Maybe she'd intended that...

You never knew with women as beautiful as Mrs. Ivory.

It began to rain again. The clouds came over the sky, but there were good headlights on the car and I thought it would take me about seven or eight hours to get down to Torquay. I looked forward to arriving just in time for breakfast. I turned off the Great West Road. In front of me was the roundabout. The road to the left led to Staines; that on the right—the Bath road—to Slough and Maidenhead. I pulled the car in on the left-hand side by the roundabout and lit a cigarette. I sat there with the rain pattering on the roof of the car, smoking and thinking about Torquay.

Of course the picture I'd seen was probably an exaggeration. All those advertisement pictures of hotels and sea fronts are always a little too good. But even if the place was something like it, it was still going to be all right. I'd always heard that Devonshire was a great county.

I started up the car and let in the gear slowly. The car began to move forward. Just for an instant I had one of those flashes—you know what I mean—a mental picture that for no reason at all comes right in front of your eyes, a reminiscent thing of something that's happened and implanted itself on your subconscious brain. It was a picture of Mrs. Ivory going out of my office. As the car moved forward I thought about her. Just in those fleeting seconds I was able to think quite a lot. I thought she was a phoney; that she didn't like telling the truth; that maybe she was a damned good actress. The whole thing possibly had been an act. But she was a very intriguing sort of woman. I wondered what the hell she was at.

Then I stopped the car.

I stopped it because I knew something. I knew I was kidding myself. I knew goddam well that if I took that left fork to Staines, and if I went down to Torquay and stayed at that hotel, and sat on the front in the sunshine and watched the sea and listened to seagulls, and took an interest in boats and things that I hadn't seen for a long time; I knew that if I did that, all the time I'd be curious. I'd be wondering about Mrs. Ivory...

And that gave me a jolt. It gave me a hell of a jolt because I realised that I was curious. I was curious about something, and I hadn't been curious about anything for years.

I knew the Torquay thing was going to be no soap. If I went to Torquay I was going to have something at the back of my brain for the rest of my life that I wouldn't be able to forget. I threw the cigarette stub out of the window and lighted another one. I started up the car again. I took the right fork—the fork to Slough and Maidenhead.

4

I STOPPED the car on the dirt road twenty yards behind the high iron gates that led into the back driveway of the house. The gates were unlocked. I pushed one side open and went through. I walked along the wide gravel path. To the left and right of me were thick shrubberies. Trees, heavy with rain, were dotted about. The path wound through a labyrinth of rhododendron bushes.

The rain had stopped as suddenly as it had started. The moon had come out from behind the clouds. I could see the house—a big Georgian affair—standing on a rise a good hundred yards away.

I looked about me. Ten or twelve yards ahead, a path ran off from the driveway on which I was standing; disappeared amongst the trees. I began to walk along it. It wound through the shrubbery. I thought maybe it would lead to one of the back entrances to the place—the servants' or tradesmen's doors.

The path led nowhere. It finished abruptly, turning off into a little clearing where the grass was thick, uncut and glistening with rain. I leaned up against a tree. I was looking at something that was very funny. A young woman in an evening frock was going through the motions of slow fox-trot underneath the trees on the other side of the clearing. It looked as if she found it difficult to dance on the slippery grass with high heels, but she seemed to like it.

She had a fur coat over one arm and an evening handbag—a large flat affair—clasped under the other. I thought she was either mad or cockeyed—maybe both. I walked across the clearing. Now the moon was right out of the clouds. It was quite bright. When she saw me, she stopped dancing. She stood, her shoulders hanging limply, the fur coat trailing on the grass, staring at me with a bemused expression. She looked to me like a girl of about twenty-five or twenty-six years of age. She might have been a little younger or a little older. She had good blonde hair which had been well-dressed before the rain got at it.

She wore a parma violet dinner frock that had been cut by somebody who knew his business, and a string of pearls. There were long sleeves to the frock and they clung closely to her arms with the weight of the rain. She was a pretty girl, with big surprised looking eyes.

She said in an odd voice: "Hallo! Who are you? And where are you going—that is if you know where you're going?" She leaned against the tree and regarded me dully.

I said: "I'm not going anywhere." I grinned at her. "You like al fresco dancing on a wet evening?"

She laughed. "Yes..." she said shrilly. "I like it. It's nice. To dance without music. We used to do that. We used to meet here in the moonlight and dance without any music and we liked it. It was fun."

"Why was it fun?" I asked her. "And what are you trying to do about it now? Are you trying to recapture the memory? That's usually due to sentiment—or misery—or jealousy. Or the whole lot. Which is it?"

She said: "You've got your nerve, Mr. Clever-dick. Telling me about what I'm trying to recapture and why and how and what. You've got your nerve, Mr. Whoever-you-are."

Her voice was thick and she enunciated with difficulty. She was tight. Her head sank down and then she pulled it up with a jerk. I should think she was finding it difficult to keep awake.

"All right," I said. "You were saying that you like to dance without music..."

She interrupted impatiently. "Yes... that's what life's like—a dance without music! A lot of people dancing about on a ballroom floor—and they don't even know that the band's gone to bed."

I said: "Maybe you're right." I came closer to her. I could see the initials in gold on the flat parma violet evening handbag—"E.R."

"My name's O'Hara," I said.

She looked at me for a little while; then she jerked her head up again. "Good evening, Mr. O'Hara. I'm Esmeralda."

"Esmeralda Ricaud?" I asked.

She said: "Yes... how did you know?"

I pointed to the initials on her handbag.

She said stupidly: "I think you're very clever." She smiled at me. Her eyes were vacant.

I said: "Look, I came here on the chance of seeing Mr. Ricaud. I have had a look at the front of the house and the whole place seems to be in darkness. I tried the frontdoor bell and nothing happened so I drove round to the back."

She said: "Quite. Everybody here uses the back gate. It's more convenient." She relapsed into silence and her head drooped. I thought she was going to fall over. I think she would have if it hadn't been for the tree. She said suddenly: "Look, why don't you and I go and have a little drink, Mr. O'Hara? Why don't you and I have a party?"

I said: "I think that's a good idea. Let's go and have a party. Where?"

She nodded towards the house. "We'll go in. I've got a key." She began to sing to herself... "I've got an invitation to a ball..."

I said: "All right. My car's on the road. What shall I do with it?"

She said: "Drive it through the gates and leave it amongst the trees. It'll be safe there. Nobody'll see it."

I asked: "Have you come down from somewhere?"

"Oh, yes... from London," she answered. "I was at a party. I got bored with the party so I thought I'd come down here."

I said: "Well, I'll go and get the car. Will you wait here till I come back?"

She nodded. "Yes, I'll wait here."

I went down the path, back to the car; drove it through the gates, off the main gravel path, in amongst some trees. I switched off the headlights and locked it. Then I went back and closed the gates. When I got back to the clearing she was still there leaning against the tree. The fur coat and the handbag were on the ground where she'd dropped them. I picked them up. I put the handbag under my left arm and draped the coat over it. When I squeezed my arm against the soft handbag I could feel the outline of the gun in it. I put my other arm round her.

I said: "Let's walk."

We began to walk. She got better every minute. Her body was well-shaped and supple but thin. She was wearing some sweet, rather heavy, perfume which I didn't like. It took us quite a while to get to the house. We reached a door at the back and after a search in her handbag she managed to find a key. We went in.

She said to me: "There's a switch in this passage somewhere on the right. You find it."

I left her leaning up against the wall while I found the switch. When I'd put the light on we walked down a long passage-way that led to what I took to be the front hall—quite a big, well-furnished affair. We went down another passage at right angles, through a door, into a room. On the way I put on lights when she told me.

It was a comfortable room—big, high-ceilinged, with good furniture. There were one or two good oil-paintings on the walls. There was a big old-fashioned sideboard against the wall with a lot of bottles on it. She moved unsteadily from the door, got as far as one of the big chairs by the side of an electric imitation fire, and flopped into the chair.

She said: "Welcome to 'Crossways,' Mr...."

I said: "The name's O'Hara."

She said: "Of course, Mr. O'Hara. What's your first name?"

I told her my first name was Caryl. She smiled vaguely. She said: "Christmas Carol... I think that's a nice name. I like it, Are you an Irishman?"

"Mostly," I said.

She said: "I like Irishmen. D'you think you might get us some drinks? And I want a cigarette."

I gave her a cigarette and lit it. I said: "Don't you think you ought to get out of that frock? You're wet through."

                                        Peter Cheyney

She looked at her thin soaked evening shoes. She said: "It doesn't matter. It couldn't matter less. I don't mind being wet."

I said: "All right."

She looked at the sideboard; then: "For me... some whisky... whisky with ginger ale. You have whatever you like... Caryl."

I went to the sideboard. I mixed myself a stiff whisky and soda. I put my forefinger in the top of the whisky bottle; ran it round the edge of a clean glass; then poured some ginger ale into the glass. That way she could smell the whisky and think she was drinking it. I carried the glass back to her. Then I knelt down and switched on the electric fire.

I said: "Well, this is very nice. What shall we talk about?"

She drank some of the ginger ale. She said: "This tastes very strange to me."

I said: "Yes? It's a very mild one. Shall I change it?"

She shook her head. "It doesn't matter. Nothing matters. Nothing matters at all... at all... at all..."

I pulled up the other big armchair so that it was opposite hers. I sat down and lit a cigarette. I said: "Tell me something, Esmeralda... why do you have to carry a gun in your bag?"

She looked at me suspiciously. "How d'you know I've got a gun?"

"I felt it when I carried the bag. Do you have to have it?"

She nodded. "But definitely!" she said. "I have to have a gun. And I have to have it all the time, because if I have it all the time, one of these fine days or nights I'm going to use it."

I said: "That's fine. You mean you can't make up your mind to get around to using it on any specific occasion. You just like to have it with you in case you feel you'd like to use it. In other words... time, place opportunity—and you've got the gun with you. Is that it?"

She said: "That's very nearly right, Caryl. I can see that you do quite a lot of thinking."

I asked: "How do you feel about me, Esmeralda. Do you like me?"

She looked at me for a long time. Then she smiled—suddenly. "Yes. I haven't known you for an awful long while, but I certainly don't dislike you. Why?"

I said: "If you don't dislike me, tell me why you have to carry a gun around always. Tell me who it is you want to kill."

She smiled again. It was a peculiar and not very pleasant smile. Looking at her now I could see that she'd been quite beautiful at one time, but her face was ravaged. Her features were good, her nose was straight, her mouth well-shaped, her teeth regular and white. But there was so much unhappiness and misery about her eyes that the beauty had become obscured.

She looked at me for a long time. The way she was sitting her face was in the shadow, and I couldn't see her expression. She seemed to be considering something.

Or maybe she was tired and cockeyed. I wasn't quite certain.

She began suddenly: "I was at a party... and what a stupid party. But then I think most parties are stupid... don't you, Caryl?" Her voice trailed away into nothingness.

"Parties can be all right," I said. "Sometimes... or not... as the case may be. You seem to have done pretty well at yours. Weren't you happy?"

She laughed. The laughter was odd. It had a peculiar lilt in it. Something not particularly good to listen to.

She said: "Parties—with me—always start the right way. Until I've had a few cocktails and a little brandy or whisky. I like brandy and I like whisky. I like any sort of drink..." She turned on the peculiar laugh again.

"But they don't stay right," she went on. "But definitely not right. When I've had just a few drinks I begin to think. Then I want to be by myself. And then I begin to think about him—in a certain way. Always when I've been at a party for a little while I begin to think about him like that..." She began to play with her glass—tilting it this way and that.

I drank some whisky. "Just what do you mean, Esmeralda?" I asked her. "What do you mean when you say you begin to think about him in a certain way. What way?"

She got up suddenly. She walked over to the sideboard and mixed herself a strong drink. I didn't like that much. I wanted her to talk. She went back to the chair.

"The way I always think about him when I'm not with him," she said. "About killing him... I like the idea... I like it now. That's why I have the pistol. So that when I feel like that and I'm brave, and when I see him when I'm feeling like that and I'm brave I'll shoot him. That's what I want to do now...You see...?"

I nodded. "By the way," I asked, "who is he?" She said: "Don't be silly... It's Alexis of course. My dear husband. Dear... dear... darling Alexis. Of course . . ."

"Of course," I said. I asked: "How did you get down here? I suppose the party was in London?"

"Yes," she said. She began to smile for no reason that I could think of. "In London... a nice party in London. I was dropped here. Somebody drove me down. That's how I got here."

I waited for a few seconds. Then I made my voice casual. I asked her: "Who drove you down, Esmeralda... someone nice?"

She looked at me. Then she smiled for a bit; then: "You wouldn't know so it wouldn't do any good if I told you. See, Caryl...? Aren't you a sweet Caryl? I like you, Caryl. I like your name, Caryl... Christmas Caryl. Tee... hee...hee..."

There was a standard lamp just behind her armchair. I got up; walked over; switched it on. I tilted the shade and the light struck her full in the face. She hissed at me.

"Damn you... put that out," she said. "I can't bear it. Put it out...!" There was a note of hysteria in her voice.

I switched off the lamp. I went back to my chair.

"What is it?" I asked her. "Morphia or heroin? I can hardly see the pupils of your eyes. You've been hitting it up tonight, haven't you? Not very clever, is it?"

"Why not?" she said. She laughed some more. "It's the shortest distance between two points and lovely... the line of least resistance... and beautiful." She began to croon some ditty to herself.

"Where'd you get it, Esmeralda?" I asked her. "Did you get it off the nice man—or was it woman—who drove you down? Come on... tell a pal..."

She became serious. She said: "So you're my pal. Palsy-walsy Caryl... Christmas Caryl... I got you off a tree... And everybody was happy ever after." She finished the drink. She mumbled a little. She dropped the glass on the floor. It smashed. She began to grind it into the carpet with her slender high-heeled shoe.

I tried a new line. "Listen... anyway, you came down here to see Alexis. Because you wanted to shoot Alexis. We'll settle for that. How did you know he was going to be here? He isn't here now, you know. Did you think he'd be here?"

She leaned her head against the back of the chair. Her hair was still beautiful. I thought she represented a waste of material that might have been originally very good.

"He'll be here," she said. "You see... he'll be here... and how. And then you'll see something, Christmas Caryl. Then you'll see..."

She drooped and fell right back into the big chair. Her shoulders and legs relaxed. One thin, wet-gowned arm hung, stupidly, over the arm of the chair. The fingers were thin, long and white.

I went over and switched on the standard lamp. She had passed out cold.

I picked her out of the armchair and laid her down on the big settee in front of the electric fire. Then I went out of the room and began a tour. I found electric light switches here and there with the help of my cigarette lighter, switched them on and, having looked, turned them off. The rooms on the ground floor were big, well-furnished. They gave evidence of taste, refinement and a lot of money.

I found the rug in a small sitting-room—probably a housekeeper's room—at the back of the house. I picked it up and went back to the drawing-room. She was lying where I'd left her. She was an odd sight. Her face was drawn and dead white. Some of the mascara had run off her eyelashes.

Esmeralda, I thought, might easily be pathetic.

I put one arm underneath her, raised her up, put her fur coat on her and wrapped the big motor-car rug around her. I picked up her handbag and looked through the contents.

Besides the gun which I had felt when I had carried it under my arm, there were the things you find in a woman's handbag—keys, a pencil, powder compact, lipstick, loose change, and at the bottom were a couple of empty phials with Chinese lettering on them. That, I thought, would be the hop she'd been using. In the inner compartment of the bag was a card: "Charles Quinceley, M.D." with an address near Belgrave Square.

I made a mental note of the doctor's name and address; put the card back. I took the automatic pistol out of the bag; put it in my hip pocket; closed the bag.

Then I picked her up and went out of the house and along the winding path, through the open glade where I'd found her dancing, to the spot where I'd left the car. I was glad when it came in sight. She wasn't heavy but she was heavy enough.

I got the door open and put her in the back. Then I locked the doors and went back to the house. I turned off the lights in the passages as I passed through; went back to the drawing-room. I mixed myself another drink and sat down in the armchair by the fire. I lighted a cigarette and did a little thinking.

Vaguely... but very vaguely... I was beginning to get the glimmering of an idea. And the more I thought about it the less I liked it.

5

I'D smoked three cigarettes when I heard the noise of a door slamming. The noise came somewhere from what I imagined to be the front of the house. There was a pause; then I heard footsteps. They indicated the walk of a man who put his feet squarely and solidly on the ground. They stopped when the walker got on to the thick carpet. Then the door opened and Ricaud came into the room.

I knew it was Ricaud all right. And he was certainly somebody. He stood in the doorway looking at me, his hand still resting on the door knob. He was about six feet three inches in height. He had broad shoulders, narrow hips, and he stood in the relaxed attitude of a man who is certain of himself and knows it. He was dressed in a well-cut tuxedo. His white shirt and collar were faultlessly laundered. He wore a black watered-silk bow. Everything about him was perfect but still not too perfect.

His face was very interesting. It was a square sort of face with a well-cut nose and lips, a small carefully-kept moustache, and naturally wavy hair that swept back from a forehead which was intellectual but not too much so. He was smiling and I could see his strong white teeth.

When you took a quick look at Ricaud you got the impression of a big, cheerful and frank personality— essentially a "big" personality—a man who would not stoop to anything little. A prepossessing person. You liked him, but to me there was something a little odd— something not quite definable. I thought maybe it was just an idea; that I was being a little too cynical.

He closed the door behind him. He came into the room. He said: "Good evening. How do you do? I'm glad you looked after yourself." He looked at the whisky and soda on the table by the side of my chair. His voice was as pleasant as the rest of him. It was low, quiet and incisive. He spoke English perfectly. It was only

Peter Cheyney

something about his head and face that gave you the impression that he wasn't quite English.

I got up. I said: "I'm sorry to barge in at this time of the morning, but I wanted to see you. I thought it was important and that you might come back. So I waited."

He said: "Of course. I'm glad you did." He seemed not at all surprised at the idea of people calling at half-past three in the morning.

He went to the sideboard and poured himself a drink; then he came back and stood in front of the electric fire. He drank some of the whisky; looked at me cheerfully.

He asked: "How did you manage to get in?"

"I got here about an hour ago," I told him. "I came to the front entrance and rang the bell but nothing happened, so I went round to the back. I found I could get in that way. I walked along a pathway and found a small door at the side of the house. It was open so I came in."

He smiled again. "Excellent. So here you are, Mr.—?"

I said: "My name's O'Hara. I'm a private detective."

He grinned at me. For the moment he looked like a schoolboy. He said: "A private detective! How interesting. So that's why you thought of going round to the back. I expect experience has taught you that people are more inclined to leave the back door open than the front one."

I said: "I've come to the conclusion that experience has taught me damned little, but I always try a back door if I can't get through one in the front of the house."

He nodded. "Looking at you, Mr. O'Hara, I should think you'd try anything once if you wanted to."

"Maybe," I said. "And twice if I liked it."

He looked at my glass. He asked pleasantly: "Why don't you have a drink?"

I said: "That's an idea." I went to the sideboard and got another whisky and soda. I went back to my chair.

He said: "Well, tell me something else. Do you know who I am?"

I said: "I take it you are Alexis Ricaud. There couldn't be two people who looked like you anyway."

He pretended to be astonished. "No? Am I so extraordinary?"

"Far from it," I said. "Most men would like to look like you."

He seemed to like that one. He said: "I don't know..." But he half-turned. He very nearly looked at himself in the mirror over the mantelpiece. He stopped just in time.

He said: "So you know I'm Alexis Ricaud, and you came down to see me and you couldn't get in at the front door, so you came round to the back, and you waited. So I take it that somebody has been talking about me, O'Hara... somebody who has told you what I was like; who told you that you'd probably find the house deserted; who told you you probably wouldn't be able to get in at the front door; that the thing to do was to try the side door. Is that right?"

"Not bad," I said. "Although all that was obvious."

                                    Peter Cheyney

He nodded. "Sometimes the obvious is the most exciting. Now, have you some business to talk to me about?"

I shrugged my shoulders. "I wouldn't exactly call it business," I said. "It might be, but I doubt it. It's more a matter of curiosity."

He said: "Ah!... So you're curious about me?"

"Not particularly curious about you," I said. "I'm curious about a lady called Mrs. Ivory."

He said: "I think that's a very charming name—a rather peculiar name, but nevertheless a delightful one. So you're curious about a Mrs. Ivory. Tell me, what can I do to satisfy your curiosity?"

I said: "I don't know. We'll see in a minute." I went on: "As I told you, I'm a private detective..."

He interrupted: "Yes... I understand that. What the English people call a private dick and the Americans an 'eye.' I think the idea of being a private 'eye' is awfully nice. One has the impression of being looked at all the time through a keyhole by an eye that never blinks—a rather protruding, somewhat bleary, eye. But please go on."

I said: "Mrs. Ivory came to see me tonight in my office. I don't know anything about her. She's an extremely beautiful woman and she seems to have a lot of money. You don't know her?"

He asked softly: "Have you come here to ask me questions?"

"All right," I said. "We'll skip the questions. I don't care whether you know her or not. Mrs. Ivory was prepared to pay me a large sum of money to come down here and see you."

He smiled quite happily. He said: "How very interesting. I wonder why she wanted you to do that."

I said: "I wouldn't know. I didn't ask her."

He nodded. "And so you came down to carry out your assignment?"

I shook my head. "No... I told Mrs. Ivory that I didn't want any part in this business. But later I got an idea that I was curious about it."

He asked: "So you want me to satisfy your curiosity, O'Hara?"

I said: "That's right, Ricaud."

He said: "People I don't know very well usually call me Mr. Ricaud."

"Do they? That must be nice for them. To me you're just Ricaud."

He shrugged his shoulders. "You have it your own way. So to you I'm just Ricaud, and you'd like me to satisfy your curiosity?"

I said: "Yes. It's just like that."

"Tell me something, Mister O'Hara..." he inquired casually, "what happens if I decide that I'm not interested in you; that I don't intend to satisfy your curiosity? What happens then?"

I finished the whisky and put the glass on the table. I said: "I hadn't thought about that. Obviously one or two things could happen. I could put on my hat and go away and do nothing about it, or I could put on my hat and go away and do something about it."

                              Peter Cheyney

He looked at me quickly. He repeated: "Do something about it? What do you mean by that?"

"Just this," I said. "If I'm curious enough to come here it ought to be quite obvious to you that if I don't find out what I want I'm going to be still more curious."

He said amiably: "I see. And you think of the two evils I should choose the lesser, Mr. O'Hara. You think I should satisfy your curiosity."

I said: "If you decide that satisfying my curiosity is the lesser of two evils, you'll do it, won't you?"

He laughed. He seemed awfully amused at that. He said: "There's a certain irrefutable logic about you that is rather fascinating. However, I might satisfy your curiosity for another reason. I might satisfy it because the idea amused me."

"I'm not concerned with your reason," I told him. "What I'm concerned with is whether you're going to do it or not. If you're not, I'll get out... maybe."

He said: "What do you mean—maybe?" He looked at me. His eyes were as cold as ice.

I leaned back in the chair; then I fished a cigarette out of my pocket and lit it. I said: "I've been watching you for quite a bit. I don't think I like you a lot."

He said: "How very interesting. Now I'm going to tell you something, Mr. O'Hara. I don't think I like you either. So now we know where we are, don't we?"

"So it seems," I said. I put my hands on the arms of the chair to get up.

He raised his hand. He said: "Please don't go. That last remark of yours has told me an awful lot."

I said: "Has it? Such as?"

"Someone's been talking to you about me," he said slowly. "Someone, who is—shall we say—not pre-disposed in my favour, has been putting a lot of odd ideas into your head. I think that, if you'd met me normally, you might have liked me very much. Now, isn't that possible, Mr. O'Hara?"

I said: "Maybe."

"But you haven't met me normally," he said. "When you came here tonight you came here to meet someone you were prepared to dislike."

I didn't say anything. I began to get an idea about Ricaud—the idea that he was more curious about me than I was pretending to be about Mrs. Ivory. That suited me all right. I played it from there.

I began: "When a woman is as nice as Mrs. Ivory—"

He interrupted. He raised his eyebrows superciliously. "How nice?"

I shrugged my shoulders. "Meaning that Mrs. Ivory isn't really a nice person?" I asked.

"If you like," he said. "Of course you couldn't decide whether she was nice or not unless you knew all about her... could you?"

"All right," I said. "I'll settle for that. Tell me about her."

He laughed. "Sometimes you are almost naif, Mr. O'Hara. Almost childlike. Or perhaps you only pretend to be like that. Perhaps you aren't so stupid after all. Tell me then... why, my dear Mr. O'Hara, are you so curious? Do you expect me to believe that your motive for being here is mere curiosity? Do you really expect me to believe that?"

I knew it wasn't any good expecting him to believe that. Because it was the truth. People seldom recognise it when they see it. I thought I'd play it another way. A way that he would like better.

I said: "I don't like Mrs. Ivory. But over this business with you—I've put myself in a rather peculiar position with her. She might make things a little difficult for me. I want to know where I stand."

He did a little thinking. I could see his brain working. I began to think that he was coming my way.

He said eventually: "O'Hara, why don't you tell me the truth? Possibly I could be of greater help to you than you know... possibly. Tell me the truth and you will find that I shall be as frank with you."

I grinned at him. I thought I'd let him have it. "All right. Here it is. She came to see me tonight and offered me a thousand pounds to come out here and scare you off somehow. I took the money and told her I wasn't going to play. I knew she couldn't do anything about it. And that was that."

He looked at me. He was pleased with life. The idea of Mrs. Ivory having been taken for her money and then told where she got off seemed to appeal to him. He was smiling. I liked him less than ever.

I went on: "Then I made up my mind to take a holiday. But outside London I began to worry a little. Supposing she did do something about it?" I looked at him. I put a worried look on my face. "I'm not looking for unnecessary trouble," I continued; "but it occurred to me that possibly she might in some way be able to get back at me."

"I understand," he said. "So you thought you'd come here and find out what you could about Mrs. Ivory. You were frightened at what you had done. You realised that after all you were only a small time private detective who had descended to swindling a woman out of a thousand pounds; that possibly she might have some friends who would make things hot for you. I understand perfectly."

I didn't say anything.

"I believe you," he went on. "But don't worry, O'Hara. Mrs. Ivory won't do anything. And, as far as I'm concerned, I'm rather amused at the idea of her losing her money. It appeals to my sense of the ridiculous."

"All right," I said. "Why did she want me to do it?"

"It's quite a story," said Ricaud. He was almost preening himself now. "I am a man," he went on, "who, for some reason which I cannot quite determine, attracts women greatly. They are invariably unable to escape from falling in love with me. Some of them become affected strongly. To an almost ridiculous extent..."

I coughed. I thought: Like hell! The one outside in the car wrapped up in the rug was an example. I thought for a moment that it would be amusing to let Esmeralda loose on him with her automatic pistol and stand in the corner and pick up the pieces.

"Some of them," he went on in a peculiar crooning voice, "become insanely jealous. Mrs. Ivory was of this type. At one time she was greatly attached to me. She

                    Peter Cheyney

was very, very jealous of me, and when the time came I was forced—rather regretfully, I admit—to tell her that it was all over; that she had been superseded by another woman. She became almost mad." He shrugged his shoulders. "I married the other woman," he continued, with a smile. "And so you can understand Mrs. Ivory's attitude. She desires revenge, but her stupidity defeats itself. She pays you a thousand pounds to try to get even with me, and you cheat her out of the money and come out here crawling, to find some means of protecting yourself against any action she may take. Don't worry, O'Hara. She will do nothing. Which is perhaps lucky for you."

I said: "Good."

He lit a cigarette. He took a long time about it. He was doing some more thinking.

"Of course you've put yourself in a rather peculiar position as far as I am concerned," he said seriously. "I could go to the police and tell them what you've told me. They might be inclined to make some inquiries about the thousand pounds you got from Mrs. Ivory, don't you think, O'Hara?..."

I said: "Nuts. Only one person could bring a charge against me. That is Mrs. Ivory."

"Possibly," he said suavely. He smiled at me. "I was only joking, of course. However, you are not pleased that Mrs. Ivory tried to make a fool of you. You have her thousand pounds and you would probably like to get some more money from her..."

My ears jerked a little. Now I was getting somewhere. I said quickly: "You bet I would. How can I do it?"

He drew on his cigarette. He said: "I suggest that you find Mrs. Ivory and tell her that unless she pays you some more money you will come to me and tell me the whole story. Tell her that."

"And you think she'll fall for that?" I asked. "You think she'll hand over some more?"

"I'm sure of it," he said casually. "Then—when she pays you, shall we say, two thousand pounds for not telling me all about it—you can come back to me and give me fifteen hundred pounds and keep the remaining five hundred for yourself. You see, I am quite generous."

I got up. I said: "I'm not sorry I came here tonight. Not really. I'm very glad I did. Do you know why?"

"Tell me why," he said casually.

"I'm going to give you a beating up," I said. "Just for the hell of it. A little softening up, shall we call it? When I've done that I'm going to talk to you. When I've put you into an agreeable frame of mind I'm going to talk to you like a Dutch uncle and you're going to like it."

He looked bored. He said: "Really... how do you propose to set about it? I think I am a little bigger and possibly much stronger than you are. You are inclined to be rather slim. Don't you think?"

I said: "Have you ever heard of judo? It's a pretty science. It was made for a son-of-a-bitch like you."

I began to move towards him.

He asked easily as if he didn't care: "Where did you learn your judo?"

                              Peter Cheyney

"Where they made it," I said. "In Japan."

I stepped nearer. I was watching him. His expression changed. He moved towards me. As his hand went up I threw out an arm lock. He avoided it easily and the next moment I was howling as he put a judo wrist-crush on my right wrist. I got out of it too late. As I flung up my left hand for an evasive blow, he dropped suddenly, flashed the "foot-throw" on me, and I crashed backwards on to my head.

I lay on the floor, shocked, half-paralysed. His voice seemed to come from a long way off.

He said: "Your judo is good... extremely good for a novice... but not against a judoka black-belt of the tenth degree. You need another fifteen years training, O'Hara."

He bent down and put his fingers in my shirt collar. He pulled my head up from the floor. His face, near mine, was smiling. His eyes were bright with sadistic satisfaction.

"I shall leave a small drink for you on, the sideboard," he said, "to enable you to get out of here and crawl to wherever it is you reside. Any time that I see you again I shall deal with you much more harshly. This will help you to understand."

He struck a back-handed slap across my face with his free hand. The floor came up and hit my head as he released his grip on my collar. Then, just for luck, I suppose, he drew back his foot and kicked me in the stomach. A nice solid kick.

A hot searing pain went right through me; then the black curtains came down and I went out.

6

THE process of coming back was not pleasant. I lay on the floor in the darkness, collecting my wits, trying to think coherently. It wasn't easy. I had a lump on the back of my head where I hit the floor. My body ached all over. I had a dull pain in the region of the abdomen that I wouldn't have wished on my worst enemy. I thought it hadn't been a particularly successful night... not very.

I lay there wondering about that. Because if curiosity had driven me to come to this house in the first place, the earlier degree of curiosity was nothing compared with that which possessed me at the moment. A curiosity that was even greater than the amount of aches and pains I was experiencing, mixed with some old-fashioned hatred.

I moved a little; started to work my legs about. I was thinking about Ricaud. An interesting type. But then, ever since I had met Mrs. Ivory at eleven o'clock, I had been running into interesting types. If she was intriguing, Ricaud was a wow. I put him right at the back of my mind in the compartment reserved for whited sepulchres, and besides my curiosity about him there was a certain cold anger which is not easy to describe.

Ricaud knew his judo all right. He was an expert. He had said that he was a black-belt of the tenth degree. I believed it. It wasn't boasting. That meant he'd been around; that he must have spent a considerable period

                                          Peter Cheyney

of his life either in Japan or in close contact with a very good master of the art.

I got up. I was unsteady, but could walk. I practised walking in small circles in the darkness, making my way slowly towards the electric light switch. Eventually, I switched it on. I looked about me. The room was as I'd seen it before, except that the sideboard had been cleared of bottles. One small lonely glass, half-filled with a yellowish liquid, stood in the centre of the sideboard. There was a piece of writing paper beside it. I went over and read the words on the piece of paper:

"Here's your drink. You'll need it. And remember what I told you. R."

I thought I could do without Mr. Ricaud's drink. I went over to the door; switched off the light; found my way out of the house; went back to the car.

As I unlocked the car I could see Esmeralda just where I'd left her. She was asleep almost. I started up the car, backed on to the gravel path, got on to the dirt road and headed for London.

After a while I began to feel better. I searched for a cigarette. I was lucky. I had one left. I slowed down; lighted it; then accelerated.

Forty-five minutes later, I stopped the car in the quietness of Cadogan Lane near Sloane Street. I went into the Pont Street call-box, dialled Joe Melander's flat. I heard the bell buzzing and waited. After a hell of a time he came on the line. I could hear him yawning.

I said: "Joe... this is Caryl O'Hara. I'm in a spot."

He said: "Anything you say, Mr. O'Hara."

I told him: "I've got a babe in the back of the car. She's not in a very good state... too much hooch and maybe a little of something else."

He said: "I know. They get that way sometimes."

I went on: "I want a place for her just for a little while. Somewhere where she can be put to bed and sleep off whatever it is she's got. I thought maybe Mrs. Melander would keep an eye on her."

"Sure," said Joe. "You bring her round. We'll look after her. She can stay as long as she likes."

I said: "I'll be with you in twenty minutes."

I drove to Vale Street; stopped outside an all-night chemists I know. I went inside and got some calomel-atropine ampoules. Then I drove to Joe's. He opened the side door—the one near the bottle-party entrance. He was in his dressing-gown. He helped me move Esmeralda out of the back of the car.

He said: "She's pretty, this one. It's always the good-lookers who do this sort of thing."

Upstairs in the sitting-room, with Mrs. Melander fussing around to get hot black coffee ready, we got to work on Esmeralda with hot-water bottles and smelling salts. When she decided to wake up she didn't look so good and probably felt worse. After she'd had the coffee she looked a little more human. Mrs. Melander was in a bedroom down the passage, getting it ready. I told Joe to go and give her a hand.

When he'd gone, she said: "What is this?" She looked about her. She was a little vague but her brain was working.

Peter Cheyney

I said: "Remember me, Esmeralda? My name's O'Hara. I met you tonight down at 'Crossways.'"

She looked at me for quite a while; then she said: "I remember. What's happened to you?" She smiled a little. It was a rueful smile. "Your face isn't quite the same."

I nodded. "That was Alexis—that was."

She said: "Yes? Did you try to do something to him? If you did that was very stupid."

"Sometimes I'm a very stupid man," I said. "Drink your coffee and listen to me. We're in London. This flat belongs to a friend of mine. You're going to stay here for a while and then I'm going to have you moved. You're going into a nursing home, Esmeralda."

She said suddenly: "Now I remember. Caryl O'Hara... Christmas Caryl..." She smiled. The smile was almost beautiful. "It all comes back to me now," she said. "But what's this about a nursing home? Who the hell do you think you are to say that I'm to go into a nursing home?"

I grinned back at her. "Never mind who I think I am. That's what's happening. I'll tell you the form. In a few minutes you're going to bed. You're going to take some medicine I've got for you. By the time you wake up I'll find some place for you to go, but you've got to behave, Esmeralda."

She said: "What happens if I don't behave? Tell me that, O'Hara. What happens if I say I'm not going into a nursing home? Why should I go into a nursing home?"

"You can answer that for yourself," I told her. "If you don't want to go into a nursing home, you can do the other thing. It's a matter for you to choose."

She asked: "What other thing?"

"I'll take you round to the police station," I said, "and hand you over as a woman who's wandering about under the influence of drugs, waving a loaded automatic pistol. They'll do something about that, you know."

She looked at me. She said: "The hell of it is I believe you'd do it too."

I didn't say anything.

She made up her mind. "If that's the case, I'm going to bed." She smiled ruefully.

"Don't worry about anything," I said, "and especially don't worry about Ricaud. Maybe we'll have a talk about him some time."

I called Mrs. Melander. I gave her the ampoules. I introduced her to Esmeralda. I said: "One ampoule when she goes to bed now—one when she wakes up. I'll probably be round sometime later in the day."

She said: "All right." She was a nice woman.

I said so-long to Joe and went. I drove to the Malinson Hotel; knocked up George, the night porter; engaged my old room; got the promise of some hot tea to be sent up, went up in the lift; undressed and went to bed. When I'd had the tea I thought: Sufficient unto the day is the evil thereof.

Which is one of the goddam silly things you think when there isn't anything else to be done about it.

　　　　　　　　　　Peter Cheyney

Before I went to sleep I thought a little about Mrs. Ivory.

She'd won the first round, I thought. Maybe she had brains as well as beauty.

CHAPTER TWO

TUESDAY — DEAD END
1

I WENT into Pell's office at twelve o'clock. I was tired and bored. With that sort of boredom that makes you wonder why the hell you're worrying about anything unimportant—such as sticking your nose into other people's business.

The girl in the outer office—a very smart number, with four-inch heels and hair darkening at the roots where the bleach was weak—flashed the tight smile at me that she reserved for people she thought she didn't like. She spoke into the intercom telephone and told Pell that I was there. After a minute she told me to go in.

Pell had a carnation in his buttonhole. He looked as if he were getting over a thick night.

I said hello and gave him the receipt for his money. He put it in the drawer.

He said acidly: "So all's well that ends well. You've got a thousand pounds and you're going to hit the high spots." He smiled sourly and showed his big teeth.

I said: "I'm not certain. I think I've been a fool about Mrs. Ivory." I lighted a cigarette. It was my first, and it tasted like nothing on earth.

He asked why.

"I've been thinking about what you told me last night," I said. "I was a fool not to hear what she wanted to say. It might have been worth while."

"That's what I told you," said Pell. He went to the cupboard in the corner and brought out the bottle and two glasses. He poured two shots of whisky.

I took the glass from him. I said: "Thanks for the drink. Where do I find her?"

He grinned at me. "So you want to see if the business is still on?" He shrugged his shoulders. "I don't know where you'll find her. We didn't take an address. There was no reason why we should. I was glad to get rid of her."

I said: "Well... it looks as if I missed a chance." I got up. "I'll be seeing you. So long." I went out.

As I went through the outer office I took a quick look at the girl. She was typing a letter. Behind her, I could see the office keys hanging on the wall. I wondered if I could trust her, and then decided it wasn't worth chancing. She looked to me like a girl who'd play along for a bit and then, when she was tired, start to talk. I didn't like the type anyway.

I said good morning to her and went down the stairs. I walked up the street and stopped at the Colour and Brush shop on the corner. I went in and asked if they had plasticine. I bought two pieces, walked round the street for ten minutes, came back round the furthest way and parked myself in a deep doorway on the side of the street opposite Pell's office.

He came out just after one o'clock. He went down the street; got into his car; drove off. I waited a few minutes; then I crossed the road and went up to the office.

I said to the girl: "Do me a favour, Miss Hynes. I want to make a telephone call, but I don't want to speak to the wrong person. Call the number for me and ask for Mr. Helley. If you get him, put him on to me. I want to speak to him personally and I don't want to be short-circuited by anyone in his office." I gave her a bright smile.

She said: "O.K. What's the number?"

I thought of a number; gave it to her; walked over and stood beside her. She had her back to the wall, and when she started to dial I grabbed the two keys off the hook, slipped them into my jacket pocket. I took an impression of each key by pressing it into the plasticine. One key for each piece.

I put the keys back on the hook while she was still trying to talk to Mr. Helley. I waited till they had told her they didn't know any Mr. Helley, said thank you, paid twopence for the call and went out.

I picked up a cab at the end of the street and drove to Steven's place off Seven Dials. Blooey was cutting a model ship out of a hunk of wood. I gave him the two pieces of plasticine; told him to cut me the keys; put them in a small parcel and leave them for me at the Malinson Hotel by six o'clock that evening. I paid him two pounds. He said he'd have the keys cut and delivered by that time.

I picked up another cab in Shaftesbury Avenue, drove to the office and kept the cab waiting. There wasn't any mail. I locked up the office, drove to my rooms in Falsom Place, packed two suit-cases and went back to the Malinson.

I left my luggage with the hall porter and told him to get the suits pressed right away. I had a word with the girl on the telephone exchange, gave her a bottle of Chanel No. 5 that I'd picked up in my rooms, and told her to be careful about telephone messages for me.

Then I had lunch in the restaurant. Afterwards I smoked a cigarette; then went down to the barber's shop and ordered a shave, a hair-trim and a face massage.

I lay back with the hot towels on my face and did a considerable amount of thinking. It didn't get me anywhere.

When the barber had finished with me, I felt a lot better. The tiredness was slipping away from me. I went up to my room, stripped, took a hot shower, got into fresh linen and clothes. Then I took a look at myself in the glass.

I thought it wasn't so bad. I saw a well-dressed serious-faced man of forty—tall, and a bit on the thin side-looking back at me out of the mirror. I thought the guy looked intelligent. I thought we'd know about that in a day or so.

Just then it occurred to me to think about what I was doing. I looked at myself in the mirror and decided that I wasn't quite certain about what I was doing. But I knew about two things. One was that I didn't like Ricaud, and the other was that I didn't like Mrs. Ivory. She'd tried to push me around mentally, and he'd definitely pushed me around physically.

I decided I didn't like that.

I went down in the lift and waited while the hall-porter got a cab. Then I drove round to Belgrave Square—to the address of Charles Quinceley, M.D.

I had to wait half an hour before I saw the doctor. I liked the look of him. He was about fifty years of age; had a lean, experienced face and greying hair. I decided that he was a direct and honest person. I thought I'd let him have it straight off the cuff and chance whether he would check up.

When I sat down in the chair in his consulting room, he took a long look at me and said: "I don't think I've seen you before, Mr. O'Hara. What can I do for you?"

·"Quite a lot," I told him. "I want to talk to you about a patient of yours—at least I think she's a patient."

He said: "Yes?" He gave me a cigarette out of a Siberian birch box; lighted it for me.

I said: "I know that doctors don't like discussing their patients' private affairs, but the exception always proves the rule. This is the exception."

He didn't say anything.

I went on: "I'm a private detective and I've been handling a very difficult case that concerns a woman who is, I believe, a patient of yours—a Mrs. Esmeralda Ricaud...."

He nodded. "She is—or was—my patient," he said. "I haven't seen her for some time."

                                        Peter Cheyney

"I don't want to go into too many details, doctor," I told him. "Because, like you, I don't like talking about my clients' business. So I'll make it as short as possible. I'm employed by Mrs. Ricaud's people to keep an eye on her. They have the idea that she's been taking drugs in fairly large doses; they believe that she's been getting them through her husband—Alexis Ricaud. They're fearfully worried because they think she's come to breaking point. So do I. You say she is—or was—your patient. I want you to do something about her."

"That's easily said, Mr. O'Hara," he said. "But Mrs. Ricaud is over twenty-one, and she's not certifiable as far as I know. Therefore I can only deal with her through her own instructions."

"Not in this case, doctor," I told him. "Something drastic has got to be done about Esmeralda Ricaud. If you tell me you're not interested, then there's only one thing for me to do. I shall have to hand her over to the police."

He looked serious. He said: "I'm sorry it's come to this. Her case has been a very difficult one for me— especially having regard to the husband—"

I jumped in on that one. I said: "just what do you mean by that? Do you mean that she has been getting the stuff from him?"

He said: "I don't know."

I grinned at him. "That's answered my question. You believe that she is getting the stuff from him but you're not going to say so officially."

He didn't say anything to that. After awhile he said: "Why do you think it necessary to hand her over to the police?"

"I'm going to do that only if you make me," I said. "The position is this: Last night I went down to a place in the country and met her down there. She was not only full of alcohol but she was also under the influence of drugs—either morphia or heroin—"

He said: "Probably heroin."

"All right," I said. "We'll settle for heroin. She was waiting about for her husband to show up and she was waving a .32 automatic pistol about. She told me that she was going to kill him. My belief is that if she'd seen him she would have killed him."

He shook his head sadly. "It's a great shame. She used to be such a nice girl. She must have slipped back during the past six months. She's not a strong type either physically or mentally, I'm sorry to say, and her heart isn't very good. If she doesn't stop racketing, she'll be seriously ill. The last time I saw her was about three or four months ago. I thought then that we might get her over the drug business, and she certainly wasn't drinking a lot. The trouble is she's very unhappy and isn't strong enough to stand up to unhappiness."

I said: "Do you expect that even a strong-minded woman would be able to stand up to Ricaud?"

He shrugged his shoulders. "I only saw him once," he said. "He's a peculiar type to say the least of it. I think he resented my endeavours to get his wife back to

                                   Peter Cheyney

normal. I think he persuaded her not to continue with her treatment. So what can I do?"

I waited for a few moments; then I said: "Look, doctor, this business can be serious. I believe that this woman is fed up to the teeth with Ricaud. I believe that she loathes the very sight of him, but that she's not sufficiently tough to kill him when she's fairly normal. So, in order that she shall be tough, she drinks—she practically told me so. And whisky and heroin aren't a good combination. One of these fine days—and pretty soon I should think—she's going to finish him off and everybody is going to get very bored with the situation."

He asked: "Have you any suggestion to make?"

I nodded. "I brought her back to London with me," I said. "She's with friends of mine. She passed out cold last night. She had a very feeble pulse and when we arrived in London she was really ill. All the usual post-addict symptoms. She's been put to bed with some mild stimulants and a couple of calomel-atropine ampoules. Now I've got to do something with her."

He asked: "What do you propose to do?"

"My idea is to put her into a nursing home. If I can do that, and you'll look after her, that's O.K. If you won't agree, I'll have to hand her over to the police."

He said: "That would be very bad for her. The idea of the nursing home is good. I would willingly do my best for her, but I doubt if she could be kept away from Ricaud. He seemed to me to be very persistent about having her with him. He's not an easy customer to deal with, I should say, and he's her husband. That makes things a little difficult."

"No," I said. "Ricaud isn't going to interfere with her. I'll see to that."

He looked happier. He said: "If you can guarantee that the patient will be left in my care without interference; if you will get her father or mother to write to me and say that they approve, I'll look after her. She could go into the nursing home at No. 12 Elham Street—just round the corner."

I got up. I said: "I'm glad I saw you. I'll deliver her to the matron at the Elham Street nursing home sometime this afternoon or early evening. Any bills can be sent to me at the Malinson Hotel."

"I'm glad you came," he said. "She used to be such a nice little thing. I'll look in and see her tonight. She'll be feeling not—so-good then. She'll be missing whatever it is she's been taking. I'll telephone the matron in a few minutes. They'll know what to do. Mrs. Ricaud's been in there before."

He came to the door with me. He said: "I take it you'll get either her father or mother to drop me a line and confirm what you've said?"

"Within a day or so," I said casually.

I picked up a cab in Sloane Street and went back to the Malinson. I paid off the cab; got the Rover out of the garage and drove round to Joe Melander's place. When he opened the flat door I asked about Esmeralda.

"She's not so good," said Joe. "She looks like hell; won't eat or drink anything. Millie says she's so depressed that she reckons if she was left alone for long she'd finish herself off."

"Nothing is ever as bad as it looks," I told him. I went upstairs and into Esmeralda's room. Mrs. Melander was sitting at the side of the bed. She got up and went away when I went in.

Esmeralda was sitting up in bed wearing a silk nightgown that had slipped off one thin shoulder. She was half-leaning against the wall on the far side of the bed. She looked like death.

I smiled at her. "Well... Esmeralda... everything's fixed. You're going into the Elham Street nursing home this afternoon. Doctor Quinceley will be round to see you there this evening. You won't know yourself in a fortnight's time."

"No?" she said very quietly. "I hardly know myself now." Some tears began to run down her face. She went on in the same low voice; "You're a fast worker, O'Hara."

I told her she was going to be all right.

"Like hell," she said. "I don't know that I want to be all right. I'd like to be dead—except that there are one or two things I'd like to see to first. Just one or two things..." She began to sob.

"Cut it out, Esmeralda," I told her cheerfully. "First of all, we've got to pick up some clothes and things for you. Mrs. Melander can do that. What about it?"

She tried to take a pull at herself. She said: "There is a bunch of keys in my handbag. It's the large Yale key.

My flat is in Montacute Place... near Welbeck Street...
No. 6 apartment at 18 Montacute Place."

I found the keys in her bag. I went outside and
found Joe. I asked him to take Mrs. Melander round to
18 Montacute Place in the car to pack some things for
Esmeralda. The sort of things she'd want in a nursing
home—and some clothes. He said O.K. They'd go right
away.

I went back to Esmeralda. She seemed to have
brightened up a little. I gave her a cigarette and lighted
one for myself.

She smoked silently for a little while. Then: "You're
a busy little bee, aren't you, O'Hara?" She laughed
weakly.

"What're you being a busy little bee for... what's it in
aid of? Why all this interest...?"

I said: "Why not?"

"What do you get out of it?" she asked. "I suppose
Leonora put you on to this. It's the sort of thing she'd
do."

"Leonora who?" I asked her.

"Leonora Ivory, of course," she said.

I didn't say anything. There was a long silence.

Then: "Are you a policeman or a detective or
something...?" she asked.

"A private detective," I said. I thought I'd let it go
at that.

But she wasn't satisfied. She did some more thinking.
Then: "Who's paying you, O'Hara?" She looked at me
sideways.

                                    Peter Cheyney

I thought: What could I lose? I said: "Mrs. Ivory."

There was another silence. Then she said very quietly: "I thought so. She's pretty good, isn't she, O'Hara?... As strong and wise as I'm weak and stupid and foolish." She began to cry again.

I thought the time had come to get somewhere. I said: "Listen, Esmeralda. All this can be straightened out. Everything will be all right. All you have to do is to steer clear of Ricaud. The rest is easy."

She began to dab her eyes. Then she looked at me. Her eyes were narrowed.

She said: "So the rest is easy. All I have to do is to keep away from Ricaud." She laughed. Out loud this time. That same shrill unpleasant laugh that I'd heard at "Crossways." She said: "It's so easy to talk about keeping away from Ricaud. It's a fine idea... if you can do it... but you can't... you can't... can't... can't... can't...!"

She was near hysteria.

I took the cigarette stub from between her fingers. I said harshly: "Lie down and keep quiet for a bit. There's nothing to worry about. Close your eyes and think of nothing. Don't be a bigger bloody fool than God made you."

She did what I told her. She lay back and closed her eyes.

I smoked another cigarette, and then I heard the Melanders arrive. I went into the sitting-room and talked to Joe, who was pouring out whisky.

They'd packed a couple of suitcases for Esmeralda. Mrs. Melander had found everything she wanted at the flat. She told me that she'd taken a good look round the place; that it was a nice place but badly looked after, and it wanted cleaning. I asked her if she'd seen any mail or telephone messages for Esmeralda. She said there weren't any.

She gave me back the keys. On my way back to the bedroom I slipped the big Yale key off the ring—the key to Esmeralda's flat—and put it in my pocket. Then I put the keys back in her handbag. By this time she was sitting up again.

I asked Mrs. Melander to get her ready for the move. Then I went and drank whisky with Joe. Half an hour afterwards Mrs. Melander came in with Esmeralda.

She looked as weak as hell, but she was wearing it all right. I gave her one small whisky and soda and she thanked everyone prettily for what they'd done for her. She seemed to be a little dazed about everything.

I'd arranged for Mrs. Melander to come with us to the nursing home. When we were starting, Esmeralda said: "O'Hara... give me my pistol. I want it."

"You don't," I told her. "You don't have to have a pistol in a nursing home. It's considered bad form to take pot-shots at the staff."

She said: "I don't want it. It isn't mine anyway. I borrowed it and I want to return it. Please give it to me. Please, O'Hara..."

I said: "No soap."

She sat down. The tears began to run down her cheeks. She said stubbornly: "Either I have the pistol or I don't go to the nursing home. Damn you, O'Hara, you know you can't make me go if I don't want to. Give me the pistol and I'll go like a lamb."

I said: "All right. I'll get it. It's in the car."

I went downstairs to the car and took the automatic pistol out of the dashboard compartment. On my way back I took a look at it. Somebody had scratched a small cross on the smooth part of the gun just under the safety catch. I thought the scratches seemed fairly recent.

Then I took out the ammunition clip which was fully loaded with ten shots, and put it in my pocket. She couldn't do any harm to herself with an empty gun. When I went into the sitting-room I took her handbag from her lap; opened it. I held the butt of the gun away from her whilst I was doing it so that she couldn't see I'd taken the ammunition clip out. I dropped the gun in the bag; closed it; put it back on her lap. That satisfied her.

I said so long to Joe and we went away.

Esmeralda said nothing at all on the way to the nursing home. She sat in the front passenger seat looking straight in front of her. But she wasn't seeing anything. Her eyes were vacant and tired.

It was nearly five o'clock when we got to Elham Street. The matron—a nice woman-told me that Quinceley had been through; that they knew what to do; that he'd told them he'd be round to see her in the evening.

I said so long to Esmeralda in the hall whilst we were waiting for the lift to come down. She looked drawn, tired to death and as miserable as hell. Her eyes were filled with tears and she was fighting to keep them back.

She said to me: "You're not a bad type, O'Hara. I like you." She tried to smile. "You're my favourite private detective. I do like you, O'Hara... Christmas Caryl O'Hara... O'Hara with the cut lip..."

They took her up in the lift. Afterwards, I wasn't sorry she'd said all that.

I drove Mrs. Melander back to Joe's place. I had a drink with Joe; then I drove back to the Malinson; put the car in the garage; told the attendant to fill the tank and level off the tyres at twenty-nine all the way round.

Then I went upstairs to my room. I took off some clothes, put on a dressing-gown, 'phoned down to the desk and asked them to give me a call at eight o'clock.

I was tired. But I wasn't so bored with things. And, anyway, I'd got Esmeralda off my hands.

I began to think about Mrs. Ivory. I remembered what Esmeralda had said about her. I wondered if I'd made a mistake about Leonora Ivory.

Supposing I had? Well... so what?

I got on the bed and went to sleep.

2

THE jangling of the telephone bell awakened me. I looked at my wrist-watch. It was just eight o'clock. I got up; ordered a double martini to be sent up to my room. Then I smoked a cigarette; dipped my face and head in cold water; dressed and drank the cocktail.

Peter Cheyney

I felt better. Until I began to think about Ricaud. Then I didn't feel so good. I concluded that there was only one thing to be done about that.

I went down to the restaurant and ate dinner. On the way, I picked up the small package that Blooey Stevens had left—the newly-cut keys of Pell's office. I put them on my key ring with the key of Esmeralda's flat.

After dinner I drove round to Montacute Place. I parked the Rover in a side street and had a look at No. 18. It was a good-class apartment block. The entrance doors were unlocked and if there was a porter he wasn't about. I found No. 6 on the first floor; let myself in.

I pulled the window curtains; then I switched on the electric lights and examined the place carefully.

It was a nice place. It consisted of a drawing-room, a small room that looked as if it had been used as a study, a bedroom, a connecting dressing-room, and a very well-appointed bathroom. At the other end of the short corridor was a kitchen, a maid's bedroom and a bathroom. Obviously, the kitchen and the maid's rooms hadn't been used for some time.

I went back to the main rooms. In the study, on the writing-table in the corner, placed in the centre of the blotter, was an envelope—with a large brass paper-weight on the corner to draw attention to it. It was unsealed and it was addressed to "Esmeralda." I opened it and read the note inside. It was written on a piece of blue notepaper with no address and it said:

My Charming, Unhappy Esmeralda,

How are you? As well as can be expected in the circumstances, I expect... Poor dear... "If there be no poppies shall the field be red?"

My sweet, I've decided that I'm bored with things as they are. Besides, I have a yen for the Bahamas and the hot sun and blue sea and skies and a beautiful and restless lady who resides in those sweet parts who is not entirely uninterested in Alexis!

So you will get what you want—if you are reasonable. Everything you want—if you are reasonable. But you must come down to "Crossways" tonight not later than ten o'clock. I am engaged at eleven-thirty but our business should not take long.

You will find that, in the circumstances, such as they are, I am prepared to be very reasonable.

Till then...

Alexis.

I put the note and the envelope in my pocket. In the drawing-room, in the drawer of a little bureau, I found some more of the blue writing paper. It looked to me as if Alexis had been to the apartment after the Melanders had left. He's been there to see Esmeralda; found she was out; left the note for her.

He's written the note at the bureau in the drawing-room. There was a clean sheet of blotting paper in the blotter on the little writing-desk. I held it in front of the wall mirror, and was able to identify the note to Esmeralda. He'd written another note too; before he'd written the Esmeralda note, because the second writing

                                    Peter Cheyney

was superimposed over the first. I could make out a word or two... "Crossways"... "twelve o'clock"... "later"...

I wondered who the second person was. Maybe that was the second appointment. He'd told Esmeralda that he was "engaged at eleven-thirty." If the second appointment had been for twelve o'clock he'd allowed ample time to get her out of the way before the second appointment. It was reasonable to tell her that it was for eleven-thirty, instead of twelve, so as to make certain of getting her out of the way. A not unusual process, as anyone knows.

I wandered about the place. I thought I might find something else. I saw nothing that interested me. The flat had a general air of untidiness that did not go with the furnishing and effects generally. I thought that Esmeralda had probably been looking after the place herself—or rather not looking after it.

I went away. I met no one on the stairs or in the entrance hall. I started up the car, lighted a cigarette and drove in the direction of Pell's office. I parked the car in a side street a couple of hundred yards away from the office and finished the journey on foot.

The street was quiet and deserted. I opened the downstairs door with the larger key; went up the stairs; unlocked the office door and went inside. I closed the door quietly; tried the door of Pell's office; found it open. Then I pulled the window blinds, switched on the light and started work on Pell's desk drawers.

Pell kept all his "private" cases under his own hand. I knew his system. He had specially-printed quarto diaries, ruled for cash, with an alphabetical index at the end. These diaries were used for addresses, confidential appointments and payments that were not intended to go through the normal office books, because these particular entries might divulge some part of an extremely confidential investigation to members of his staff.

After twenty minutes' work I got the locked double drawer open. I took the diaries out and examined them, beginning with the current year. There was no entry in the alphabetical index either under "I" or "R." I looked at the diary for the previous year—1945. I found it. Indexed under "R" was the name "Mrs. Alexis (or Leonora) Ricaud, née Ivory." The date under the index was "12th September, 1945." I turned to the 12th September page and found the note: "Mrs. Alexis Ricaud (or Ivory) of Steynehurst, Wych Cross, Sussex. Divorce pending. Husband's address Chilverton Arms, Fifth Avenue, New York City, N. Y. Attorney Hyram C. Metzling, Metzling & Fearns, Attorneys, Maerrick Building, New York City, N.Y. Paid cash on account as retainer £1,500."

This closed the entry. So Mrs. Ivory had been to see Pell as far back as September 1945; had paid him £1,500 in cash as retainer.

I looked through the books. Right at the back of the drawer was an alphabetical address book. I began to look through it. I'd got as far as the "B's" when I came across the name Birk. I remembered Birk. Birk had left Pell early in 1946 to work for the Transcontinental

Peter Cheyney

Agency in Maddox Street. His address shown in the book was 17, Ferndale Apartments, Albany Street, and the telephone number was Albany 98765.

I gathered from the entries that Mrs. Ricaud, as she was then, had been to see Pell about three or four months after she left Ricaud in America; that she was still calling herself Ricaud and that therefore her divorce from Ricaud had not then been completed. It would be some time after that that Birk had left Pell to work for the Transcontinental Agency. Birk, I knew, was a good operative, and Pell had been sorry to lose him. I thought Birk might know something about Mrs. Ivory.

I made a note of what I wanted; put the books away; relocked the desk drawer with the "spider" key I had used to open it; closed up the offices and went away. I walked back to the car and sat in the driving seat thinking.

I looked at my watch. It was eleven o'clock. I started the car, drove round to the all-night Post Office in Charing Cross Road and sent a cable:

```
CALEY   JERRIS.   JERRIS   RESEARCH   AND
INVESTIGATIONS      176      TWENTY-SECOND
STREET,   NEW   YORK   CITY,   N.Y.   RUSH
ALL  AVAILABLE  RECORDS  INFORMATION  RE
ALEXIS  RICAUD  BACKGROUND  ASSOCIATES
ALSO  MRS.  ALEXIS  RICAUD  BORN  LEONORA
IVORY  MARRIED  NEW  YORK  STATE  BETWEEN
JANUARY  AND  JUNE  1945  STOP  DIVORCE  SUIT
IVORY  RICAUD  BEGUN  APPROXIMATELY  THREE
FOUR  MONTHS  AFTER  MARRIAGE  STOP  CHARGE
```

After I had sent the cable I drove out to Notting Hill Gate. I found Sado's house and rang the bell. It was a long time since I'd seen him, and I hoped he hadn't moved off somewhere. I need not have worried. He opened the door himself and stood, looking at me, his lined brown face creased with the usual smile.

He bowed. He said in Japanese: "Greeting, O'Hara. The patient reed bends before the wind."

I bowed gravely, and said in the same language: "Greeting to you, Sado. Because the reed bends it does not break." This was a gag from the old days.

We both laughed. I went inside after him.

Sado was a good guy. He was good Japanese. He had all the virtues of his race and none of its vices. Or if he had, they weren't apparent. He'd done some good work for British Intelligence in Japan during the War. And when I say good I mean just that. If the Japanese had got him they would have boiled him alive.

We went into his sitting-room which looked a cross between East and West, with a little U.S.A. thrown in. He looked just the same. A thin, wizened, brown face that was as ageless as time, small constant eyes that looked straight in front all the time; the relaxed hanging arms and fingers of the judoka; the thin supple body of a man who could get through two days on a handful of rice.

I said: "Sado, last night I used judo against a bad man. He told me afterwards he was a Black-Belt of the tenth degree. I can believe it. I was useless against him."

He looked at me gravely. He asked: "Why, O'Hara?"

I told him. I told him how Ricaud had put a wrist crush on me before I could even get started against him. I described what he had done to me.

He said: "O'Hara, this man is well-trained in the faith of judo. Is he a very bad man?"

I said yes.

Sado said: "The faith of judo embraces the science of giving way before attack and defeating the aggressor by the going away from him. But against the evil-doer the faith of judo allows for atimi—the secret blows—but only for good. Swear to me, O'Hara, by your ancestors that if I teach you some part of the atimi you will use it only against the evil-doer."

I swore the Japanese oath.

He showed me three atimi. They were "attack" blows. Their simplicity, intensity and results were startling.

It was twenty minutes to twelve when I left Sado. The roads were clear and I thought I should make Maidenhead in an hour. I was looking forward to seeing Ricaud again. I began to feel a little sorry for him.

3

I WAS on the other side of Maidenhead by twelve forty-five. When I reached the dirt road behind "Crossways" I switched the car lights off. I left the car on the road a hundred yards from the back entrance to the house in the shadow of some bushes. I went through the iron gates at the back, along the gravel drive, and turned off into the path through the trees. When I passed through the clearing where I'd found Esmeralda dancing I thought about her. I thought maybe she'd had a lot of hard luck. I thought that life could be not-so-funny for women like Esmeralda. Some people had all the breaks; others—whom you'd expect to have all the breaks—got a poke in the eye. Money wasn't everything. Esmeralda may have had money, but I'd an idea she hadn't had much else. Now she hadn't even got the money. Life had seen her coming; had given her a tough deal.

The back door—the one that she and I had used the night before—was open. I don't know why that surprised me but for some reason I'd expected it to be locked. I went in; closed the door very quietly behind me; made my way along the passageway. There was no doubt in my mind but that I should find Ricaud at home. I thought that maybe he might even have his second visitor with him—that is if my guess at the writing I'd looked at in the mirror at Esmeralda's flat had been right.

Well... I wouldn't mind that. The situation would be very funny. The idea of giving Ricaud a bigger beating up than he'd given me appealed to me a lot—and I knew that with the three new tricks I'd learned from Sado he was mine.

And if his visitor was there to see the fun so much the better. I was pretty certain that I knew who that visitor was going to be. I rather liked that too.

When I approached the drawing-room I saw the light under the bottom of the door. I went in. I stood inside the room with my back to the door. Ricaud was lying on the settee in front of the electric fire. He was alone. One arm lay indolently along the back of the settee. The fingers were relaxed. He was asleep.

I said: "Good evening, Ricaud. Remember me? I'm O'Hara."

I walked across the room. I expected him to get up. He didn't. When I got near I saw why. He wasn't asleep. He was dead. From where I was standing by the side of the fireplace looking directly at him, the sight wasn't pretty. There was a lot of blood all over the settee, which was very close to the fire. His right hand was hanging down over the edge of the settee which was a low one. The fingers were actually touching the off-white rug. Just beneath them was an automatic pistol. I could see it was a .32 Colt.

I went close and had a look. Then I saw the note. The note was on the floor just near the gun, but two-thirds of the sheet of octavo paper was hidden under the settee. I took my handkerchief out of my pocket, put it over my fingers, drew the note out and read it. It said:

My delightful wife,

So you won't play.

But my time has not been wasted. I have had time to think and I have come to the conclusion that I am sufficiently tired of you, of the Ivory, of the world in general—and two or three people in particular—to want to deal with things in an adequate manner.

And so I am going to deal with it. I am going to deal with it in a way that I hope will make a great deal of trouble for all of you. And this is the way....

I put the sheet of notepaper back where I'd found it. I looked at Ricaud closely. It was suicide all right. I could see the powder burns round the inlet hole where the bullet had gone in. The flesh was badly burned. The gun had been held very close to, if not right on, the head. From where the gun was I could see how his hand had fallen away after death and the gun had dropped out of it.

I was disappointed. I was disappointed because I didn't want Ricaud dead. I had wanted him alive. I had wanted to deal with him myself because he'd beaten me up. Well, I wasn't going to do it.

I looked round the room. Over in the corner, in front of the curtained windows on the left-hand side of the room facing the doorway from the fireplace, was a writing-table. The desk lamp was still on. I went over and looked at it. On the blotter, in the middle, was an octavo writing-pad of the same paper that the suicide note was written on. There was a fountain pen with the cap off lying by the side of the pad. I picked up the pen with my handkerchief and ran the nib over the palm of my hand. The ink was still flowing. The nib hadn't had time to dry off completely. The pen had been used within the last couple of hours; otherwise the flow

                                    Peter Cheyney

would have dried off and the pen would have required shaking before it would write. I put the pen back.

I went back to the fireplace. I came to the conclusion that there is some sort of justice or retribution, or whatever you like to call it, in the world. I thought of Esmeralda. This would be good news for her even if it was a tough ending for Ricaud.

And there was nothing else for me to do. I don't know why but as I stood there looking at the defunct Ricaud—who was a rat if ever there was one—I felt an odd wave of regret come over me just because there was nothing else for me to do.

I lighted a cigarette; put on my hat which I had thrown on a chair when I came into the room; walked over to the door; went through. I was in the passage with the door nearly closed behind me when I stopped. I thought of something.

When you're in my business you make a habit of mentally photographing things; of getting a quick picture of rooms and people. Standing there in the darkness, a little voice in my mind told me there was something wrong with the set-up. I went back into the lighted room. I stood by the door looking around me. Then I got it. The settee on which Ricaud was lying was too near the electric fire. The sense of incongruity in my mind had arisen from the fact that when I was kneeling down examining his head I'd felt my leg being burned by the heat of the fire. When Ricaud had committed suicide he'd been lying on that settee and it would have been too hot, even for a would-be suicide.

I went back to the fireplace. I got the idea. Somebody had moved that settee nearer to the fire after Ricaud was dead. Why? There was only one reason I could think of. Situated as it was at the moment, the heat from the electric fire would delay rigor mortis. No doctor, with that fire going for some hours, would be able to state definitely the time of death.

I came to the very quick conclusion that Ricaud had not committed suicide. Somebody had shot him. I thought for a moment about the second caller—the person with whom Ricaud had had an appointment at twelve o'clock. It was too late for them to arrive if they hadn't already arrived. The time was nearly ten minutes past one. I thought I was fairly safe in taking things easy.

I went back to the car, taking care to keep in the shadows in case anyone should come along the road, although that was unlikely at this time, and got my electric torch out of the dashboard compartment. I went back, through the drawing-room where Ricaud was, and went over the house.

I started upstairs because I thought that Ricaud would probably only have used a couple of rooms if he were there alone—a bedroom and the drawing-room downstairs. So I concentrated on the bedroom. I found his room fairly quickly. I found it because the electric fire was half on.

The curtains were drawn and I switched the light on. I went over the room with a fine-tooth comb, but I didn't find anything that mattered until I came to the table set up against the wall opposite the bed. It had been used as a writing-table and the single drawer was unlocked. I opened it. Inside was Ricaud's passport, a letter signed by a woman and sent from an address in Nassau in the Bahamas—a more than affectionate letter, and Ricaud's airplane tickets dated the following day. He hadn't lied in the note he'd left for Esmeralda at her flat in Montacute Place, for he was going to the Bahamas. That made the suicide thing more improbable than ever. Now I was certain he'd been murdered.

I stood looking down at the passport, the letter and the tickets. Then I got an idea. I didn't think it was true, but I thought it just might be. I picked up the passport, the letter and the tickets; put them in my inside breast pocket. I turned off the electric fire, using my handkerchief on the switch. I switched off the light the same way. Then I went back to the drawing-room.

Ricaud had been shot and somebody had framed it to look like suicide. And Ricaud himself had contributed to that scheme—unwittingly but effectively. I began to get a lot of ideas about that. I bent down to the bottom of the settee, got my hands underneath it; raised it off the floor with an effort; moved the bottom part three feet away from the fire. I repeated the process with the top end. Now the settee was in its normal position.

I moved back to the front of the fireplace. Then I got down on my hands and knees so that I could get a look along the floor. Then I found it. Under the edge of the off-white rug which had been hidden by the settee when it was near the fire was a spent cartridge case. I picked it up and smelt it. It was the discharged case from a .32 Colt automatic. Whoever it was had tried to turn Ricaud's murder into an apparent suicide had moved the settee over the edge of the rug, effectively concealing the discharged cartridge case. So that there wouldn't be anyone's finger-prints on it. I put it in my pocket. Now I had my prints on it.

I went over to the sideboard, opened it, got out the whisky and a glass, gave myself a drink. I held the bottle and glass with my handkerchief; wiped the glass after I'd had the drink; put them back. Then I put on my hat and went out.

I went out of the back door and along the path towards the clearing. I could have gone one of two ways—either by the path I was on, or by taking the wider path that led from the side door to the main gravel drive leading to the back entrance gates. The moon was out and I walked slowly. My idea was to get down on to the back drive at the point where the path left it, and that was all I was thinking about. I was nearing the clearing when my foot kicked something hard under the shadow of a rhododendron bush. I picked it up.

It was a .32 Colt automatic. I looked around me; went into a thick coppice behind some trees. I put the gun on the ground; knelt down by it; sheltered the gun with my coat and put the torch-light on it.

I was right. The gun I had kicked was Esmeralda's. There was the cross scratched on the butt that I had seen that afternoon. And that was that!

I put the gun in my pocket; continued on my way. I kept my eye on the ground for anything else that had been dropped. I saw nothing. When I got to the point where the path ran off from the gravel drive, I walked along the grass verge, looking at the drive. What I saw was quite obvious in the moonlight.

There were two distinct sets of tyre tracks. I spent a lot of time crawling about the grass verge that ran alongside the gravel drive, and when I'd finished I came to this conclusion: One car had been driven up to the garage; had later been reversed out of the garage and driven away. Then another car—a lighter car—had arrived. I could see where the tracks of the second car crossed the going-out tracks of the first car. The markings on the tyres of the first car were regular. I should say they were balloon Dunlop tyres. The markings of the tyres of the second car were distinctive. Three of the wheels had fairly small tyres with a vertical tread, but the fourth tyre—the rear near-side tyre—was an odd one. It had a regular diamond tread all round it.

I went back to the drawing-room. I gave myself another drink, using the same technique with the bottle and glass as I had before. I sat down in a chair not far from the late unlamented Ricaud, and did a considerable amount of thinking. I must have been there for a quarter of an hour. At the end of that time I thought I knew as much as I wanted to know, and what I didn't know I could guess. So I had to do something about it.

I went out to the garage. I went in—the doors were open—switched on the electric light and started work. First of all I took from my pocket the spent cartridge case that I'd picked up from the rug in the drawing-room—the case of the bullet that had killed Ricaud. I stood the case up on its end and knocked the open end inwards with a spanner which I found on the work-bench. I put that cartridge case carefully on one side. Then I took Esmeralda's pistol out of my pocket. I handled it very gingerly with my handkerchief. I smelt the barrel. The gun had been fired. Using my finger-nail so as not to mess up any prints, I worked out the ammunition clip and wiped it. It was a ten-shot clip and it contained nine live shells. I pushed them out of the clip one by one. Then I took out a penknife and got busy. I worked out the lead slugs out from each cartridge case. When I'd got the nine slugs I put them in my pocket. Then I knocked the open ends of the empty cases inwards with the spanner. Then I put the empty cases back in the ammunition clip using my finger and thumb in such a manner as to leave my fingerprints on them. Then I put the clip back in the automatic. I'd handled the gun earlier that afternoon when I had given it to Esmeralda so one set of my prints would be on it somewhere underneath the prints of the person who'd used it afterwards. But there would only be one set of prints on the cartridge cases. They would be mine.

I switched off the light; went back to the drawing-room. I took the cartridge case which I had picked up from the rug, the open end of which I had now knocked in to match up with its fellows in the ammunition clip in Esmeralda's gun. I placed it just under the edge of the rug where it would be found if somebody were really

                                    Peter Cheyney

looking for something like that. Then I gave myself another drink; put the bottle and glass away; took a final look at Ricaud and went away.

I went back along the path towards the clearing. I dropped Esmeralda's gun and kicked it under the rhododendron bush where I'd found it. It would take a great deal of searching to find that gun. I continued on my way, slipped through the iron gates, started up the car, lit a cigarette and drove towards London. On the way back I checked over what I'd done.

I might have made a mistake but I didn't think so.

4

I STOPPED the car at the telephone call box at the Great West Road intersection. I looked at my watch. It was a quarter to three. I looked up the number of the Elham Street nursing home and called through. After a bit somebody answered.

I said: "I'm sorry to bother you so late, but I've an urgent message for Mrs. Ricaud. I wonder if you could give it to her in the morning."

The voice at the other end said: "Who is that, please?"

I said: "I'm Mr. O'Hara. I brought Mrs. Ricaud to the nursing home this afternoon."

The night sister said: "Oh, yes, Mr. O'Hara... but I'm very sorry to tell you that Mrs. Ricaud isn't here. She left tonight—we think about ten o'clock."

I made my voice sound astonished. "What!... She's left? But why... I don't understand?"

"Neither do we," she said. "She must have slipped out when the night nurse in charge was in the service-room. We're all terribly upset about it."

I asked: "Have you done anything about it?"

She said: "What could we do? Matron has telephoned Doctor Quinceley and told him."

I asked: "Had Doctor Quinceley seen her before she left?"

"Oh, yes," said the night sister. "He came in about eight o'clock. He saw Mrs. Ricaud and he was very pleased with her. He had a long talk with her and left her much more contented. We're all fearfully upset about her going away like that. You see, she's not at all well. It's very worrying."

I said: "You're telling me! Thanks, sister, I'll get in touch with Doctor Quinceley."

I hung up-the receiver. I went out of the telephone box; got into the car; started up the engine. I thought that was that.

I drove back to the Malinson Hotel; put the car away in the garage; went upstairs; went to bed.

Because there wasn't anything else to do. Nothing that I could think of.

CHAPTER THREE

WEDNESDAY — CLIMAX
1

I WOKE up at nine o'clock, ate breakfast and telephoned through to Birk at the number I'd got out of Pell's address book. He was just leaving to work on a case he was handling for the Transcontinental people. I made a date for him to have lunch with me at the Premier in Albemarle Street at one o'clock.

I spent the morning quietly in the lounge at the Malinson, which is a good, slightly old-fashioned hotel. I read the papers and magazines and did a lot of thinking. I was sorting things out but only up to a point.

When I arrived at the Premier, Birk was sitting on a high stool at the lunch counter downstairs. He was a man about forty-five years of age who had been free-lancing in the detective business from the time he was thirty until he took his present job on the staff of the Transcontinental Agency. At the time he was working for Pell in 1945 he had worked as a free-lance when he wanted to and when the money offered was good enough. He was a keen, reliable man with a good record.

We ate lunch and afterwards, at my suggestion, drove along to a quiet café I knew near Regent Street. Birk didn't ask any questions because he knew that I hadn't telephoned him to ask about the state of his health. He was waiting for me to talk.

When we were in the café, drinking our coffee, I pushed two five-pound notes across the table. He folded them up; put them in his pocket.

He said: "So this is business, O'Hara?" He grinned at me. "By the dough it looks like a nice case. Is this just a little on account? You know I'm tied up with the Continental. I can't work outside."

I said: "Just a few questions. And the answers are easy. And to me they're cheap at ten pounds."

He grinned again. "That depends how useful they are to you. Go ahead."

I said: "You were working for Pell on some jobs in October, November and December 1945 and in January and February 1946. I did some jobs for him in the last months of 1945. We met about that time. Right?"

He nodded.

"What did you think of Pell?" I asked.

He shrugged his shoulders. "I think he was too clever. He thought too much of the money and not enough of the job. He used to try and cut down on his own staff and the outside men he used. He was mean."

I asked: "Why?... Wasn't he making money?"

"He made big money," said Birk; "but he never had enough of it to please him. He was nuts about dough. I've known him fall down on a damn good commercial case where he'd been paid a hell of a retainer just because he was trying to make on expenses. He was that sort of mug—money mad and mean."

I asked him: "Did you ever hear of a Mrs. Ivory?"

"Sure," said Birk. "I heard of her and I saw her. Some woman. She had everything. She was a lovely piece, with a lot of money."

"What did she want with Pell?" I asked.

He shrugged his shoulders. "Search me. You know how damn close he is about jobs he handles himself. I saw her once or twice sometime towards the middle or the end of 1945. It was just before Pell went to America on some case. He was away a couple of months, I believe. Soon after that I stopped working for him. I got fed up with being stuck on the tough stuff that he didn't care to handle, being paid damn-all and knowing that he was getting away with big fees. So I signed off his free-lance list and went to the Transcontinental as a staff man."

I finished my coffee and got up. I said: "Thanks, Birk. I'll be on my way."

"What I've told you is dear for a ten-spot," he said. "Anything else I can do?"

I said no. We said so-long and I went.

I drove round to the nursing home in Elham Street and saw the matron. She was fed up and worried about Esmeralda. She wasn't used to that sort of thing. Nursing homes are run on pretty regular lines and they don't like the customers taking a run-out powder just when they feel like it. Especially when they're dope-addicts.

She told me all about it. She talked because I suppose Quinceley had told her I was working for the family.

She said: "After you'd gone yesterday afternoon, Mr. O'Hara, I saw Mrs. Ricaud. She'd been put to bed in a pleasant room on the second floor. We knew about her because she'd been here as a patient before. She wasn't very well, but after a while she seemed to pick up. Her pulse was steadier; she seemed brighter and was obviously trying to make the best of herself.

"Doctor Quinceley came to see her at eight o'clock. I think he'd come prepared to prescribe a reduced dose of a barbituric drug for her, but she said she'd rather try to do without it. She told him that she was fed up with the way she'd been living and that she was really going to try and take a pull at herself.

"I think he believed her. He gave her a long comforting talk and said that he would leave some sedative tablets for her in case she couldn't get off to sleep easily—although she was very exhausted and should have been able to sleep and that he would come and see her again in the morning. He told her that if she felt bad then he would prescribe a reduced quantity of heroin. I think he was trying to get her to go as long as she possibly could without recourse to drugs.

"After he'd gone, she seemed to settle down nicely. She seemed to be dozing, the nurse on duty said, and eventually appeared to go off to sleep. I say appeared because there is no doubt that she took this opportunity to get out of bed, put on her underthings which had been put away in her room and get back into bed with her night-gown over them.

"The night nurse came on at ten o'clock. At about a minute after that time, Mrs. Ricaud rang her bell and when the nurse answered it, said that she would like to take the sedative tablets. The nurse fetched them, with a glass of water; then Mrs. Ricaud asked if she might have some tea. She knew the night nurse would have to go to the service room at the end of the corridor to make the tea. Whilst the nurse was away Mrs. Ricaud must have put on the rest of her clothes, slipped downstairs and out of the front entrance. Unfortunately, owing to the shortage of staff we have no night porter."

I said: "So she left about five or six minutes past ten?"

"Yes," said the matron, "about then. It's a most distressing thing to have happened. Directly the matter was reported to me I telephoned, at once, to Doctor Quinceley, but of course there was nothing he could do. Do you think you'll be able to find her, Mr. O'Hara?"

"I hope so," I said. I wondered just where she thought I was going to start looking for Esmeralda. I told her I'd go and see Doctor Quinceley as soon as I could and went off.

I got into the car and thought for a bit; then I drove in the direction of Pell's office. I parked the car some way from the office and walked quietly up the street looking for his car. It was parked in its usual place. I looked at the rear near-side tyre. The other three tyres were of a kind, but this one was an odd one—a fairly new one—and it had a diamond tread on it.

So now I knew. I knew that the tyre marks I'd seen on the back carriage drive at "Crossways" were the marks of Pell's tyres. And as these tyre-marks were the top ones it meant that he'd been there last. Somebody had driven in and, probably later, driven out again, and then Pell had arrived.

And that was that. And it meant a lot. The pieces in the jig-saw were beginning to fit.

I walked back to the car and drove round to Montacute Place. When I got there I rang the entrance bell and waited inside the hall for the porter.

After a minute he appeared from somewhere downstairs. He was an elderly man with grey hair, an intelligent face and one arm—an ex-service type from the 1914 War, I thought.

I said: "I'm a private detective. My name's O'Hara. I'm trying to find Mrs. Ricaud. She got out of a nursing home last night about ten o'clock and disappeared; she's very ill and ought not to be out. D'you know anything about it?"

"Why, yes, sir," he said. "She came here last night. I spoke to her. I thought she looked very ill. But she didn't leave word where she was going. She—"

I interrupted. "What time did she get here?"

"It would be about a quarter past ten," said the hall-porter. "She couldn't get into her flat. She said she'd lost the key off her key-ring. I opened the door for her with my pass key. She seemed sort of excited and funny-looking."

I asked: "What happened then?"

"I gave her the telephone message I'd received, just a few minutes before she got here."

                                      Peter Cheyney

I took out my wallet and gave him a pound-note.

"What message?" I asked.

"The message I'd received from Mr. Ricaud," he answered. "He came through on my line downstairs, sir. He'd got through to my office because he couldn't get any reply from the flat. He said that he'd expected to see Mrs. Ricaud at ten o'clock; that he'd left a note for her at the flat during the afternoon. I told him that she hadn't been in and so she couldn't have had it."

"What did he say to that?" I asked.

"He seemed a bit put out," said the hall-porter. "As a matter of fact he seemed angry about something. He said: 'Oh, very well... you can tell her if you see her tonight that I shall be writing her. She'll get my letter sometime to-morrow, and you can tell her that I hope she likes it.'"

"What happened when you told Mrs. Ricaud that?"

"She stood in the hallway of the flat looking at me," he said. "She looked sort of... well, stupid... if you know what I mean, sir. Then she told me to go down and telephone to the Lynn Garage just near here and tell them to send a hired car round at once, and then she asked me if I could get her some whisky."

"You got the hired car?" I asked.

He nodded. "It was round in a few minutes, sir. I went up to the flat to tell her and to take up half a bottle of whisky I'd got for her. The flat door was open and I could hear her in the bedroom opening and shutting drawers. I could hear her cuss when she couldn't get the drawers open. Then she came out and I gave her the whisky. I told her that the hired car was here. She said all right, and then, she began to complain about the telephone. She said she'd been trying to get a number but couldn't even get the exchange—the 'phone's been a bit funny lately. When I said I'd try, she said no, it didn't matter."

"Did she seem any better?" I asked.

"Yes, she did, sir," he said. "I was surprised at the difference. She seemed to have more life about her. And her hands weren't shaking like they were when she came in."

"Then what?" I asked.

"I went downstairs to tell the car to wait. She came down about five minutes later. She got into the car and went off. She didn't leave any message and she didn't say where she was going."

I gave him another pound note. "I'd like to take a look round the flat," I said.

He thought for a moment or two and then said all right. I followed him up the stairs. He opened the flat door with his pass key.

I said: "You'd better go downstairs and wait in the hall for a bit. There may be some C.I.D. men coming along from Scotland Yard. Bring them up here when they come."

I had to pull that one. I knew he wouldn't have left me alone in the flat if I hadn't. But that satisfied him. He went off.

I took a quick look into the drawing-room. It looked as if Esmeralda had been throwing things about.

Probably she'd been trying to find the note from Ricaud. The one I'd taken. The telephone was off its cradle. I put it back. Then I went into the bedroom. I went round the room trying to find a drawer that wouldn't open easily. The drawer that had caused Esmeralda to curse at its stiffness.

I found it. It was one of the small, upper drawers in the dressing-table. I had to coax it open. When I looked inside I saw what I wanted to see. There was an empty heroin ampoule and a syringe. There were one or two feminine knick-knacks. And there was a fully-loaded ten-shot magazine clip for a .32 automatic pistol in a small cardboard box that was made to take three clips.

I thought I knew about those three clips. One of them was the one I'd taken out of her gun before I'd given it back to her the previous afternoon. The second was the one she'd reloaded into the pistol when she came to the flat; and I was looking for the third one.

I thought that wasn't so good.

I put the cardboard box with the ammunition clip in my jacket pocket and closed the drawer. Now I knew all about it—more or less.

I went back into the sitting-room and had another look. I found the half-bottle of whisky stuck down at the back of the settee. Half of it was gone. I sat on the settee, the bottle in my hand, and thought about what had happened.

It was easy. She'd never intended to stay in the nursing home. She knew she'd got some dope at the flat and she intended to get it. She knew that if she stayed in the nursing home, Quinceley would put her through a cure and she wasn't going to stand for it. She'd had that before. So she'd got out and she'd gone back to the flat and given herself a shot of heroin. Then she felt better.

Then she began to think about the message that Ricaud had given to the hall-porter. She went into the drawing-room and tried to get him on the telephone, but she was impatient and wouldn't wait. She slammed the telephone down, went back into the bedroom, opened the drawer again, took out one of the clips of ammunition, loaded it into her gun and put the gun in her handbag. She closed the drawer and went back into the hall, complained about the telephone, went into the drawing-room and took a swig at the whisky.

I could hear her voice saying the words she'd said to me at "Crossways" the first time I'd met her. I could hear her saying... "When I've had a drink I begin to think... I think about him in a certain way... the way I always think about him when I'm not with him... about killing him... I like the idea..."

I took a look at the neck of the half-bottle of whisky. There was lipstick on it. I thought it was goddam funny that no matter how tough things were with a woman she'd always think about putting on some lipstick. Even if she had on her mind what Esmeralda had on hers.

I wiped the neck of the bottle with my handkerchief and took a pull. I felt better.

I closed the flat door and went down to the hall. The hall-porter was waiting.

                                        Peter Cheyney

I asked him: "Leaving last night out of the question, when did you see Mrs. Ricaud last?"

He scratched his head. Then: "It would be Monday, sir... last Monday. She was in during the afternoon and evening. She'd ordered some sandwiches to be sent up at nine o'clock in the evening because she was going to a party and wouldn't have time for dinner. I think somebody came to see her after nine o'clock—before she went out."

"Who came to see her?" I asked.

"I don't know," he said. "But I went up to the flat to bring down the tray after she'd gone—she went out about ten o'clock; said she'd be coming back before she went to the party. And I noticed there was two glasses on the sandwich tray. Somebody else had had a drink with her."

"D'you know who?" I asked him.

He shook his head. "People come in an' go out. It's not like the old days when we always had a porter on duty. I don't know who it was."

"Did you see her when she came back?" I asked. "Before she went to the party."

"Yes," said the hall-porter. "She was out about half an hour, and during that time I came into the entrance hall after going down to the basement, and found someone had left a parcel there for her..."

I interrupted. "What was the parcel like? And how was it addressed?"

"It was a small cardboard box about eight inches by three," he replied. "And the address was typewritten on a label. I took it up to the flat," he went on, "and gave it to her when she came in. She was in a funny state then... worse than ever...."

I said: "And then she went off to the party?"

"Yes, sir," said the porter, "about ten minutes after that, I should think. And I didn't see her again until last night..."

I said: "Thanks.... I've telephoned through to Scotland Yard. The C.I.D. men won't be coming here tonight after all."

He said: "Thank you, sir. I hope you find Mrs. Ricaud. She's always very nice to me. Everybody likes her. I hope she'll be all right."

"She'll be all right," I said, "I hope."

I meant it too.

2

I DROVE back to the Malinson; put the car in the garage; then I went into the cocktail bar at the back of the lounge; I drank two whiskies and sodas. The bar was full of people who seemed to be enjoying themselves.

After a bit I went upstairs; took a hot shower, lay down on the bed and smoked a cigarette.

I didn't think it looked very good for Esmeralda, and I thought it was a damned shame. As far as I could see she was a person who'd never had very much brains and perhaps not a great deal of character—one of those young women who go for lush romantic novels when they are young and never really grow out of the stage.

Peter Cheyney

As far as I could see she'd only done one thing in her life that was really wrong, and that was marrying Ricaud, and she'd done that because she'd loved him; because she thought he was a great guy; because at that time he'd seemed everything in the world that had mattered to her.

Well, you couldn't blame her for that. A much cleverer, stronger personality could have thought the same thing. A much cleverer and stronger personality had thought the same thing. Mrs. Ivory had thought it. Mrs. Ivory, who was no fool, had been attracted to Ricaud; had thought he was good enough to marry. If he could pull the wool over her eyes, what chance had Esmeralda got? I thought about her as I'd seen her last—a weak, trembling, shattered thing, standing by the lift gate in the nursing home trying to keep back her tears. I thought that although I wasn't given very much to sentimentality, it wouldn't be very difficult to be sentimental over Esmeralda, even if she had killed Ricaud; even if she was a murderess. Because it seemed to me that even if the law doesn't allow it, some killings are justified. I hoped the jury would feel like that too.

I got up; walked across to the telephone; rang down for The Evening News. It came up in a few minutes. I got back on the bed and looked through the paper. I found it on the front page. They'd given it about four inches. It said:

WEALTHY MAN FOUND SHOT DEAD
PISTOL AND NOTE BY BODY

With an automatic pistol by his side, Mr. Alexis Ricaud was found shot dead in his home, "Crossways," Maidenhead, this afternoon.

The discovery was made at three o'clock by Mrs. Eliza Frampton, employed at the house as a daily cleaner.

Mr. Ricaud is believed to have been of foreign extraction and to have come to England from the United States. He had been the tenant of "Crossways," a fine Georgian house and one of the show places of the district, for the past year.

His body was found by Mrs. Frampton on a settee in the drawing-room, one of the few rooms in use in the house. The pistol was on a hearth rug by the settee and nearby was a note apparently written by Mr. Ricaud.

The Divisional Police Surgeon who examined the body is satisfied that Mr. Ricaud shot himself. The inquest will be held on Saturday.

So that was that!

I put my head back on the pillow; looked at the ceiling and smoked. I wondered if Esmeralda would get away with it. I didn't see why she shouldn't. That depended on where she was and how much she'd talked if she had talked. I thought she stood a chance, but only a chance. I thought about the hall-porter at Montacute Place, and Quinceley. I began to wish I hadn't talked quite so freely to Quinceley, but maybe that would be all right.

The telephone jangled. It was the girl on the switchboard. She said brightly: "There's a cable for you, Mr. O'Hara. Shall I send it up?"

I asked her to send it up at once. For some reason which I couldn't quite determine at the moment I was a little bit excited to read that cable. Jerris had worked quickly.

The boy brought it up. I took the envelope from him; gave him a shilling. He went away. I opened the cable. It was from Jerris all right. It said:

LEONORA IVORY MARRIED ALEXIS RICAUD QUEENS COUNTY STATE OF NEW YORK 5TH MAY 1945 STOP WIFE BROUGHT DIVORCE SUIT AUGUST 1ST PLAINT AND SUMMONS IN SUIT SERVED ON RICAUD AUGUST 10TH BUT NO FURTHER PROCEEDINGS TAKEN NO RECORD OF HEARING OR DECREE BEING GRANTED OR PETITION DISMISSED STOP HAVE CONTACTED ATTORNEYS METZLING AND FEARNS CONFIDENTIALLY AND ASCERTAINED THEY RECEIVED INSTRUCTIONS TO STOP DIVORCE PROCEEDINGS STOP ALEXIS RICAUD BACKGROUND SOMBRE TWO CHARGES BLACKMAIL ONE STATE OF NEW YORK ONE ILLINOIS BOTH ABANDONED AFTER PROCEEDINGS HAD BEEN BROUGHT IMAGINE COMPLAINANT SCARED TO PROCEED IN EACH CASE STOP RICAUD CHARMING CLEVER PLAY-BOY NO KNOWN MEANS OF SUPPORT STOP BELIEVED TO HAVE LIVED ON WOMEN EVIDENCE OF VARIOUS LARGE SUMS RECEIVED FROM DOWAGER TYPES STOP WILL RUSH FURTHER INFORMATION IF POSSIBLE GOOD LUCK COLEY JERRIS.

So that was that! Mrs. Ivory had brought suit for divorce against Ricaud on the 1st August 1945. The original petition, which the Americans call a plaint and summons, was served on him on the 10th August, but nothing further had been done. The case had been dropped. I thought I knew the answer to that one.

With regard to the information about Ricaud, I wasn't surprised. It all fitted in.

Now, I'd got to do something about it. The time had come when I had to have a talk with Mrs. Ivory. I swung my legs off the bed and sat there, in my underclothes, thinking about seeing Mrs. Ivory.

I dressed, went down to the restaurant and ate dinner.

3

DRIVING a car at night when the roads are clear and the weather fine makes it easy to think. You can keep your eyes on the road and drive almost automatically, with most of your brain available and undisturbed.

I began to think about the holiday that I hadn't had. I thought about the railway folder in my desk drawer, in the office the folder with the picture of the hotel in Torquay, with its quiet and peaceful-looking garden, and the sea-front. I wondered whether I would ever get around to that holiday. I'd had the idea of going there ever since I'd picked up the folder one day—a hell of a time ago, it seemed. But something had always turned up to stop it. A job of work or being hard up or a woman or something.

And usually it hadn't been a woman. Because women were things that I was inclined to keep away from. Except to think about. You can do a hell of a lot of thinking about women. The feminine sex will always provide food for thought; especially in my business. In ninety-nine cases out of a hundred you'll find a babe at the root of any trouble—whatever it may be. The character who said Cherchez la femme only knew half his stuff. Because usually you don't have to look for them. In any spot of real grief they're usually sticking out a foot.

Another thing, I'd probably been a little too selective. I knew why that was. Most of my time as an investigator had shown me that most of the trouble in the world is due to some man slipping up somewhere about a woman. A beautiful woman. The number of men who come to grief over ugly women is so small that it practically doesn't matter.

And as I don't go for ugly women much I'd shied off getting in too deep with any of them. There was another reason for my being choosy about them. A very simple one.

When a man is stuck in a hole like I was for over three years with damn all to do but think, he puts in a hell of a lot of time thinking about women, believe you me. And the women he thinks about are easy to look at. Of course if he has one of his own he is inclined to think about her. In that case absence really does make the heart grow fonder—especially in the place I was thinking about. But if he hasn't—as I hadn't—he's inclined to go in for feminine idylls in a very big way. The women who'd played leading parts in some of the dreams that had run through my head during those three years had been just dreams. Anyhow, they were probably too good to be true.

I found the house easily enough—between Wych Cross and the coast. It was a romantic-looking place; big—but not too big. And it had an air. If the inside was as good as the outside, I thought it was a pretty good frame for the picture that Mrs. Ivory made.

It was just before eleven o'clock when I parked the car at the end of the wide drive and rang the bell. An old boy—looking rather like a stage-type butler—opened the door. I told him I wanted to see Mrs. Ivory.

He looked vaguely shocked. He said: "I'm sorry, Sir, but I'm certain that she won't see anyone."

I said I'd got to see her.

He still wasn't playing. "I'm very sorry, Sir," he explained, "but I'm afraid it isn't possible. I am sure that Mrs. Ivory has retired for the night."

"If you mean by that that she's gone to bed, she'll have to get up," I told him. "You go and tell her that Mr. O'Hara wants to see her. Tell her that when he says he wants to see her he means he's going to see her. Just tell her that. Then come back here and wait for me. I'll be back here in five minutes."

He looked almost hurt. He said: "But, Sir!"

"Go and do it," I said.

                              Peter Cheyney

I must have sounded tough because he said weakly: "Very well, Sir..." He went away. He seemed very unhappy about everything.

I followed the carriage drive round the house and found the garage at the back. It was locked and padlocked. There was a twelve-inch square window at one end of the low brick building. I pushed it open and flashed the torch through. There were three cars in the garage. A well-kept, highly polished Rolls, with a sedanca de ville body, a just-as-well-kept Armstrong-Siddeley "Typhoon" coupé, and a not-so-well-kept saloon—I couldn't see the bonnet—with a badly crumpled front off-side wing and a scraped side-panel.

That would be it, I thought. That would be Ricaud's car.

I went back to the porticoed entrance. The butler was waiting.

He said: "Will you come in, please, Sir. Mrs. Ivory will see you."

I went after him, across the wide hall, into a carpeted corridor on the far side; then into a room. It was a pleasant room, exquisitely furnished and with two or three fine paintings on the walls. A small fire was burning.

I went over and stood looking into the fire. The butler went away. A minute or so passed and then she came into the room.

When I turned to look at her I felt a slight shock. I knew what she looked like. I'd had ample opportunity to study her when I'd seen her last—on Monday night at my office.

But you only half-remember a woman like that. You couldn't keep the complete picture. It was too good.

I stood looking at her. Giving my eyes and my brain the first piece of rest they'd had for days.

She wore a crimson velvet house-coat, built high in the neck, with the top buttons undone suggesting a wisp of chiffon beneath. A wide sash of the same material was tied at her waist. The sleeves were wide at the wrists, edged with sable.

The colour of the house-coat showed up the whiteness of her skin, and the soft lights of the room caught the bronze tints in her brown hair. But beneath, her eyes were dark shadows. She was tired... worried....

She said: "Well... Mr. O'Hara?"

"I'd like you to sit down," I said. "I want to talk to you."

She stood—three yards away from me—looking at me coldly. Her eyes told me that I looked to her like something scraped off the underneath side of a low bridge after the flood season.

She said: "I should like to know exactly why I should talk to you."

"There are two reasons," I told her. "The first is you're scared sick, and I've got the second one in my pocket. I think that, at the moment, the second reason is probably the most important, so I'll dispose of that first of all."

                                              Peter Cheyney

I took the quarto envelope in which I had placed her thousand pounds out of my pocket and put it on the table. She picked it up; opened it: saw what was inside.

She said: "Why have you brought this back to me? Did you think that was necessary?"

"No." I said. "I didn't think it was necessary. I just thought I'd do it."

She moved a little. She asked: "Why did you take it in the first place?"

I said: "I'll be happier if you'll sit down. You'll have to sit down eventually, because I've quite a lot to say to you. And you'd better relax. It isn't going to do you—or anyone else—any good at this moment to stand there indulging in a good hate. Which is what you're doing. And you'll have to relax, because you've got to think, and you can't think if your mind is running around like a squirrel in a cage—which is what it's doing just now. So sit."

She looked surprised. But she sat.

I said: "First of all about the money. It doesn't really matter, but you'd better know about it." I grinned at her. "The time has come when you and I had better stop having secrets from each other. When I saw you in my office on Monday I didn't like you very much. In fact, I disliked you a lot. I was entitled to."

She raised her eyebrows. "Why?" She was almost interested.

I said: "You told me that you came to me because you wanted somebody who was unscrupulous. I suppose you thought I had to be unscrupulous. I had to be like that because that afternoon Pell had told you I'd been involved in a tough divorce case; that Counsel for the other side had been having a good time at my expense that day. I suppose it didn't occur to you that I might have been doing a quite decent job—such as getting some woman who'd been tied up to a swine for years out of a rotten marriage. Just as you tried to get out of your marriage to Ricaud at the end of 1945. I suppose you hadn't thought about that?"

She started to say something. I stopped her.

"Another little thing," I went on. "I know Pell. I was entitled to think, and I did think, that Pell would never have the nerve, off his own bat, to stop payment of the thousand he owed me. I thought that you'd gone to his office and bribed him to say that he wouldn't pay me that money so that I'd have to work for you. Because I wanted the money. I was entitled to think that because I know Pell, and because I didn't believe that a woman like you would come to my office with a thousand pounds—just like that—unless the business was very odd and peculiar and somewhat crooked. That's what I thought. Your attitude told me I was right."

She asked tensely: "What do you mean?"

I said: "I was entitled to think, after I'd told you that I wasn't going to do anything about it after I'd taken your money, that, if the business was straight and above board, you'd do something about it—such as talking to Pell; threatening me with the law; or something of the sort. You didn't. You just accepted the situation."

I stopped talking. I said: "Do you mind if I smoke?"

                                        Peter Cheyney

She shook her head. She got up and went to a table at the end of the room and brought a box of cigarettes. I took one. It was the same brand as the fat Egyptian cigarette she'd smoked in my office. I lighted it and drew some smoke down into my lungs.

"It was only yesterday evening," I said, "that I came to the conclusion that you weren't being crooked with me; that you were just being a fool. A very beautiful, very attractive fool, but nevertheless a dyed-in-the-wool damned fool."

She flushed. Then she said in a low voice, not looking at me: "Why do you say that?"

"Because you hadn't enough sense to tell me the truth—all of it," I told her. "Because you hadn't enough sense to know that if you're in a spot and you want someone to help you, the least you can do is to tell the truth, the whole truth and nothing but the truth. Because you came to my office and told me just what Pell had intended you should tell me; because Pell has been playing you as a fool from the start. That's why I say that."

I paused to give her a chance to be rude. She didn't say anything, so I went on: "I can guess what happened between you and Pell last Monday afternoon. You went to Pell and asked him to help you about Esmeralda, and he said he couldn't do it. He said he was too busy, or that he didn't like it, or something like that. All that was lies. I know why he couldn't do it. Pell charged you some money for his advice, because he has to have money all the time, because that's all he thinks of—money. So you paid him some money for his advice, and he told you that if you came to me with a story that he would suggest—a story about his intention not to pay me what he owed me—and if you offered me a thousand I'd have to do the job. Is that right?"

She said in such a low voice that I could hardly hear her: "Yes... that is right."

I grinned at her. "Actually I did what you asked me to do. I did it for three reasons. One conscious reason and two other reasons that, at that time, were subconscious ones. The conscious one was that I was curious—very curious—and it was a new sensation."

I threw the cigarette into the fire. I don't like Egyptian cigarettes. I lighted one of my own.

She said, still in the same low voice, still looking away from me: "What were the other reasons?"

"The subconscious ones?" I asked. I smiled at her. "Well... I suppose one was that I'd taken your money and told you to go to blazes, because I thought then you'd deliberately stopped Pell paying me what he owed me—with malice aforethought. But he did pay me. He paid me that night. He was too scared not to. After that, I suppose I thought I ought to try and do something for the thousand I'd taken you for. That was the second reason. The third doesn't matter."

She asked: "Why not?"

"Because it's purely a personal thing between you and me," I said. "So it doesn't matter."

                              Peter Cheyney

She looked at me. She said: "I want to know everything. Now... I must know everything. What was this personal thing between us?"

I took a lungful of cigarette smoke. I thought she'd better have it straight. I suppose I was curious to see what she'd do or say about it.

"The third reason was you," I said. "I haven't ever seen anyone like you. You fascinate me. I know that now. I didn't know it then. I suppose—thinking about it now—that that was the main reason."

She said: "Oh..." She folded her hands in her lap. She looked uncomfortable. For some vague reason I rather liked that.

"I went down to 'Crossways' that night," I told her. "I met the unfortunate Esmeralda. She was in a not-so-good condition. You probably know about the state she gets into. She said her little piece to me and passed out. I parked her in the back of my car and waited for Ricaud. Then we had a little talk. I didn't like Ricaud much. Not a lot. Having seen Esmeralda, and after I'd talked to him, I thought I understood how she'd got like that. I thought he was responsible. So I decided that a beating-up might do him a lot of good."

She looked at me. There was a shade of interest in her eyes. "Do you mean you thrashed him?" she asked. I could see her white fingers twining and untwining in her lap.

"I'd like to say yes to that," I said. "But I can't. Ricaud beat the living daylights out of me. I can still feel what he did to me. I didn't like that at all. But after that, I was in this business—personally. Not because of Esmeralda, or you, or money or anything else, but just that..."

She said slowly: "Mr. O'Hara, why was a thrashing from Alexis Ricaud more important to you than Esmeralda, or what I had asked you to do, or money? Why?"

I shrugged my shoulders. "The reason doesn't matter. It doesn't come into the story."

"But I would like to know," she said. "Will you tell me... please?"

It was the "please" that did it. And the way she said it. I thought for a minute, and decided that I was saying nothing about it and then... well, it came out. It was just one of those things.

"I spent over three years in a Japanese prisoner of war camp," I said. "One of the bad Formosa camps. Maybe you've heard about them. The Japanese didn't like me much." I grinned at her. "They didn't go for my type. I used to get a beating up most days, and I didn't like it. I did a lot of thinking about it. And I had a lot of time for thinking. I made up my mind that if ever I got out of that dump nobody was ever again going to lay a finger on me. I suppose I'd developed some sort of inferiority complex about it."

I looked at her. Her hands were still now. She was interested and her eyes were not cold any more.

"Near the field where I used to work in the day, the Japs were running a judo (some people call it ju-jitsu) instruction class for young soldiers. I used to watch. All

                    Peter Cheyney

the time I had one eye on what was being taught. After that, one of the Japanese people who were working with our Intelligence out there, and who made contact with me in the camp, taught me a few things. His name was Sado. He was a great guy. So after a bit I began to feel better. I began to feel that although I couldn't use it then, I'd got something extra that I could fight with if I had to fight. It was a great feeling. Can you understand that?"

She nodded.

"I tried it on Ricaud," I said. "And I got a surprise. Believe it or not, he was much better at judo than I was. He'd forgotten more than I'd ever learned. And what he did to me was nobody's business. I didn't like that at all. It wasn't good for the inferiority complex. I realised next day that if I didn't go back and give Ricaud something worse than he'd given me, then I'd find myself back mentally in the camp at Formosa. It was something that had to be done... for my own sake."

There was a pause. Then she said: "I think I understand."

I said: "Have you read the evening papers?"

She nodded her head. "He's dead," she said. "He killed himself."

"Which is very good for everyone concerned," I told her. "Especially for you."

She said in a low voice: "Why especially for me, Mr. O'Hara?"

I threw my cigarette stub into the fire.

"In May 1945," I said, "you married Ricaud in New York. You left him three mouths later. You had told him that you were going to start divorce proceedings against him. You instructed your lawyers in New York to do that. Then you came back to England. Is that right?"

She said: "Yes... that is right."

"But you didn't trust Ricaud," I went on. "You knew him too well. You wanted someone to keep an eye on him to see that he didn't try any tricks. You were recommended by someone to go to the Pell Detective Agency. You went to Pell, paid him a retainer of £1,500 and instructed him to go to New York and see that the divorce went through. Well?"

She nodded. "Yes..."

"Pell went to New York," I went on. "He met Ricaud and he sold you out. Ricaud was already planning to get after Esmeralda's money. And he wanted to be revenged on you. He was, as you know, a nasty, sadistic type. He thought up a very cute scheme and he talked Pell into it. Pell went to your attorneys in New York—and, remember, he was your accredited agent—and instructed them that you did not wish to continue with the divorce suit; that you had changed your mind... ."

She got up. She stood looking at me. Her eyes were wide. "But I have the decree.... I received the decree from the Court... I—"

I shook my head. "That decree never came from the Court," I told her. "Pell or Ricaud obtained an official Form of Decree which anyone can get. Then they had the Court seal forged and stamped on the form. Then

                                          Peter Cheyney

Pell had the material matter, the names and the decree filled in, and it was sent to you in England. Naturally, you accepted it at its face value. You had no further communication with your New York attorneys because that was unnecessary. Pell had been there acting for you so you knew everything was all right."

She said: "Oh, my God... so... so..."

"So you were Mrs. Ricaud until some time yesterday night," I said. "Until he committed suicide... if he did commit suicide."

"What do you mean?" Her voice was strained. Her fingers gripped the arms of the chair.

I sank my voice. "Ricaud was killed. If the police are satisfied with the suicide idea, so much the better. But he didn't kill himself. He was murdered."

A small sound almost like a sob came from her. She sat in the chair looking straight in front of her as if she were seeing something. Something not pleasant. For a moment I thought she was going to faint.

I said: "Why don't we have a drink?"

She took a pull at herself. She said: "But of course." She got up; pressed the bell button by the fireplace. Then she stood, one hand on the mantelpiece, looking at me with dark troubled eyes.

The butler came in.

She ordered whisky. When he'd brought the drinks and gone away, I said: "Drink some whisky slowly and relax. Nothing ever is as bad as it seems." I grinned at her. "It could be a great deal worse."

She drank a little of the whisky; put down the glass. She asked: "How could it be worse?"

"It could be worse two ways," I told her. "If Ricaud were alive, he'd be on his way to the Bahamas now. Once he got there you'd have a hell of a job getting free of him. You probably wouldn't be able to do it. It's one thing starting a divorce in New York when both parties are domiciled there, but it's a hell of a different proposition when one party—the one wanting a divorce—is in England, and the other—the one who is going to play all sorts of tricks—a few thousand miles away. Before you'd got that divorce from Ricaud you'd have had to pay plenty. He knew that."

She nodded. "I understand..." Then: "What other way could it have been worse?"

"You might not have an unscrupulous private detective working for you," I said.

She tried to smile at that and nearly succeeded.

I went on: "The situation isn't good. With luck it may be all right. Esmeralda was at 'Crossways' last night. That isn't very good. And she's here now. Ricaud's car is in the garage. The car she drove here in the early hours of this morning. The car with the crumpled wing and the scraped side-panel. Tell me about her."

She came closer to me. She said, almost in a whisper: "She got here between half past two and three this morning. God knows how she managed to get here. She's terribly ill. She's been unconscious for hours."

"Has a doctor seen her?" I asked.

                                    Peter Cheyney

She nodded. "He can't do a great deal at the moment," she said. "All we can do is to wait. She has a nurse with her." She looked at me piteously.

"Don't let them come here... or try to take her away..." she said. "Whatever she's done... whatever she's done... she's suffered so much... so terribly."

I stopped her. "Listen. This is no time for sentiment. Things may be all right. The police may be satisfied that Ricaud committed suicide. Does anyone here know who Esmeralda is?"

She shook her head. "She's never been here before. When I've seen her it has always been in London. I didn't tell the doctor her real name. I gave him her maiden name. Her name before"—she hesitated—"before she thought she had married Ricaud...."

I said: "Good. Then there's no immediate need to worry. Look after her and hope for the best. There's nothing else you can do."

"Supposing they find out that she was there?" she asked. "Supposing that... what can they do? Mr. O'Hara, could they... could they...?"

"Don't let's meet trouble," I said. "You'll have to do what I say. There's a good chance that the suicide theory will hold. But when Esmeralda recovers consciousness don't let her talk."

"I'll do my best," she said in a low voice. She looked at me for a long time. "I think I've been stupid about you."

I smiled at her. "That evens things up," I said. "Because I'm still stupid about you. But I expect you're used to that."

She said nothing. She went back to her chair; sat down. She began twining and untwining her fingers again. She was thinking about Esmeralda.

After a while she said miserably: "What am I to do? What am I to do?" Her eyes were dark and troubled. They moved restlessly from my face to her fingers clasped nervously in her lap.

I said: "What's to be done must be decided by me. You wanted me to work for you in the first place. Now I'm working and it's got to be my way. Tell me some things. I'm going to do a little guessing. Don't interrupt me unless I make a mistake that matters. Do you understand?"

She nodded her head.

"Last Monday afternoon you went to see Pell," I said. "You went to see him because you knew that things had come to a head between Ricaud and Esmeralda; because you knew that she was broke and miserable, and you knew that she'd start drugs and drinking because she was broke and miserable. And you were afraid she'd do something to Ricaud. She's probably threatened that a dozen times—publicly. You were scared of her. You asked Pell to see Ricaud and throw a scare into him—to try to get him away. Right?"

She nodded again.

"Pell told you he couldn't do it. He probably gave you some reasons that sounded good. Then I imagine he

                    Peter Cheyney

pretended to do a lot of thinking and said that he might
be able to advise you. You jumped at that and paid him
some money. Then he asked you some questions. He
wanted to know where Esmeralda was and whether she
had any money or not. Right?"

She said: "Yes. I told him her address. I told him that
I knew she had no money; that I'd wanted to help her
but that she wouldn't see me; wouldn't even talk to me
on the telephone."

"Then," I went on, "Pell began to talk to you about
me. He said that I was the man to handle your work,
but that I was difficult; that I wouldn't take a case unless
I liked it a lot or unless I was broke. He said I wasn't
broke because he had to pay me a thousand pounds.
Then he got a big idea. He suggested to you that you
came and saw me; that you told me that he wasn't going
to pay me because he thought there'd be trouble about
the case I'd handled for him; that you offered me a
thousand to work for you. He said that he'd hold up
payment to me so that I'd have to work for you. He
advised you to see me as soon as possible and get me
to see Ricaud as quickly as I could. He told you that I
invariably went back to my office late at night to see if
there was any mail; that he'd often left messages for me
late at night. He told you to go to my office and wait for
me and tell me the story he'd suggested, and to make
it sound tough as if he really meant not to pay. Is that
right?"

"Perfectly right," she said. "He asked me if I'd ever heard from Ricaud since he had married Esmeralda and I said no."

"Has Pell ever met Esmeralda—as far as you know?" I asked.

She shook her head. There was silence for a bit. I stood, in front of the fire, looking at her. I could have gone on looking at her. To me she was a perfect view.

She said: "Mr. O'Hara... do you think that there's a chance that the police will be satisfied that Ricaud committed suicide?"

"A very good chance," I told her. I couldn't very well tell her that I knew damn well that the police wouldn't be satisfied. That I wasn't going to let them be satisfied. I'm fairly tough but I just couldn't do it. It would have been like taking bread from a starving child.

I said: "I must be on my way."

She got up. She put out her hand. "Thank you for everything," she said. "You've been very kind. I rely on you absolutely. No one else can help me."

"I'm staying at the Malinson Hotel," I told her. I wrote the address and telephone number down in my notebook; tore out the page; gave it to her. "Telephone me if anything happens. If anything happens at my end that you ought to know I'll call you here."

I said good-night. I went to the door.

I had my hand on the door-knob when she spoke. I turned and she came close to me. A suggestion of her perfume reached me. I remembered Birk's description of her—"a lovely piece." I thought that Birk's description was an understatement.

She said: "Will you please have the money—the thousand pounds? You might need it. Please have it."

I smiled at her. I said: "Not yet... So long, Mrs. Ivory."

I walked into the hall; got my hat from the butler; went outside; started the car; drove towards London.

I thought her thousand pounds could wait. And the idea of working with Pell's money was amusing. That would have pleased him if he'd known it.

He'd know it one day.

The night was fine and the road was good. I pushed the accelerator down. Ten miles away I stopped to light a cigarette.

I re-started the car slowly. As it gathered speed, I wondered if I could do it. If I could get away with it. But I was going to try.

I wondered why. I wondered why I should take the chance. Because it was a chance—a hell of a chance.

If I fell down on it... I thought that wouldn't be so good.

But I was going to try and it was no use kidding myself about why.

I began to think about Mrs. Ivory. I thought about her, with her heart-shaped, lovely face and her crimson velvet house-coat, and small gold sandals, and her long fingers that trembled and her eyes that were scared.

Then I knew goddam well why I was going to take the chance.

4

IT was nearly two o'clock when I got back to the Malinson. The night porter gave me a note—a telephone message that had come through earlier in the evening. I put it in my pocket and asked him to send a pot of tea up to my room; then I went upstairs. I was thinking about Mrs. Ivory and a lot of other things. I didn't like the situation very much. It was tough—so tough that it was scaring, especially having regard to what I had at the back of my mind.

I undressed and took a warm bath. I'd still got a few bruises from my encounter with Ricaud on Monday night. Monday night seemed a hell of a time ago—years ago—and it was only two days. I thought that time was a funny thing; that one's idea of time depended mainly on the things that happened during any given period. I seemed to have crowded a lot of life and death into the last few days. I thought about Esmeralda. What had happened was pretty obvious.

Esmeralda had never intended to stay in the nursing home, but she wasn't going to tell me that. She didn't know that I was bluffing when I'd told her that if she didn't go into the nursing home I'd hand her over to the police. She'd thought that I'd meant it. So I had to be kept quiet. Then, when Quinceley had gone there to see her, she'd pulled an act on him. She knew that even if Quinceley allowed for the more than cunning mentality of a dope addict he'd never guess what was in her mind. She'd told him that story about not wanting drugs; of

                                                      Peter Cheyney

trying to take a pull at herself. It was on the cards that Quinceley had believed her. He'd believed her because first of all he'd want to believe her, and secondly because there wasn't anything else he could do.

She must have lain in that bed thinking things out. I wondered what she could have been thinking about. But not for very long. Esmeralda hadn't had any dope for some little time. She'd suffered a certain amount of shock. She was ill. She'd got to have some drugs of some sort and she knew she had that ampoule of heroin at Montacute Place. She wanted to get there. So she pretended she was going to sleep and when the day nurse had gone out of the room she had slipped out of bed, put on some of her clothes, put her night-gown over them, got back in bed and pulled a fast one when the night sister came on.

She'd got out of that place, taken a cab and gone straight round to the flat, and when she arrived there she got the message from the night porter. That must have shaken her a little. For two reasons. She wanted to know what Ricaud wanted with her. My bet was that after she'd told the porter to go and telephone the hired car people, she'd gone straight to her bedroom and given herself a shot of heroin. She'd left the little drawer open. Then she'd gone back to the drawing-room and moved everything about the place trying to find the note that Ricaud had said he'd left. But I think she had a pretty good idea what that note was about. She'd been trying to get away from Ricaud for a long time and Ricaud had stopped the process very easily. He'd stopped her getting away from him not because he wanted her, but because he wanted her money. He'd kept her with him by means of giving her drugs, and she'd got to the state when she couldn't go on without them. That was the Ricaud technique and it couldn't fail to work. But now he knew she hadn't got any money, and she probably knew that Ricaud knew that too. She knew that he wasn't going to hang around without money. So she probably guessed that he'd found another woman; that he'd be going. She wanted to know about that.

She couldn't find the note so she gave up the idea. Then she thought she'd talk to him, but she couldn't get through. And she was impatient and ill—very ill. And the shot of heroin wasn't helping a lot because she'd probably reached the stage where the drug is merely an irritant and makes things worse instead of helping. So she got fed up with trying to telephone. She dropped the receiver on the table without even worrying to put it back on the cradle.

She went back into the bedroom and saw the little drawer in her dressing-table open. She went over to shut it; then she saw the cardboard box with the two ammunition clips. By this time she'd have noticed that I'd taken the ammunition clip out of the automatic pistol when I gave it back to her before she went to the nursing home. She would have had to open her handbag in the meantime to pay off the taxi-cab or other things. She'd see that I'd removed the clip, so she took one of the ammunition clips out of the box, leaving the third one that I'd found, and then she had heard the hall

                    Peter Cheyney

porter coming back to say that the hired car was there. She tried to shut the drawer quickly but she couldn't do it. It stuck, but she'd got it shut eventually. Then she went back to the hall, took the half-bottle of whisky from the hall porter, told him to go and tell the hired car that she'd be down in a minute, went back to the drawing-room and had a last look for Ricaud's note. She couldn't find it. Then she sat down on the settee, took the stopper off the half-bottle and took a long drink. She put the stopper back, dropped the bottle on the settee where I'd found it, went down and told the hired driver to go to Maidenhead.

I wondered how much the driver of the hired car was going to remember. But I wasn't worrying about him a great deal. Supposing he'd read the evening papers and seen the news about Ricaud's suicide. People believed what they read. He'd think nothing of Esmeralda having gone down there. Besides which, it was possible that she'd stopped him, and sent him back, some way from the house, but even if she hadn't he wouldn't think very much of it.

If the newspaper had said murder it would have been different. He would immediately have connected driving that odd, tired-looking woman down to Maidenhead that night. But the newspaper hadn't said murder. I thought, having regard to all things, that I needn't worry too much about the driver of the hired car.

But I was worried about something else. There was another aspect of the case I didn't like. I heard the night-porter take the tea into the bedroom and go away. I went out of the bathroom into the bedroom, began to pour out a cup of tea. When I was doing it I saw my coat lying on the bed where I'd thrown it. That reminded me of the telephone message. I put the teapot down; walked over to the bed; fished the folded piece of paper out of my pocket. I opened it and read it. It said:

Doctor Quincely rang through at 11 o'clock. He would be grateful if Mr. O'Hara would get in touch with him as early as possible tomorrow, Thursday morning.

That wasn't so good. I didn't like it. I'd been hoping against hope that Quinceley would not see the report of the Ricaud suicide in the evening paper. He had seen it.

I drank my cup of tea; lighted a cigarette; began to walk up and down the bedroom thinking about Quinceley, wondering what sort of man he was. Although, I knew Quinceley was a typical general practitioner, and those people are usually pretty good and damned straight. They have to be. I thought regretfully that I was going to have trouble with Quinceley.

I switched my mind back to Esmeralda. I could visualise the scene that had happened the night before at "Crossways." It was all plain as daylight. Ricaud had been down there in the drawing-room walking up and down in his flowered dressing-gown, thinking with a certain amount of sadistic pleasure about his final scene with Esmeralda, because he'd intended it to be his final scene, when she arrived at ten o'clock.

He knew she'd come. He knew she had to come; that she'd want to come; that she'd want to know what was going to happen. He knew when she'd read his note and heard that he was going off to the Bahamas to some other woman, she'd know that was true and she'd feel sorry and glad. Sorry because she would wonder where she was going to get further supplies of drugs from—although, Ricaud would think, she would try to believe that in certain circumstances he'd tell her. And she would be glad because a situation had arisen which was forcing her to part from Ricaud, and God knows she hated him enough. No one knew that better than he did.

So he knew she'd come down. And ten o'clock came and she didn't come. Then he began to get angry—that nasty vicious temper, that sadistic cruelty of the mind which lurked under his charming exterior, that impatience to get his own way, began to work. He went over to the telephone and called through to the Montacute Place flat. I could imagine him sitting at the table drumming on it with his free hand, waiting for Esmeralda.

But there was no reply. After a bit he got tired of that. His temper by this time was worse. He hung up and called through again—this time to the hall porter. He asked if Esmeralda had had his note; was told that she hadn't been to the flat. Then he left his message that he was going to write to her; that she'd get the letter tomorrow; that he hoped she'd like it. The fact that he'd said she would get the letter tomorrow proved that he was going to leave it at the flat himself; that he was coming to London, because it was too late to catch the post.

By this time Ricaud had begun to think about his second appointment—the one for twelve o'clock. He thought he'd clear the decks for action. He thought he'd get the letter to Esmeralda written. I expect he spent a certain amount of time walking up and down and thinking just what he was going to tell her. He was picking his phrases, working out what he could write that was going to hurt her most. Eventually, after quite some time, he sat down at the table and wrote the note. He wrote:

My delightful wife,

So you won't play.

But my time has not been wasted. I have had time to think and I have come to the conclusion that I am sufficiently tired of you, of the Ivory, of the world in general—and two or three people in particular—to want to deal with things in an adequate manner.

And so I am going to deal with it. I am going to deal with it in a way that I hope will make a great deal of trouble for all of you. And this is the way....

As he wrote those words he'd come to the end of the first page on the writing pad. On the next page he was going to explain just how he was going to do it, but he never got to the next page. He heard the door of the drawing-room open. He put down his pen and turned round, and Esmeralda came into the room.

I think Ricaud was very pleased with that. He was going to have his little bit of sadistic satisfaction after all and he knew he could be much more cruel by word of mouth than by letter.

I could imagine the scene.

He walked over and laid himself down on the settee. Esmeralda would be standing by the side of the fireplace looking at him.

Then he told her. He told her that the next day he was going up to London; that some hours afterwards he was leaving for the Bahamas. But, he told her, she had sufficient time in those few hours to raise some money for him. He suggested for instance that as she hadn't any, she might get it from her friend Mrs. Ivory. He told her that if she agreed to raise some money for him he might consider being kind enough to tell her where she might get some more supplies of dope. He said that if she didn't he was going to make things very uncomfortable for her—not only uncomfortable for her but for her friend Mrs. Ivory, the lady who had once been very rude to him, and who had tried everything in her power to stop Esmeralda from marrying him. I don't know what Esmeralda said to that. Ricaud had a dominating personality. She probably stood there looking at him with those big eyes of hers—rather vague, slightly stupid, trying with her small fuddled brain to work it all out.

Then he'd told her some more. He'd told her that it was rather amusing—the idea of having entreated him so often to let her have a divorce. That must have been the cream of the jest to Ricaud. He told her that she didn't need a divorce; that she was free; that she was free because she wasn't married to him. She wasn't Mrs. Ricaud at all.

I think that must have shattered Esmeralda. Her brain was shocked into action. She probably asked him what the devil he was talking about. So he told her. He told her that he'd never been divorced from Mrs. Ivory; that the decree which Mrs. Ivory had received from the New York Court was fake. He told her how he'd got an official Form of Decree; had the seal of the Court forged; how Mrs. Ivory had accepted it because she'd trusted her New York attorneys; and she'd trusted the man she'd sent out there to look after her interests—Pell.

That was too much for Esmeralda. This was the last straw. The last insult. This was the ultimate thing. She could endure no more. She opened her handbag. She took out the pistol. I think that as she did so Ricaud, scared for the first time in his life, raised himself from the couch. But he was too late. By this time she'd got the automatic pistol at his head. She squeezed the trigger.

That was the end of Ricaud.

I could see Esmeralda standing there, the pistol in her hand, looking at what she'd done, seeing the grim finale of all her dreams of love and romance, of all the sweetnesses and kindnesses that she had thought would come with love and marriage, instead of the appalling cruelty to mind and body which she had suffered.

She must have walked out of the room in a daze, along the dark passage, through the side door, along the winding path through the trees towards the clearing where, in the old days, when she had thought she was going to be happy, she had danced with Ricaud without music because "it was such fun." She had lurched against the rhododendron bush. The automatic pistol had fallen from her hand. I could visualise her leaning up against the tree gazing blankly before her, wondering what she was going to do.

A lost soul with nowhere to go.

And she remembered Mrs. Ivory. Mrs. Ivory, of whom she had said that she was as strong and as wise as she, Esmeralda, was weak and stupid. Leonora Ivory— her only friend.

She had walked back to the garage; started up Ricaud's car; driven out on to the gravel drive and away. Heaven only knows how she steered that car to Wych Cross. She'd hit something badly on the way. The crumpled wing told that story. But she'd made it. And when she got there her last strength was gone. She had reached the haven, and the peace of unconsciousness had descended on her.

I had some more tea. These ruminations, I thought, got me nowhere. There were some hard tough facts to be dealt with. If I was going through with this business I'd got to be prepared for all sorts of surprises.

I went to bed. And I was asleep in five minutes.

CHAPTER FOUR

THURSDAY — ANTI-CLIMAX
1

I GOT up at nine o'clock, took a hot and cold shower, ate my breakfast and walked round to Quinceley's place. On my way there, I thought about him and the line I was going to take.

I was shown straight into his consulting room when I arrived. I said good morning with just the right amount of nonchalance and then asked him what the trouble was about.

He looked surprised. "Didn't you read the evening newspapers last night?" he asked.

I nodded. "You mean that business about Ricaud killing himself? A damned good thing. Good riddance to bad rubbish." I grinned at him. "Now you'll be able to get to work on Esmeralda without any come-back. You'll be able really to cure her now."

He didn't say anything for a bit. Then he got up and began walking about the room.

Then: "I'm worried about this thing, Mr. O'Hara," he said. "I'm a doctor and I have to think about what is my duty. I don't like it at all."

"Don't like what?" I asked him. "Don't tell me that you're sorry that Ricaud committed suicide!"

"I'm not concerned with Ricaud," he said. "That isn't the point. He was an appalling type and all the worse because he looked entirely unlike what he was. I know quite a lot about Ricaud. I've talked to him on more than one occasion, and I loathed the sight of him. I've talked to his wife too. And she's told me one or two things as between doctor and patient that weren't good. He must have given her a very bad time. But that isn't what's worrying me now...."

"All right," I said. "So something's worrying you now. What is it?"

He sat down at his desk. He said: "I've been practising medicine for thirty years. I've come into contact with all sorts and conditions of people, and in the process a doctor has to be a really stupid specimen if he doesn't learn to weigh people up. I weighed Ricaud up. I formed an estimate of his character on what his wife had told me about him when I was trying to get her off drugs the first time, and also on what I noticed about him when I saw him and spoke to him. I've never met a type less inclined to commit suicide."

"What's in your mind, doctor?" I asked him. "Surely you're not trying to suggest—"

He interrupted. "I'm not trying to suggest anything. I'm just saying that. I don't like it. I don't like it because on Tuesday you were here telling me that you found Mrs. Ricaud waving a pistol in a very excited and neurotic condition; that she had threatened to kill Ricaud; that you believed that unless something drastic was done she would kill him. On the strength of that she's put into a nursing home and I said I'd look after her. She got out of that home the same evening. It's my considered opinion that she never intended to stay in it for a minute longer than she had to. She made a fool of you and a fool of me."

"What do you think she was after?" I said.

"Ricaud," he said. "You interrupted her in the process of wanting to kill him and she intended to continue with that process as soon as she could. I'm not saying that she did. But I'm saying that the whole business is very odd and that I feel I ought to say something about it."

"To the police?" I asked.

He nodded.

I smiled at him. I made it a very knowing sort of smile. Then I considered for a moment. I put on a thinking act intended to convey to him that I was wondering just how much I could tell him about something that I didn't really want to talk about.

Then I said: "Look, doctor, this is a bit difficult for me because I want to play fair with you and at the same time there are some aspects of my client's business that I'm not entitled to discuss. So all I'm going to do is to tell you this: Ricaud committed suicide. If he didn't commit suicide and somebody killed him, then it wasn't Mrs. Ricaud. I happen to know that it couldn't have been her."

"You really mean that?" he asked.

"Of course," I told him. "Why should I tell you if I didn't?"

                                    Peter Cheyney

I lighted a cigarette. "I was as fed up with this business as you are," I went on, "until I found that Esmeralda hadn't been anywhere near Ricaud. She couldn't have had anything to do with it. I'm absolutely positive about that. I can't say any more at the moment without breaking a confidence, but that's how it is."

He said: "I'm very glad to hear it. You see, Mr. O'Hara, from my point of view it is quite obvious that the Coroner will want to know something about the dead man. He'll certainly want to know if there are any relations. He'll certainly find out about the existence of Mrs. Ricaud, and he may ask some very difficult questions. Not so difficult now that you are able to state that she couldn't possibly have had anything to do with this. But she's been threatening publicly to do something like this for some time. I shouldn't be at all surprised if someone didn't inform the Coroner of that fact. Then—unless suicide is absolutely proved—he would have to make further inquiries. In the circumstances the authorities might well believe that I had not done my complete duty. They might well say that I should have communicated to the Coroner or the police what I knew about Mrs. Ricaud and her husband."

He had to be headed off. I saw that. There was only one way to do it. Anyhow, all I wanted was time. Just a day or so.

I said: "I quite see your point, and I agree with it. But there's no need for you to start something that might do Mrs. Ricaud a lot of harm and set her back more than ever. You'd hate to do that—especially when it was made plain to you that your trouble had been unnecessary and possibly—even if unintended—a little mischievous. You wouldn't like to do that, would you?"

He said: "Of course not. But—"

I interrupted. "Then it's all right. The inquest is on Saturday afternoon. You won't mind waiting until then... will you?"

I said it in a voice that showed him I thought he was being a little bit of a busybody.

He reacted.

"Of course not," he said. "I'm very fond of Esmeralda Ricaud. I'd like to see her well and strong and happy."

"All right," I told him. "Then don't worry. Just wait until you see the result of the Coroner's inquest on Saturday. You'll know all about it then. And if you're not completely satisfied in your own mind—then go ahead and do what you want."

He looked relieved. He said: "I'm not trying to make any sort of trouble... you know that."

"Of course," I said. "I'm in exactly the same boat as you are. I know all the things she's been saying and doing too. But I also know that she had nothing to do with Ricaud's suicide... in any way. If I thought that I wasn't going to be absolutely satisfied with the Coroner's inquest on Saturday I'd probably be feeling the way you do."

He said: "I rely on what you say, Mr. O'Hara. I shan't even consider doing anything about this until I've had another talk with you—if that's necessary—on Saturday."

We shook hands and I went away.

Outside, I breathed a sigh of relief. I'd stalled him till Saturday. I thought that would be all right.

I walked back to the Malinson garage and got out the car. I drove round to Mack's place; bought some petrol and oil, waited while they washed the car.

Then I drove down to Brighton.

2

BRIGHTON'S a hell of a place. It's "one of those places"—if you know what I mean. It has a peculiar atmosphere, half gay, half macabre. The top surface is nice and clean and obvious, but after a bit you think it is too temperamental to be just like that. In the old days, whenever I went to Brighton I always felt that I wanted to start scratching under the surface. Just to see what really made it tick over.

But I liked being there. It was good to be away from places where I knew people and had to talk. I wanted to think.

I parked the car and walked about for a bit. There was a good breeze from the sea. I ate lunch at a place on the front and afterwards did some more walking. I came to the conclusion that there were too many people about. After a while I went back to the car park, started the car and drove out of Brighton towards Rottingdean. Half an hour afterwards I turned off the main road and drove towards Alfriston.

There was practically no traffic on the roads. I parked the car in a lane and walked about the fields. It was quiet and peaceful and easy to think.

Mainly I was thinking about Mrs. Ivory. About Mrs. Ivory and a lot of other things which seemed, for no accountable reason, to be mixed up in my mind; to need sorting out.

I thought about the P.O.W. camp on Formosa and the other place they'd moved me to and my escape. I had been lucky to get out. So far as I know I was the only one who had and I shouldn't have pulled it off but for Sado.

Then my mind switched on to the detective business and the way I'd drifted into being a "free-lance" and working for the London agencies. And my first meeting with Pell. I thought about some of the cases I'd handled.

But I'd never struck a case like this. There was no doubt that the Ivory-Ricaud case was going to be a star effort. Either that or a complete flop and the end of me—one way or another.

I knew that this case was important to me. If I pulled it off I was going to be all right. With myself I mean. If I didn't pull it off I had a nasty idea I was going to slip back into what I called that Formosa feeling. The way I used to feel—sort of dull-witted and no account—when I was being kicked around by those goddamned Japs in the camp.

Of course I knew that I was stuck on Mrs. Ivory. I suppose I'd known it from the first time I saw her.

Even when I thought she was pulling a fast one on me. I hadn't consciously realised it then but that's how it was.

Not that it meant anything so far as I was concerned. I had too much common sense not to know that there was no possible point of contact—except a professional one—between us.

All the same I didn't mind the idea. The idea that I was just a little bit crazy about her. I had to be. If I wasn't I ought to be put into a looney bin for doing what I was planning to do.

I began to think about all the people I'd met and talked to since Monday night when she'd come to my office and waited for me to turn up. Esmeralda and Alexis Ricaud and Pell and Mack, Quinceley and the hall porter with one arm at Montacute Place; the telephone girl at the Malinson—to whom I'd given the Chanel No. 5. I fitted them all into the picture with Mrs. Ivory and myself.

Some picture... .

I lighted a cigarette and came to the conclusion that I liked being in the country. It was quiet and it was only when you were away from the noises of London that you realised that you don't like London a lot. Even if you thought you did.

I walked back to the car. I got in and smoked another cigarette. Then I drove back to London.

3

AT eight o'clock I had dinner; drank two whiskies and sodas; went up to my room and telephoned Pell. When he came on the line I said:

"This is O'Hara. I'd like to see you, Pell. I'm worried."

He said: "Who isn't these days? But what's the trouble in particular?"

"I don't want to talk about it on the telephone. It's about this Ivory thing."

He said: "Oh... that..." He laughed. "Did you manage to find her after all?" There was a pause; then: "Come on round and see me. If I can do anything for you, you know I'll do my best."

I said: "Thanks, Pell." I hung up.

When I got round there I was let in by the same character in the alpaca coat. I went into the room where I'd seen Pell before. He was standing in front of the fireplace, smoking one of his small but very good cigars.

Looking at Pell you wouldn't have thought he was a private detective. He didn't look the part. He was big and burly and although his face was lined and old-looking, especially when he'd been drinking and had a hangover, he exuded an air of good nature. He liked good clothes too. He might have been anything. A well-to-do man in the city. He might even have been a country squire.

He said: "Give yourself a drink, O'Hara—and a cigar or a cigarette; the boxes are on the table. Then tell me what all the trouble's about." He grinned at me. "You've

 Peter Cheyney

caught me in a good humour. You may not know it but I don't dislike you. You're a damned good operative even if you are a peculiar sort of cove."

I said: "I'm worried, Pell. I've made a goddam fool of myself."

"Yes? Well, everybody does it sometime or other. But what's it got to do with Mrs. Ivory? How have you made a fool of yourself over her? Don't tell me you've been trying to make love to her or something." He laughed at his own joke. "She's a hell of a piece, isn't she? I've never seen anything like her in my life. A really beautiful woman—not one of those with a beautiful face and a bad figure or a good figure and a face like the back of a cab—but everything. Brains too, I should think, if she wanted to use 'em."

I said: "Maybe. If she's got brains she's better off than I am. I've come to the conclusion I haven't any at all."

He asked: "What's the trouble? What's worrying you?"

"Look," I said, "I haven't been quite straight with you. I've got myself into a spot and I'm a bit scared. When I told you on Tuesday that I didn't know what Mrs. Ivory wanted to talk to me about the night before; that I'd sent her about her business; that wasn't the truth. She'd told me what she wanted but I just didn't feel inclined to do anything about it."

He asked: "Why not?"

I shrugged my shoulders. "She told me some story about you not paying me that thousand pounds; about your having an idea that there'd be an intervention or something. I knew it was a lot of rubbish. Then she offered me a thousand to work for her. I thought she'd stopped you from paying me so that I'd have to work for her."

Pell said: "I get it. You got the needle to her. You're a funny chap, aren't you? So you sent her away?"

"That's right," I said. "And would I be glad if I'd let it go at that?"

He raised his eyebrows. He drew on his cigar. "So you did something about it?"

I nodded. "When she'd gone, I became curious. I don't know why, but... well, I was just curious. That's all I can think of. So I got myself a car and drove down to Maidenhead. I saw a man called Ricaud. This was a man that Mrs. Ivory married way back in 1945 and divorced soon afterwards. The story was that he'd come to England and married Mrs. Ivory's best friend—a piece called Esmeralda—out of spite. Mrs. Ivory's story was that this Ricaud has been feeding Esmeralda drugs; that what with that and drinking she was in a bad state and liable to finish off Ricaud if she got a chance. What she'd wanted me to do was to go down there and scare him off."

Pell said: "I see. So you went down there and scared him off. Did he go quietly?" He grinned at me.

"It wasn't a bit like that," I said. I helped myself to one of his expensive Virginian cigarettes and lighted it. "When I got down there I found this Esmeralda person hanging around in the grounds with a .32 Colt automatic in her bag. I had a talk with her and she told

                                        Peter Cheyney

me that her idea was to take a shot at Ricaud any time she felt brave enough to do it. It seems she felt brave enough when she was a little high, so all she wanted was to be high and to have Ricaud at the end of a gun and then she was going to squeeze the trigger."

Pell said: "I know... they often talk like that, but they never do it."

I didn't say anything.

After a bit he asked: "What happened next?"

"She passed out," I told him. "So I put her in the car and waited for Ricaud to show up. He and I had a few words. It seemed he didn't like Mrs. Ivory a bit and guessed she'd got me working for her. We talked generalities and were pretty rude to each other. Then I thought I'd try a little judo on him just to keep me in practice."

Pell said: "I bet he didn't like that. I was watching you when you were working on Lennet in this room. You know, you're good, O'Hara."

"I wasn't good enough for him," I said. "He beat hell out of me. He knew more about it than I did."

Pell roared with laughter. "That's the funniest one I've heard. So you took a beating up?"

"And how!" I said ruefully. "What a beating up! Anyway, I thought that the thing for me to do was to look after Esmeralda. That way, I thought, I was going to be doing the friendly thing to Mrs. Ivory. I thought that Mrs. Ivory might reciprocate in the usual way."

He said: "You've got brains, haven't you?"

"I wonder," I told him. "Anyhow, I found a doctor's card in Esmeralda's handbag. So I brought her back to London; went and saw the doctor—a guy called Quinceley—a nice guy. Apparently, this doctor had been looking after her before when she got herself into a bad way. So we put her in a nursing home. That was on Tuesday."

He said: "You've been busy, haven't you? I think you're one of those fellows who never lets his left hand know what his left hand's doing," he added humorously.

I said: "A man can be too clever. I think I was. You remember I came to you on Tuesday and tried to get Mrs. Ivory's address. I thought now was the time to go and see her and tell her what a good fellow I'd been. Well, you couldn't give it to me because you hadn't got it."

"That's right," said Pell. He drew some cigar smoke down into his lungs; blew it through pursed lips slowly. "What did you do about that?"

"I didn't know what to do about it," I told him. "Eventually, I thought I'd take a chance. Mrs. Ivory had wanted to pay me a thousand pounds. She'd wanted to pay me a thousand pounds on Monday night, when I'd turned the job down. I'd refused to take it."

Pell said: "That was silly, wasn't it?"

"It was very silly," I told him. "But now I wanted it. You see, I spent seven hundred and fifty of your thousand on buying a motor car."

He said: "Are you funny? You get a thousand pounds and you have to pay seven hundred and fifty of it on a car."

"I've always wanted a car," I said. "Anyhow, my main idea was to find out where she was. As far as I could see there was only one way I could do it. I could get her address from Ricaud. I could go down there, eat humble pie, tell him some story and by some means find out where she was."

Pell said musingly: "I see. Did you go down there?"

"Yes. That's what I'm worried about. Pell... I didn't know it but I was walking into a bunch of trouble."

He asked: "How come?"

"When I got down there," I told him, "a side door to the house was open and I went in. I found Ricaud in the drawing-room where I'd seen him before, lying on the settee. He was dead. He'd committed suicide."

Pell said: "I know. I saw it in the papers. What are you worried about?"

"Just a little thing," I told him. "Naturally, I was curious. I knelt down and had a look at the body. There was a note too. I didn't touch it. He'd written a suicide note—or so it seemed. I thought I'd get out. I was going away when something funny struck me."

Pell asked: "What?"

"When I was kneeling down by the settee, I didn't think about it at the time, but my leg was being burned by the electric fire which was just behind me. I was almost on top of that fire. When I was going away I realised that that settee was too near the fire. I got the idea that somebody had moved it there after Ricaud was dead. I got the idea that Ricaud hadn't committed suicide. I thought somebody might have killed him. And if somebody had killed him, I had a pretty good idea who it was. It was his wife—Esmeralda Ricaud."

Pell considered the matter. He bit on his cigar. I could see his big teeth. "Well, I still don't see what you're worrying about. You didn't kill him, did you?" he asked humorously.

"No," I said. "I didn't kill him. But look at my position, Pell. I'm a private dick—a 'free-lance.' I'm all right as long as I keep my nose clean, but if I don't what's going to happen to me? If I get mixed up with the police in some lousy killing case? I'm going to get a black mark against my name at all the agencies. See what I mean?"

He said: "That's true enough. But I still don't see what you're driving at?"

"This is it," I said. "When I went down there on Monday, I didn't know where the place was. I had to ask. I asked at that coffee stall that's on the other side of Maidenhead—on the Henley road—that sort of shack place where drivers pull in. They told me where 'Crossways' was. If the police start asking questions, the man at the coffee stall is going to remember me. Who's going to believe me when I say that I went back on Tuesday night to try and get somebody's address from him? It sounds a bit screwy, doesn't it? Truth always does sound screwy. I know all this doesn't add up to anything, but I'm scared. There's the Coroner's

                                   Peter Cheyney

inquest on Saturday, and I've got the wind up about that damned doctor."

Pell said: "You mean the Quinceley bird—the one who put Esmeralda in the nursing home?"

"That's right," I told him. "You see when I saw him he didn't want to play. I had to pull a pretty strong story on him to get him to help me. I told him about Esmeralda having been down there on Monday night waving that gun about, wanting to kill Ricaud. Well, Quinceley knew all about that. She's been saying that sort of stuff all over the place for some time. He knows that the inquest on Ricaud is being held on Saturday. He's wondering whether it is his duty as a doctor to come forward and say something. If he does, he's got to talk about me."

Pell said: "It's one thing for a woman to go about saying she's going to kill her husband and another thing for her to do it. You've got to prove murder, if not by direct evidence then by very good circumstantial evidence."

"That's just it," I said. "There's some damn good circumstantial evidence. We put her in that nursing home on Tuesday in the afternoon and she got out of the goddam place at ten o'clock on Tuesday night. It's known that she went down to Maidenhead. It's all the tea in China to a bad egg that she killed Ricaud. My evidence about what she was doing on Monday night, and the fact that she got out of the nursing home on Tuesday and went down there is pretty good circumstantial evidence. With one or two other things it's almost direct evidence. I know the story and I know what I ought to do. I ought to go to the police."

Pell rubbed his chin. He said: "Now I see what you're getting at. You think this doctor is going to start talking and this suicide theory is going to be exploded. Then you think the cops are going to start running around and looking for something. You think that when they start looking they're going to find something. You think they're going to find you. You think they're going to be very rude to you; that they might get tough about that old-fashioned Metropolitan Police Act—'withholding evidence, etc.'?"

"That's right," I told him. I gave myself another cigarette out of his silver box. "I don't know what the hell to do?" I said. "If it weren't for Quinceley, I think I'd keep my mouth shut. But if I keep my mouth shut and Quinceley talks, I'm in bad. I don't want to start anything unless I've got to. I don't give a damn who killed who or why. I'm thinking of me."

Pell said: "You really think this doctor bird is going to talk? Why don't you go and see him and sound him out?"

"I've done it," I said. "And I don't like the look of it. My guess is that he'll go down to that inquest on Saturday and see how things are going. My guess is he's going to get scared. He may shoot his mouth any time. You know what these doctors are. Even if he waits till Saturday before he talks, the Coroner will adjourn the inquest, and the police will get busy. The next thing is

　　　　　　　　　　　　　Peter Cheyney

I'm going to be a star witness. I don't fancy myself in that role. It wouldn't do me any good."

"No," said Pell. "It probably wouldn't."

There was a pause; then I said: "It's a funny business, Pell—this killing. I've got an idea in my head that somebody was down at that place after Esmeralda left there—after she left and before I arrived. I'll bet anything you like that Ricaud wasn't lying on that settee right close up to that electric fire. Somebody moved that settee—somebody was down there."

Pell said: "I wonder how the police will like to hear that. Ninety-nine per cent of your evidence hangs this killing on to Mrs. Ricaud, who looks to me as if she's the person who did the job. The other one per cent casts a shadow of doubt and brings in some other suspect— somebody who messed around with the evidence. Maybe it'd be a good thing to keep quiet about the settee. Let 'em find it out for themselves."

"I wish I could," I said. "I did another damn silly thing."

He raised his eyebrows. "Don't tell me you've done some more silly things. What else did you do?"

"I don't know what made me do it," I said, "but I moved that settee back to its original position—where I'd seen it on Monday night. It was just one of those things. I wish I knew why I'd done it."

"It's understandable enough," said Pell. "I can understand it. You had the idea first of all that it was suicide. Then, when you thought it was murder, you wondered if suspicion would fall on you. I could tell that by the way you were talking a few minutes ago. So you moved the settee back. If you'd thought, you'd have realised that it was a silly thing to do, but you didn't think. People don't think in those circumstances, or if they do, they think too quickly."

"Maybe you're right. But I'm in a spot. If you were me what would you do?"

He shrugged his shoulders. "I don't know. I'm not you, so I can't say. The thing is what do you think you're going to do? You've got to decide between two things. If you tell the whole truth about this business, it's not going to do you a lot of good as a private detective. I mean, as you've said, the agencies might take it into their heads to blacklist you. On the other hand, if you don't do anything about it and this doctor talks, you might be in a spot with the police. It's for you to decide. It's a pity about that doctor, isn't it?"

I said: "Yes...." I thought for a moment. Then: "Maybe I'll have another talk with him. Maybe I can get him to keep quiet. It's worth trying anyhow."

Pell said: "You'll have to move quickly, won't you? When are you thinking of doing that?"

"I'll have to see him tomorrow morning. I've got to make up my mind one way or another." I poured myself out a drink. I went on: "It's funny... ever since I've been in the detective business I've managed to keep my nose clean. I've made some good money and I've done some good work. Now here's a case which I didn't even want; I turn money down for it and then have to stick my nose into it out of curiosity. And look where I've landed myself."

Pell said: "That's the way it goes." He looked serious. I could see he was thinking hard. He said: "Well, you'll have to work it out for yourself, O'Hara, and I hope it comes out all right for you."

I said: "Well, it was nice of you to listen to me. I've been worrying about it. It's done me good to talk about it. I'll see this doctor tomorrow morning. I'll make up my mind then after I've heard what he's got to say."

He said: "All right. I wish you luck. Have another drink?"

I had another drink. I told him I'd left my rooms; that I was staying at the Malinson Hotel. Then I went away. On my way down the street to where I'd parked the car I thought I wasn't dissatisfied. I thought I'd said my little piece without any slip-up. I thought I'd be all right.

4

I WENT on the town. I went on the town because I was bored, a bit scared, and very depressed. I'd started something now that I couldn't stop even if I wanted to. I'd got to go on with it. All the way.

I told myself that it was "one of those things "—which is what you do when you're trying to kid yourself that you don't really mind what happens.

I started off at the Gay Nineties in Bruton Street. I drank a couple of large whiskies and sodas and wise-cracked with the two behind the bar—Terry and Dodo.

Dodo thought I was in very good form and said so. She thought I was very funny. I didn't. To me I sounded like something on its way to a funeral. The whisky didn't do anything to me at all.

Then I walked around for a bit. Most of the time I was thinking of variations of the main theme in my mind—a process which didn't get me anywhere, I dropped into one or two places that I knew and drank whisky without getting any kick out of the liquor.

It was eleven o'clock when I went to Griselda's. Griselda's—just in case you don't know—is a bottle party. One of the better ones. It differs from most of the others inasmuch as they keep some air on the premises and the one or two turns that they put on about eleven-fifteen are good. I did a job for Griselda once which she thought was a good business and she's always made things very nice for me at her place.

I sat down at a table and ate a sandwich and drank some more whisky. After a bit they put the house-lights out and the band swung into a rhythmic number. Some babe with a sweet and inquiring face, a frock that looked as if it had been pasted on to her and a streamlined chassis that was built for speed rather than safety, wandered on to the floor and started to vocalise the customers with a voice that would have been out for the count if it hadn't had her legs behind it. She crooned... 'When he don't talk baby talk any more. When he don't kiss like he used to before. It's time you added up the score...' And a lot more like that. When she finished she got a nice hand from one and all. And all I can say is that if

                                    Peter Cheyney

she thought the boys were applauding her voice she was looking at life with blinkers on and no mirror in the bathroom. She didn't have to have a voice anyway. She didn't need a voice.

She sang another little piece in the direction of a plump sugar-daddy at one of the edge-of-the-floor tables. It was called 'What could I do for you.' After she'd got through one verse and the refrain the old boy ordered a bottle of champagne and looked soulful. Maybe he was thinking of his boyhood, or his wife or something... maybe...

I got up and went out. It was a nice night and I thought I was bored with whisky and walking around. I went back to the Malinson Hotel.

It was near midnight and I was tired. Thinking about it I concluded that I'd done a lot since last Monday night. I went up to my room, stripped and got under the shower. Then the telephone began to ring in the bedroom. I wrapped a towel round me, went into the bedroom and answered it.

It was the night porter. He said: "Mr. O'Hara, there's a gentleman down here at the office wants to see you particularly. He's Detective-Inspector Gale from Scotland Yard. He says that his business is urgent."

I thought: This is it. This is where the fun begins.

I said: "I'm taking a bath. Ask him to sit down and wait in the lounge for ten minutes or so. I'll call you when to bring him up."

He said: "O.K., Mr. O'Hara."

I went back to the bathroom and finished the shower. Then I dressed myself, lighted a cigarette and telephoned down to the night-porter.

5

THERE'S an awful lot of nonsense talked about police officers. It's only during the last year or so that the public have been getting an idea as to what they do and what they're like.

Most of the time people think that they're either like Sherlock Holmes with an answer for everything, or else that they're so stupid that they positively creak. In quite a lot of detective fiction the police officer is made to be so moronic that he ought to be certified and put in a looney bin. This is done so as to make some other type in the story seem all the more brilliant by comparison.

By and large police officers—especially C.I.D. men—and more especially the boys from the Central Office—are intelligent men with one speciality. The speciality is that they know about life and they're used to talking to all sorts of people. And when I say they know about life I mean just that. Nine-tenths of the people in any big city know sweet nothing about the tenth tenth. Nothing at all. If they did they'd be very surprised.

But the experienced detective—like the experienced crime reporter—is never surprised at anything. He knows where to look for things. He knows where to find certain sorts of people. He knows all about the odd things that go on in the city. The things that never make

Peter Cheyney

the news pages for no other reason than the fact that they never make the news pages. And they never will. No matter who's running the newspaper. Just because life is like that. And he knows it.

Fifty per cent of the crime that happens isn't due to this or that or any of the things that nice people like to think are responsible for crime. It's due to certain basic things that lurk in the minds of all sorts and conditions of people in all classes.

If a detective officer knows that a clever job has been pulled off he doesn't delude himself that the boys who did it got busy because they wanted to stand themselves oysters and champagne at the Savoy. Or because they wanted a trip to Switzerland. He knows that usually the job was pulled because the boys who planned it wanted some quick money for a reason—and the reason is—in ninety-nine cases out of a hundred—a skirt. A skirt with a nice shape inside it; a skirt that likes things that cost money. If they ever want to write a motto over the entrance to Scotland Yard they know what it ought to be—just three words 'Cherchez la femme'—and the three words mean the same in any language—including Chinese.

That's why a successful detective officer is a man who knows quite a bit about women and likes them; a man who can talk to a woman; a man who can talk as if he really meant it; a man who can kid some baby that her boy friend—who is a police suspect—is making a pass at some other frail. You'd be surprised at the number of people who've pulled really nice jobs, get hauled in for them and spend a number of quiet years inside pondering on why they were stupid enough to talk to the girl of the moment. By the time they get out they've realised that they talked to the girl of the moment because they thought at the time that she was the one and only girl; that there wasn't going to be another one.

But now they think they're wiser. And they know they're never going to talk to a woman again. Not about business. And six months, or a year or two years later, some pleasant-spoken detective officer has a cup of tea with a nicely-shaped girl, and the boy friend goes inside again. History repeats itself.

Because human nature is like that. If it wasn't there wouldn't be any fun in anything at all.

That's how it is. The normal good citizen you see walking around is a normal good citizen walking around because he wants most of all to be just that. But he mustn't delude himself about it. If he does he may catch himself out one day. If he does he may run into some sweetie-pie with that cute appeal—that special appeal that he likes—that he wants more than anything else. Even more than being a good normal citizen walking around. See what I mean?

A lot of men think that they've been unlucky because they've never met the woman they've dreamed about. They don't know the half of it. Maybe they've been more lucky than they know. Supposing they had met her and she'd wanted some quick money very quickly. Very badly. Just supposing... what would they have done?... Think that one out.

                    Peter Cheyney

Whoever it was said: "There but for the grace of God goes so-and-so" must have had a pal who was a C.I.D. man from Central Office.

6

THE Detective-Inspector was a thin type with horn-rimmed glasses. He wore a well-cut, double-breasted, blue, pin-stripe suit and a close-shaven, keen and amiable expression.

I asked him to have a drink and he said yes. Which told me quite a lot. Police officers don't usually drink when they're on duty. If they do, it's only because they think it's going to help them; that it's going to make you feel easier and happier about everything.

It told me that Detective-Inspector Gale was doing a little reconnaissance on me and what I knew. It told me that this was going to be a nice informal conversation with me doing my duty as a good citizen and helping the police; and that underneath all that Gale was watching points like a cat over a mouse-hole. It told me that there'd been a telephone conversation between Scotland Yard and the Berkshire Chief Constable. Scotland Yard had told the Chief Constable just what somebody had told them within the last four to five hours. The Chief Constable had been a trifle surprised and had promptly—being a wise man—asked for co-operation from Central Office. That meant that a Chief-Detective-Inspector had being appointed to the Ricaud affair. The Chief-Detective-Inspector had done a little quick thinking about this and that and had come to the conclusion that Detective-Inspector Gale was the man for the job. Because Gale was a nice, amiable person who looked so pleasant that nobody was going to feel odd or unhappy or scared. The Chief-Detective-Inspector knew that Gale wouldn't make any mistakes and that he had a memory like a shorthand notebook and that what I said to him would stay in his mind— almost word for word.

I turned on the electric fire and he drank some of his whisky and soda and got to work.

He said: "Mr. O'Hara, you've probably seen the newspaper reports about the death of a man called Alexis Ricaud at a house called 'Crossways' near Maidenhead?"

I said yes and he went on: "We believe that there's more in this thing than meets the eye and we believe that you can help us. Naturally, we have to check on all angles—even if we don't quite believe that there's anything in what we're checking. I know you understand that?"

I said yes and drank some more whisky.

"The Berkshire police have asked us to make one or two inquiries," said Gale in his nice soothing voice. "We've discovered amongst other things that on Monday night last you asked where 'Crossways' was. You asked at the coffee stall on the other side of Maidenhead. The man who told you remembers you well."

I nodded. "How does he remember my name? I didn't tell him that?" I grinned at Gale.

                                    Peter Cheyney

He said: "Quite "—which, if you think about it, was a good answer. The only answer he could think of to that one.

He continued: "Actually—and I'm going to put my cards down flat on the table, Mr. O'Hara, there is a suggestion that this Ricaud bird didn't commit suicide; that somebody killed him. Of course you know that in an inquiry into alleged murder any citizen who has any knowledge that may help the police is bound, by law, to produce it. But please don't think that we're taking that attitude with you." (I thought: Oh... no... like hell you're not.) "I've come to you because I thought you might be able to volunteer something—no matter how slight—that might help us."

I said: "I don't know. It depends on what line you're taking in your enquiry. When I know that I'll know if I can tell you anything."

He said: "Quite."

I got the idea that when he wanted to do a little rapid thinking he said "Quite." It was a nice word and gave him two or three seconds.

He went on: "Our line is that Ricaud was killed. We have to take that line, not necessarily because we believe it, but because it's been suggested. By the way, did you go to 'Crossways' last Monday night?"

I nodded. "Yes," I told him. I got up and began to walk about the room. I looked worried for his benefit. Then I said; "Won't you have another little drink?"

"Yes, please," he answered. "I never drink much in the day but it's nice to have a drink at this time. And this is nice whisky."

I poured out two more drinks. Then I began to walk up and down with my glass in my hand. After a bit I said: "The best thing I can do, Mr. Gale, is to tell you what I know in my own way. It may add up to something from your point of view. Incidentally, I'm glad you came along because I've been worried about whether or not I ought to have gone to Scotland Yard and talked before."

He said: "Quite." Then: "Why didn't you... if it's not a rude question?"

"An obvious reason," I told him. "I didn't want to start something that might be unfair to anyone."

"Of course," he said. He drank some whisky and let it go at that. Then, after a bit: "Would it help you if I made note of what you'd like to tell me? I write shorthand so it wouldn't take a lot of time. Perhaps it would help."

"No... it wouldn't," I said.

"Don't you think it might?" he asked. "But perhaps you've a reason for not wanting it."

"I have," I told him. "I'm going to tell you what's in my mind. Right off—without even thinking much about it. And I know that when I've talked to you it will be necessary for me—some time or other—to make a proper statement. When I do that I'd like to write out the statement myself. You see? I think it would be better that way."

                                        Peter Cheyney

"Of course," he said. He was feeling happier now. I was coming along nicely, he thought.

I said: "I went to 'Crossways' last Monday night to see Ricaud. I went to see him on some business that a client had asked me to see him about. I'd rather not discuss that if you don't mind. When I got there I couldn't get any answer at the front of the house so I had a look round at the back."

I stopped talking and finished the whisky.

Then I said: "By the way, when the Berkshire police went to the house after the suicide report, and when the mortuary ambulance went there to take Ricaud's body away, did they use the front carriage drive or the back?"

He said: "The front. And the back gates were locked this morning. Nobody's been in that way since the first report. Why?"

"Because you'll want to photograph the back gravel drive," I said. "So you won't want anyone walking about on it. See?"

He said: "I see." Now he was looking very interested. He lighted a cigarette from a neat leather case.

"I went in the back way—the gates weren't locked," I went on. "I went into the grounds and I met a woman—I know now that she was Esmeralda Ricaud—Ricaud's wife. She was high. She'd had a lot of whisky, I should say, and she looked to me like a dope. When she dropped her handbag on the grass I picked it up—I felt the gun inside it—an automatic pistol. And I didn't think she was the type who ought to be walking about with a gun."

He said: "You're telling me." He was listening intently. Everything, he thought, was going to be much easier than he'd expected. He could already visualise me in the box—the star witness for the prosecution—'Rex 21. Esmeralda Ricaud on trial for Murder.' He was feeling happy all right. And why not? It's a policeman's business to arrest murderers. And he could see himself arresting one, he hoped, very shortly.

He stubbed out his cigarette in the ash-tray. I told him to help himself to another drink. He said no thanks; he'd have another cigarette instead.

I went on: "I thought it my business to head her off. I thought she was a little dangerous "—he smiled at the understatement—"more especially as she didn't like her husband very much and said she'd like to kill him. I believe she's been saying that quite a lot. And by what I know of him she was dead right. Somebody ought to have done Ricaud a long time ago."

He nodded. He was too patient, too well-trained, to tell me to stick to the story and cut out the frills.

"I put her in the back of my car. That was easy because she'd passed out. I brought her back to London and put her up with some friends of mine for the night. Next day I got her into a nursing home—"

He interrupted. "Mr. O'Hara, when you were at 'Crossways,' did you see and talk to Ricaud?"

I jumped in on that. I intended to run this thing my way—not his. I said: "Listen... I told you that it's obvious to me that I shall have to make a statement. When I do, I shall expect to be cross-examined on it—maybe in Court. But not here. Be a good guy and skip the questions. I'm trying to think."

He smiled apologetically.

"When she was in the nursing home I thought she'd be O.K.," I went on. "Besides which, I was rather bored with her. I never fancied myself as a nurse for dopes. Before I took her to the nursing home I saw the doctor who'd been looking after her before—a doctor named Quinceley. You know him. He's the person who told you about me, isn't he?"

He said: "Does it matter? The point isn't really material."

"To me it is," I said. "Either you answer that question or I stop talking. I'm entitled to some sort of consideration. I'm saving you a hell of a lot of work." I made my voice sound a trifle peeved.

He said: "Well... actually, it wasn't Quinceley. This is the first I've heard about him."

But he hadn't told me who it was. And if he could have told me he would have done so, just to seem nice and open and honest. He hadn't told me because he couldn't. I knew why, so I skipped the point. I'd found out what I wanted to know.

I lighted a cigarette. I went on: "That night I went down to 'Crossways' because I wanted to see Ricaud. What I wanted to see him about doesn't matter just at this time. I'll get around to that point when I write out my full statement. And, anyway, it isn't material at the moment."

"All right," he said. "Just go ahead. Stick to the main story. It's very interesting."

"And how!" I said. "When I got down there—and it was pretty late—I went round to the back gate—like I did before. I found the side door—the one not far from the garage—open, and I went in. I went into the drawing-room and I found Ricaud lying on the settee in front of the fire. At first I thought he was asleep—until I had a look. Then it was obvious. He had committed suicide."

"Suicide! You really think that?" he asked.

"At that moment I did," I told him. "And so would you and so would anyone else. Anybody would have been satisfied that it was suicide. There was the gun, the powder marks round the inlet wound; there was the suicide note—and you can take it from me Ricaud wrote that note—I know his handwriting and I'd swear to it—everything pointed to suicide. I knelt down and took a close look at him and that was how it seemed to me."

He said musingly: "So he did write the suicide note?"

"Of course he did," I said. "But it wasn't all that he intended to write. It was only the top page. He'd intended to go on writing some more. The note looked finished but it wasn't."

He whistled softly to himself. He'd heard the wording of the note—probably from the Berkshire police—and he got what I meant.

"I was satisfied that it was suicide," I said. "And I thought the thing for me to do was to get out while the

Peter Cheyney

going was good. I wasn't keen on getting myself mixed up in a suicide inquest at that time."

"No," he said, with a grin. "You wouldn't want that at that particular time, would you?"

"Meaning what?" I asked him.

"Meaning that you didn't go down there to see Ricaud to inquire after Ricaud's health. You went down there to see him about something else—something connected with a client of yours—obviously. Which is why you didn't want to get mixed up with a Coroner's inquest. That's quite understandable. O.K. Go ahead with the story."

I thought: That's one to you, Gale. There weren't any flies on Detective-Inspector Gale. And he wanted me to know that. He wanted me to know that he'd guessed I was down there on some client's business that I didn't want to talk about. He was indicating that providing he got what he wanted about the main story, nobody was going to ask me questions on matters that could be considered immaterial if I didn't want to volunteer the information. Gale was no fool.

I said: "I was on my way out when I remembered something. I remembered that when I was kneeling down by the fire in order to get a look at Ricaud—a close look—I'd felt my leg being burned by the electric fire. I realised that the settee was too near to the fire. Then I got the idea that somebody had moved the settee up to the fire to confuse the medical evidence."

He nodded. "To delay rigor mortis," he said. "But I don't get it about this settee. The Berkshire police never said anything about a settee being moved out of its normal position."

"No," I said. "They wouldn't. Because I moved it back."

"Why did you do that?" he asked.

"To make sure that it had really been moved in the first place." I said. "When I'd moved it I saw that the position into which I'd pushed it was the normal position. I didn't bother to move it back again because by now I really was scared. Damned scared."

He drew on his cigarette. He was watching me. He was concentrating. He asked: "What made you so scared?"

I shrugged my shoulders. "I didn't like the set-up. Because it looked to me as if somebody had moved that settee and framed the job to look like suicide. I didn't like that at all. And I didn't want to get mixed up in a murder job. That's understandable, isn't it?"

He nodded. "What did you do then, Mr. O'Hara?"

"I got out," I told him. "Good and quick. I went back to my car that I'd left out on the road behind 'Crossways' and went back to London. I stopped only to make a telephone call."

"To whom?" he asked. There was a certain decision in his voice.

I hesitated for a moment, then: "What the hell!" I said. I shrugged my shoulders. "You're going to find out anyway. If I don't tell you, Quinceley will. I stopped to telephone the nursing home..."

"To ask if Mrs. Ricaud was still there?" he queried.

                                            Peter Cheyney

I nodded.

"And was she?" he asked.

I shook my head. "She'd got out just about ten o'clock. She took a run-out on them. They didn't know where she'd gone."

"And you think she went to 'Crossways'?" he asked.

"I don't know," I said. I gave myself a cigarette. I needed it. Then I helped myself to another drink.

He said: "I didn't ask you what you knew about Mrs. Ricaud's movements. I asked you if you thought she went to 'Crossways' after she left the nursing home?"

I shrugged my shoulders.

He didn't say anything for a bit. He took a cigarette out of his case and lit it. He took plenty of time. He was thinking. He was thinking whether it would be better to start work on me then and there and try and fill in the gaps I'd left in the story; to try and find out my reasons for being at "Crossways," what the job was and all the other things he wanted to know, or whether it would be better to talk to Quinceley first, get his story and then start in on me again. That's what he was thinking about.

But he said: "Mr. O'Hara, I appreciate very much the information you've given me. It's going to be a great help to us. Because, as I told you, we've got to take a serious view of this business. Especially now that we've heard your story. There's one thing that you might be able to tell me that would be of the greatest assistance to us. I hope you'll do your best to give me just one more piece of information."

"Such as?" I asked.

He said: "Where is Mrs. Ricaud?"

I replied: "I don't know."

There was a silence. One of those silences. He looked at the glowing end of his cigarette and did some more thinking.

Then: "Mr. O'Hara. You say you found Mrs. Ricaud in the grounds on Monday night. With an automatic. Was it loaded?"

I said: "I don't know. I didn't look."

There was another pause; then: "You say that you brought her back to London and put her up for the night with some friends of yours; that next day you took her to a nursing home and got her doctor—Quinceley—to go and see her. Did she give you his address?"

I said: "No. I found his card in her handbag—after she'd passed out."

He asked: "Had you any reason for taking such an interest in Mrs. Ricaud? When you went to 'Crossways' on Monday night, did you expect to find her there?"

I said: "No."

He nodded. "Of course not. You went there on other business, didn't you?"

I didn't say anything.

He asked: "Why did you feel that you had to bring Mrs. Ricaud back to London; to put her up for the night with friends; to get her into a nursing home next day; to go and see her doctor about her; to get him to go and see her; and then, after your return to 'Crossways' on Tuesday night when you found Ricaud's body—why did you, as soon as you'd got well away from the house, telephone the nursing home to find out if she was still there? Why did you do all these things?"

I grinned at him. "I wouldn't know," I said.

He grinned back at me. He got up and opened his cigarette case; held it out to me. I took a cigarette, lighted it and said thank you.

He sat down again. He said: "I know that it's considered professional ethics on the part of you private dicks not to discuss a client's private affairs with anybody, but—"

I interrupted. "Who told you that I was a private dick?"

That one got him. It got him for quite twenty seconds. He smiled and said: "We know all the private detectives in London. We have to. And there's only one O'Hara."

I thought that was a very quick recovery. I gave him full marks for that one.

He went on: "I wanted to ask you if Mrs. Ricaud was your client?"

I said: "No. I'd never seen her before Monday night."

He said: "I see. And you don't know where she lives?"

I said: "No."

"And you don't know where she is at the moment?" he asked.

I said: "No."

"You brought her back from 'Crossways' after she'd passed out on Monday night," he said. "And you brought her back to London in your car—"

"I brought her up to London," I said. "Why back to London? I've never suggested that she came from London to 'Crossways.'"

He grinned at me approvingly. "You know all the answers, don't you? I think if I ever needed a private detective I'd be inclined to brief you."

I said: "Thanks. I'd be glad to do your business—if I liked it."

"All right," he said. "Well... anyhow, you brought her up to London, and I suppose some time or other she came out of the pass-out?"

I nodded.

He said: "Are you telling me that after that, when she found you'd brought her up to town, she didn't talk to you? Are you suggesting that she did what she was told and went into a nursing home, and generally behaved herself like a good little girl and never once told you where she lived?"

I said: "Yes, I am suggesting that."

He asked: "When you were taking her to the nursing home didn't she need some clothes—some night stuff and toilet stuff? She would have to take some things in with her. Where did those things come from?"

I said: "I never thought about it. Maybe the nursing home sent for some things for her. I wouldn't know."

He asked: "Where was the nursing home?"

I told him.

He got up. He said: "Well, Mr. O'Hara, you've been very helpful, and I'm very much obliged to you for your assistance. I think I ought to tell you that the Berkshire

                                    Peter Cheyney

people have handed this business over to us at the Yard; and I think you ought to know that as the result of the additional information we have received, my superior will be inclined to inquire very closely into the matter of the death of Alexis Ricaud."

I said: "Yes... They'd be nuts if they didn't."

He threw me a quick look. "I think you ought to know that we shall subpoena you as a witness in the event of inquiries necessitating an arrest on a charge of murder. I suppose you won't be thinking of going out of London for a day or so?"

I said no.

He picked up his hat. "I shall report the full gist of our conversation to my superior, Mr. O'Hara, and I take it that if called upon you will be prepared to make a statement on the lines you've indicated to me."

I said: "Yes... of course." Then I grinned at him. "Without prejudice..."

He looked mildly surprised. "Without prejudice to what?" he asked.

I gave him another grin. "Mr. Gale, you and I have had a conversation. Just that. I haven't been giving evidence on oath. I've just been doing what I consider to be my duty as a private citizen who is requested to give information to the police. I've given you the information. I've given it without prejudice to my right as a citizen to withdraw, amplify or amend such information at any time I make a statement in writing."

That shook him a little. But only a little.

He said in a nice, quiet and friendly voice: "Mr. O'Hara, I think you're much too clever a man to fall out with the authorities. You're too clever to do that because you know it wouldn't do you any good. Not in your business. I'd like you to answer me one question—and really it's not a question that I'm entitled to ask; I tell you that frankly. This is a question just between you and me. If you answer it, you'll help me. If you don't answer it, I'll know why you haven't answered it."

I grinned some more. "So either way you've got me. I'm getting scared. What's the question?"

He looked seriously at me. He said: "If, as a result of the inquiries I make during the next twenty-four hours, my superiors should consider it necessary that a warrant for the arrest of Mrs. Ricaud be issued, do you consider that your evidence would be evidence for the police?"

I said yes.

That satisfied him. He put on his hat, said good-night and went.

I shut the door after him; gave myself another drink; smoked two cigarettes and went to bed.

I read the Evening News for ten minutes and switched off the light.

I thought that as a police officer Detective-Inspector Gale was pretty good.

Then I went to sleep.

　　　　　　　　　　　Peter Cheyney

CHAPTER FIVE

FRIDAY — APEX
1

I GOT up at ten o'clock. I rang down for breakfast; ate it; dressed; wandered about my bedroom. I was restless. I concluded I was entitled to be restless.

After a bit I got sick of walking about the bedroom. And the idea of sitting about downstairs in the comfortable lounge, reading the magazines and papers, didn't appeal to me. I went out and walked about. I walked around Leicester Square, Regent Street, Bond Street, aimlessly—not even bothering to notice things.

After a bit I found myself walking towards the West Central district—towards my rooms in Falsom Place.

I'd had those. I was fed up with those rooms. I was beginning to think that I was fed up with everything. But I made up my mind about one thing. After this business was over I was going to have a new set-up. I was going to get myself some new rooms and a new office. In an odd sort of way this Ivory business had done me good. Whatever happened my morale had improved. I had thrown off that "Formosa" feeling.

When I got to my rooms I packed up my remaining things, saw the Manager of the block downstairs, paid him his money, took a receipt and got out. He arranged to send my things on to the Malinson.

Then I walked to the office. There was some mail—two or three letters. Somebody wanted me to investigate some cash leakages at an hotel in North Devon. Then there was an Insurance job. I liked that. I'd always wanted to start working for Insurance Companies. It's good business. If you do the job well you can get plenty of work from those boys, but at this moment I didn't want it. I couldn't take it anyway—not as things were. I got out the typewriter and wrote a letter and told them so.

Then I looked round the office and concluded that I liked it less than ever. I started going through the drawers in my desk. There wasn't very much in them—only odd paper clips, bits of sealing wax and the usual things that a man collects. But in the bottom drawer——the one I used to keep the whisky bottle in—I saw the Railway Company's folder—the folder with the picture of the hotel in Torquay. The folder was stuck in the drawer, so I pulled the drawer right out; then I saw there was another half-bottle of whisky right at the back—something I'd forgotten! I liked that a lot.

I pulled the stopper out and gave myself a drink. Then I sat back in my desk chair looking at the folder. It was a nice-looking hotel—not too big—and with a garden at the back that looked out on to the sea-front, and another one at the side. It was a big rambling old-fashioned house that had been converted. It had atmosphere. It looked friendly, and in the picture you could see that the sun was shining and you could see the sea. And right at the end of the picture you could see

                    Peter Cheyney

the bandstand with the band playing. I put the folder in my pocket. I thought maybe with luck I'd get around to that hotel one day.

I wrote a letter to the office landlords telling them that I'd be giving it up by the end of the quarter; that I'd call around some time next week and give them a cheque. When I'd finished the letter I locked up the office; went out; posted my letters; went back to the Malinson and had lunch.

I'd nearly finished when a page boy came in and told me I was wanted on the telephone.

I took the call in the box in the hall. Somebody asked who I was. When I said I was O'Hara, they told me that was the office of Selby, Rourkes and Selby, and would I hold on. I said yes. Then a voice came on the telephone. It was a nice, crisp voice.

It said: "Good afternoon, Mr. O'Hara. I hope I haven't interrupted your lunch. But my business is rather urgent."

I said yes and waited.

The voice went on: "I am Mr. Selby. We are solicitors for Mrs. Leonora Ivory. I believe you know her."

I said yes that was right.

He continued: "I'm very sorry to tell you that a rather tragic situation has happened this morning. I don't want to discuss it on the telephone but I think I ought to give you some idea of what it is. It seems that the police think that a friend of Mrs. Ivory's—a Mrs. Esmeralda Ricaud, the wife of an individual who died three days ago—is somehow implicated in what they allege to be a murder."

I said: "Yes? That's the Ricaud suicide thing. So the police think it's murder?"

He said: "Yes, Mr. O'Hara. The point is that I would very much like to talk to you. I might go so far as to say that it is essential that I talk to you. I need not tell you that any demands we make on your time, which I am sure is valuable, will be adequately recompensed."

I asked: "When would you like to talk to me?"

"As soon as possible," he said. "I wonder if you could come round to the office now. Our address is at 129a. Lincoln's Inn Fields."

I said: "I'll be with you in ten minutes, Mr. Selby."

I went back and finished my lunch. Then I got the Rover out of the garage; drove round to Lincoln's Inn Fields. I found the place in two or three minutes—nice old-fashioned family lawyers' offices.

Selby was a good type—about sixty with white hair and keen, penetrating eyes. He looked very wise. He gave me a big leather armchair at the end of his desk and a cigarette; then he said: "Mr. O'Hara, I'm not going to waste time—either yours or mine—with long explanations. I'm going to come to the point as quickly as I can. Briefly, the situation is this:

"Mrs. Ivory, whose solicitors we are, has instructed us to represent her friend Mrs. Esmeralda Ricaud, who, it would seem, is at the moment under suspicion of having murdered her husband Alexis Ricaud last Tuesday night at a house called 'Crossways' near Maidenhead.

"We have had only vague instructions from Mrs. Ivory. In fact, she has been unable to tell us very much about this matter. It seems that Mrs. Ricaud is at the present moment very ill at Mrs. Ivory's house at Wych Cross in Sussex. She has been more or less unconscious most of the time since she arrived there in the early hours of Wednesday morning, and the doctors will not allow her to be questioned. They consider she is in a very serious state of health. The police are of course behaving with their invariable courtesy in the matter. But there is a detective officer at the house in case Mrs. Ricaud should recover sufficiently to be able to answer some questions, and of course he will stay there for the time being.

"Naturally, Mrs. Ivory is extremely perturbed at the situation. She instructed us an hour before I telephoned you and we are in fact watching the case as carefully as we can. You understand all that, Mr. O'Hara? I am sure you can realise exactly what the position is."

I said: "Yes. It's not a very good one from your point of view. You're working in the dark, aren't you?"

"Not entirely," he said. "I've been through to Chief-Detective-Inspector Millin who, I believe, is in charge of the case, and he has very kindly informed me of the things which he thinks it is right for me to know. Amongst other things, I have discovered that some sort of verbal statement was made by you last night to Detective-Inspector Gale—an officer junior to Chief-Detective-Inspector Millin and working under his direction. I do not know of course what lines this statement followed, but Mrs. Ivory has told me that you are aware of certain facts which would certainly mitigate the very harsh circumstances which seem to be pressing upon Mrs. Ricaud at the moment. I thought, therefore, I should like to have a heart-to-heart talk with you to find out as much as possible about this unfortunate affair. Naturally, anything that is said in this office is between you and me and in the most complete confidence."

I said: "Of course. Ask anything you want, Mr. Selby."

He said: "Mr. O'Hara, is it your considered opinion that Mrs. Ricaud may have killed her husband?"

"Yes... I think it is."

He asked: "Do you think, if she did so, it was accidental or deliberate and premeditated?"

"I don't know," I replied. "I wasn't there."

"But you do believe that she did kill him?"

I said: "I couldn't swear to that in a witness box. Before I'd swear that Esmeralda Ricaud killed her husband I should have to know she did it—that is I should have to have seen her do it. I didn't see her do it, so I can't answer that question."

"Then you have other things in your mind—shall we say some circumstantial evidence—which leads you to believe that she might have killed him?"

I said: "Yes, there's a lot of circumstantial evidence and most of it isn't very good for Mrs. Ricaud."

He said: "Mr. O'Hara.... I wonder if you'd talk freely to me on this subject."

"Surely," I said. "I haven't anything to hide. The position is this: Last Monday night Mrs. Ivory came to see me at my office. She was very worried about Esmeralda Ricaud. She was worried about Esmeralda because apparently she's heard from Mrs. Ricaud's friends, or from somebody, that Mrs. Ricaud was in a very bad state. She'd been drinking a lot and taking drugs."

He nodded. "I realise that's a very important point. Please go on, Mr. O'Hara."

I went on: "I understood from Mrs. Ivory that this Ricaud bird was pretty bad medicine. I have my own reasons for believing that what Mrs. Ivory told me about him was true. I think he was a man of the very worst type—a blackmailer, a sadist, a man who had preyed on women for most of his life. Mrs. Ivory told me that in her considered opinion, Ricaud had merely married Esmeralda for her money; that he'd had most of it; that she was desperate. In other words, she thought that in the condition in which Esmeralda was she might do something very stupid."

"Such as killing Ricaud?" he asked. "Did Mrs. Ivory suggest that?"

"No," I said. "She didn't suggest that. That was my idea."

"I see. You came to that conclusion on no facts at all? You had no real reason to believe that Mrs. Ricaud had thought of killing her husband?"

"I hadn't" I said. "Not then. But I had a few hours later."

He raised his eyebrows. He looked at me enquiringly.

"Mrs. Ivory's idea was that I should go down to 'Crossways' and endeavour to talk sense to this Mr. Ricaud," I went on. "She thought that if I told him that we knew that he'd been supplying his wife with drugs, and generally threw a scare into him, he'd get out. She thought that would be a good thing for one and all.

"I went down there. That's where I met Esmeralda. I met her in the grounds. She was cock-eyed, and I think she'd been taking dope. She had an automatic pistol in her handbag and she told me that she was waiting for Ricaud; that she was going to kill him. She told me she always wanted to kill him when she was tight."

He jumped in on that one. "Only when she was drunk did she feel like that? She didn't feel like it when she was her normal self?"

I said: "I don't know. I've never seen her when she's been normal."

He asked: "Would you like to go on, Mr. O'Hara?"

I continued: "On Tuesday I put Mrs. Ricaud into a nursing home. I'd already seen her doctor—a Doctor Quinceley—and told him the circumstances. Quinceley didn't like Ricaud either. I'm pretty certain that Quinceley had an idea in his head that Ricaud had been the source of the drug supply to his wife. Anyway, she went into the nursing home, and on Tuesday night Quinceley went and saw her there. She got out of that nursing home on Tuesday night about ten o'clock. She went back to her flat. She had some more drink and she got a hired car. I believe she went down to Maidenhead."

                    Peter Cheyney

He said: "You're not certain?"

"Of course I'm not. I didn't see her there."

He asked: "You went down there again on Tuesday night?"

I said: "Yes... and when I got there Ricaud was dead."

"Mr. O'Hara, have you reason to believe that Mrs. Ricaud went there on Tuesday night?"

I nodded. "Every reason. I have direct evidence to that effect."

He asked; "Would you tell me what it is?"

I said: "No."

"Have you given that evidence in the verbal statement you've made to Detective-Inspector Gale?"

"No..." I said.

He asked: "Why not?"

"I suppose I just didn't think of it."

"Do you propose to make a further statement to the police?" he asked.

I nodded. "Yes.... I shall have to."

He said: "In that statement do you propose to refer to this direct evidence that you say you have—evidence that shows that Mrs. Ricaud went down to Maidenhead on Tuesday night?"

I said: "Yes, I shall have to do that too."

"Then why, Mr. O'Hara, cannot you tell me what this evidence is?"

"I could tell you," I said. "But I'm not going to."

He didn't like that. He was quiet for quite a bit. Then he said: "Mr. O'Hara, let us for the sake of argument adopt a theoretical basis to work from. Let us imagine that Mrs. Ricaud did go down to Maidenhead and did kill her husband. Do you think that if and when she did that she was responsible for her actions?"

"I'm damned certain she wasn't. I don't believe that Esmeralda Ricaud was responsible for her actions at any time that I've known her. Certainly not on Monday night. In my opinion she was drunk and under the influence of drugs. On Tuesday, before she went into the nursing home, she was very ill—physically and mentally. When she was in the nursing home she had no sort of drugs or stimulants. She said she was trying to do without them. That would make her feel worse. I don't know if you know anything about a drug hangover but it's a pretty bad thing. People who are used to taking drugs have got to have them or they go a little funny in the mind. She must have been like that when she got out of the nursing home."

He said: "Quite. And probably she would have taken something else to try and steady herself before she went to 'Crossways'—that is if she went to 'Crossways.'"

I said: "I should think she would have."

"So," he went on, "when she got there she wouldn't be responsible?"

"I think that might easily be," I said. "She'd just go down there because... well, she was drawn to this man Ricaud by this peculiar attraction he had for her."

He said quickly: "Almost hypnotic possibly?"

"Call it that if you like," I said. "But she felt she had to go down there."

"Has it occurred to you, Mr. O'Hara, that she might possibly have carried that pistol for self-protection?"

I said: "Yes... it has occurred to me."

"And," he continued, "do you think that's why she carried it—because she thought Ricaud might attack her?"

I said: "No... I don't think that. Ricaud wasn't the sort of person who went in for attacking people. He was a sadist but a mental one. He gave her enough hurt in the mind without worrying about knocking her about. In any event, he'd succeeded in doing that by means of drink and drugs, because I believe it was he who introduced them to her."

He said: "I see. Tell me, Mr. O'Hara, would you like to give me a description in your own words of Mrs. Ricaud? Would you like to tell me what you think about her generally?"

"Yes," I said. "I think she's a poor thing. I think she's never had a dog's chance. I think she was a pretty decent girl till she met Ricaud. But after he'd been working on her for two or three months I don't think she'd have a hope. I should say his technique was to get hold of a woman who was good-looking and had some money; to get the money; to wreck her mentally and physically and throw her aside and find another one."

He asked: "Do you think he'd found another one, Mr. O'Hara?"

I said: "How do I know? A man like Ricaud is always on the look out for another one. Men like him like to have a string of them if they're lucky enough to find them."

He thought for some time. Then he said: "Mr. O'Hara, I'll tell you what's in my mind. It is my firm and unbiased opinion that if by any chance, when she recovers, Mrs. Ricaud should be arrested for the murder of her husband and brought to trial, no jury will find her guilty of murder. I think that in the circumstances they will reduce the charge. Manslaughter in some degree possibly... but murder—no. And I think that when the Court hears this story—this terrible story that you have outlined to me—it is doubtful if any Judge would be able to give this unfortunate woman more than a nominal sentence."

I said: "Maybe you're right."

He went on: "I'm very glad I've talked to you, because you know all about Mrs. Ricaud. You know what had happened to her. You are the impersonal trained observer. You heard her unfortunate story. When you saw her the first time, you saw the terrible results of this story. You realised that the woman was in no circumstances responsible for her actions. It is my belief, Mr. O'Hara, that your evidence will save Mrs. Ricaud from anything but the lightest penalty which the law can demand."

"If I give it," I said.

He sat back in his chair. Even he was surprised by that one. He said: "What do you mean... if you give it?"

I said: "You ought to know, Mr. Selby. I'm a witness for the prosecution. Of course I may be cross-examined

                    Peter Cheyney

by the defence and all sorts of things may or may not come out in that cross-examination."

He said: "I see." There was another pause; then he went on: "Mr. O'Hara, am I right in saying that you've merely had a verbal conversation with Detective-Inspector Gale; that you have not yet made a full and complete statement?"

I nodded. "That's right. I'm going to make that statement today some time. I felt I wanted to sit down and type it out in my own words—in my own way." I smiled at him. "I always feel more comfortable sitting in front of a typewriter knocking the keys down with two fingers. The words seem to come more easily. I shall type that statement some time today and I shall hand it over to the police."

He smiled. He said: "You know, Mr. O'Hara, from what you've told me we ought to have a copy of that statement now. I think you're a witness for the defence."

I said: "Sorry... but I don't think I am."

"I see... I must say I find it a little difficult to understand your attitude, Mr. O'Hara."

"Sometimes," I said, "I find it difficult to understand my own attitude." I grinned at him.

He said: "I'm all the more surprised because Mrs. Ivory told me that she was certain we should receive the most sympathetic co-operation at your hands."

"Well, it looks as if Mrs. Ivory was wrong, doesn't it?"

He said: "I'm afraid it does. I wonder if you'd forgive me if I brought up a point which might not seem—"

"You go ahead," I told him. "Say just what you like."

He asked: "Is it money that's worrying you, Mr. O'Hara? Possibly you believe that your financial dealings with our client up to the moment—I mean as between you and her—nothing whatever to do with Mrs. Ricaud—have not been satisfactory. It might be that you feel that possibly our client hasn't been particularly generous up to the moment, but I assure you if you do think that, you are wrong. Mrs. Ivory is a wealthy woman and a very generous one."

I grinned at him. "That must be very nice for her."

He said: "What I meant was that you needn't worry about a more than generous settlement for the services which you have rendered to Mrs. Ivory."

I said: "Did I say I was worrying about it?"

He sighed. He was beginning to feel that he didn't like me very much. Not a lot. Because he couldn't understand my attitude. I didn't want money and I didn't want to talk as much as he'd like me to talk. I'd mentioned a lot of things that were in Esmeralda's favour, but not enough. He thought I was holding out on him. And he couldn't understand why. In the back of his mind he was already getting ideas about regarding me as a potentially 'hostile witness.'

I felt damned sorry for Selby. Because he was trying hard. He was doing his best for his client.

And I knew that when I'd gone he was going to telephone Mrs. Ivory. He was going to tell her all about it. And she was going to be very burned up about me. She was going to think that she'd been right about me

                                    Peter Cheyney

the first time—that I was unscrupulous; that I was playing my own game. She was going to think that I was the complete louse.

That is if she ever thought about people in that language. And if she didn't this might be a good time for her to start.

Selby said: "Mr. O'Hara, let me try, once more, to put this whole thing in a nutshell. I believe that you can save this poor unfortunate woman, Mrs. Ricaud, a great deal of additional misery and unhappiness. I believe that if you are prepared to talk freely and frankly with me—to give me the truth—the whole truth as you know it; in other words if you are prepared to tell me exactly, and in full, just what you are proposing to tell the prosecution in the written statement that you intend to prepare for the Scotland Yard authorities today about the events that led up to this unfortunate affair; about Mrs. Ricaud's state of mind; about the conversations that you had with Ricaud; about his character as you know it, then I believe that I shall have a case which can be submitted to Counsel tomorrow which would enable me, before we go to trial, to make it plain to the prosecution that the lines of our defence will be such that they, in their discretion, will be ready, and willing, for a reduction of the capital charge."

He paused to get some breath. I thought that he'd put up a hell of a good speech.

He said: "Isn't it your duty to do that? Isn't it? As an ordinary, decent humane citizen. And won't you do it, Mr. O'Hara?"

I said: "No." I got up. "Well, thanks for the cigarette, Mr. Selby. I'm sorry I haven't been able to be of more use to you."

He shrugged his shoulders. "Candidly, Mr. O'Hara, I'm extremely disappointed. After my conversation with Mrs. Ivory on the telephone, I thought that we could count on you for a hundred per cent support. You'll forgive me for saying again that I can't understand your attitude, and I don't like it."

I said; "Well, that's how it is. Is there anything else, Mr. Selby?"

He looked at his desk. He said: "No, I don't think there's anything else, Mr. O'Hara." The tone of his voice told me that he thought I was a first-class heel, a louse and a sonofabitch.

I said: "Good afternoon." I went out.

The sun had gone in and it was a grey September afternoon.

I didn't think I liked the weather either.

I drove back to the Malinson, went upstairs, took off my top clothes, lay on the bed and went to sleep.

2

I GOT up at seven o'clock. I rang down to the desk and ordered a double Martini and the Evening News. When the boy came up I drank the Martini slowly, and looked at the newspaper. I found it on the front page:

SHOT MAN NOW BELIEVED TO HAVE BEEN MURDERED

MURDERED

ARREST EXPECTED IN MAIDENHEAD TRAGEDY

Scotland Yard detectives investigating the mysterious shooting of Mr. Alexis Ricaud, who was found dead with an automatic pistol and a note by his side, in the drawing-room of his home "Crossways" near Maidenhead, now believe that he was murdered.

Mr. Ricaud's body was found at three p.m. on Wednesday by Mrs. Eliza Frampton, a daily cleaner, and the police theory is that he was murdered some time after ten o'clock on Tuesday night. The medical report is unable to state the exact time owing to delay in rigor mortis due to the proximity of an electric fire.

Chief-Detective-Inspector Millin, of Scotland Yard who is in charge of the case, is now in possession of some important information which is expected to lead to an early arrest.

And that was that!

Detective-Inspector Gale hadn't wasted very much time. But I didn't expect he would. He'd moved pretty quickly after he'd seen me the night before. He'd seen Quinceley, the nursing home people, the hall-porter at the Montacute Place flat. Then they'd found Esmeralda—a process that would not be difficult. They'd sent a man down to Wych Cross first thing that morning to have a heart-to-heart talk with Esmeralda, but the doctor had stopped that. And the police officer was still staying there waiting his chance.

Then Mrs. Ivory had got through to Selby. I wondered just what Selby would have said to Mrs. Ivory on the telephone since I'd left him. I could imagine!

I took a shower, shaved and put on a freshly pressed suit of clothes. When I was dressed I took a look at myself in the glass and came to the conclusion that I was suitably dressed for the part. I found the idea amusing.

I went downstairs and ate dinner. Then I went round to Joe Melander's flat. When we were upstairs in his sitting-room having a drink, he said:

"I see the police have got the idea that that suicide at Maidenhead might be a murder."

I said: "Yes. Are you curious?"

Joe shrugged his shoulders. "Milly and I were talking about it. We just happened to remember Mrs. Ricaud's name."

"She's the widow of the dead man." I said.

Joe didn't say anything.

I went on: "Listen, Joe... about this thing—this Ricaud killing or suicide or whatever it is—it occurred to me that the police might want to ask you a few questions."

"Yes?" he said. He wasn't very much surprised. When you've been in the bottle party business as long as Joe has, it takes a lot to surprise you.

I said: "It's only a small point, but they might want to ask you about it."

He asked: "What is the point?"

"You remember when your wife went and got Mrs. Ricaud ready to leave here just before we took her round to the nursing home? You remember when she was sitting in that chair over there and she asked me for the gun?"

Joe said: "Yes. Milly and I noticed that you didn't want her to have it."

"Do you remember what I said?"

"Sure," said Joe. "You said something about her not wanting a gun in the nursing home—something about nursing homes not liking people to take pot-shots at the staff. You didn't want her to have it."

"Anything else?" I asked.

"Yes," he said. "She got stubborn about it. She said if she didn't have the gun she wouldn't go into the nursing home, because she wanted to give it back to the friend who'd lent it to her, or something like that."

"That's right. And what did I do?" I asked.

He said: "You went downstairs and you got the gun out of the car."

"Did I give it to her, Joe?"

"No... you didn't actually give it to her. You took up her handbag off her lap, opened it and threw the gun in."

I asked: "Did you think anything about that?"

He thought for a moment. Then: "Well, if you ask me I did. So did Milly. We talked about it afterwards." He grinned at me. "I've never known you change your mind about a thing once it was made up. We wondered why you gave the gun back to her after you'd said you wouldn't. Milly said she thought it might be dangerous in the state she was in. She might do something to herself."

I asked: "What did you say?"

"I told her not to worry; that you always knew what you were doing."

I said: "You don't know how right you are."

He asked: "Look, am I being too curious? What's the point?"

"Nothing much," I said. "Maybe they won't worry you about it, but if they do, and you tell them that—which is just what happened—that's O.K. by me."

Joe said: "All right. Have a drink?"

I had another whisky and soda and went.

I walked around for a bit; then I went into a call-box at Piccadilly Circus Underground and rang through to Pell at the flat. He answered the telephone himself.

I said: "Look, Pell... I'm sorry to be a nuisance but I'd like to see you again."

He said: "Of course. Some more trouble, O'Hara?"

"Nothing I didn't expect," I answered. "The police came round last night and saw me about this Ricaud thing."

He said: "I wonder how they got on to that."

"It's obvious," I said. "Quinceley—the doctor—must have talked. I thought he might."

He said: "Yes. I remember you saying that. Well, I hope you told them the truth. It's the only thing to do."

"Yes, I did... more or less. But I'm not happy. I thought I'd like to have a talk to you about it."

He said: "All right. Why don't you come round? But not for a bit because I'm going out. I've got a date and I shan't be back until well after eleven."

                              Peter Cheyney

"That suits me. I've got one or two things to do myself. Say half-past eleven."

He said: "All right. I'll expect you."

I hung up.

I started to walk towards the office. Now it had begun to rain—the sort of odd shower of rain that you get sometimes in September. It was dark and the street lamps were lit.

When I got into the street where the office was I took a look at it; saw the street lights gleaming on the shiny asphalt of the road. I thought it looked like a river. Then I remembered that I'd thought that on Monday night when I was going back to the office; when I didn't know that Mrs. Ivory was waiting there for me.

When I went up the dusty stairs and along the wooden-floored corridor, with the sound of my footsteps making the echoes that they do in an empty place, I felt glad that I wouldn't be going there a lot more. I was tired of that dump. There was something depressing about the street, the office and the whole set-up.

I went into the office, switched on the light in the inner room, took a swig at the half-bottle of whisky and got out the typewriter. I put it on the desk with a pile of foolscap typing paper. I thought that when I took a new office I'd have to have a new typewriter. I put a sheet of paper in the machine and started to type:

20th September 1946.

This is a statement made by me, Caryl Wylde O'Hara—private detective—at present residing at the Malinson Hotel, London, W.C.1.

On Monday evening, September 16th, I returned to my office at about eleven o'clock...

I stopped typing because I thought I heard something. The night was quiet. I'd been right and I had heard something. And I recognised what the sound was. I'd heard it last Monday night—the sound of Mrs. Ivory's high heels going down the wooden corridor when she'd gone away. But this time they were approaching.

I sat back in my chair, fished a cigarette out of my pocket and lighted it. I heard the outside door open. She came in. She stood in the doorway of the inner office, looking at me.

I don't know whether the sight of some people ever makes you think of certain words, but whenever I saw her, for some reason which I couldn't understand, the word "ecstasy" came into my mind.

I thought that was a nice word "ecstasy." That's what she reminded me of.

She was wearing a grey frock of some sort of smooth wool with a touch of colour at the collar, and over it a long grey velvet cord coat. She had on a grey pull-on felt hat with a ribbon. She looked good enough to eat.

I got up. "Good evening, Mrs. Ivory." I pushed the big chair forward. "Would you like to sit down?"

She said: "I don't know that I want to sit down." Her voice was strange and cold. There was a note in it that I hadn't heard before.

"Well, you do what you like about it." I was still smiling at her.

She said: "I shan't take up much of your time. I've come here because at the moment I'm so terribly worried with everything that's going on, and about Esmeralda, that I feel it's not possible to have any more worries. I couldn't bear it. I came here because I thought I would like, for my own satisfaction, to know something about your extraordinary attitude—"

I interrupted. "Why is my attitude extraordinary?"

She said: "When the police came to my house this morning to question Esmeralda it was a most terrible shock to me. It came into my head that you must have been responsible, but I wasn't certain. I couldn't bring myself to believe that it was you. Now I am prepared to believe anything."

I drew on my cigarette. "Yes... why?"

She said: "This morning, after I'd talked to the detective who came to the house, after the doctor had said that he couldn't in any circumstances be allowed to talk to Esmeralda at the moment, and after he'd indicated to me what the police thought, I telephoned my lawyer, Mr. Selby. I asked him to get in touch with you. I said that I was certain that he could rely on getting all the facts in this terrible business from you.

"He telephoned you and he says you went to see him. He says that your attitude was most unsatisfactory; that you were proposing to make a full statement for the police; that you wouldn't let him know the lines that statement was going to take. He said that he almost regarded you as someone who might be considered to be a hostile witness."

I said: "That's fairly natural. If I were Selby I'd probably think the same thing."

She asked: "What are you trying to do? Don't you think that Esmeralda needs every bit of help that she can get? Everything you do is odd and contradictory and strange."

"Don't you believe it, Mrs. Ivory," I said. .

"It is," she went on. "I spoke to Doctor Quinceley this morning. He told me about the trouble you'd taken to get Esmeralda into a nursing home. I thought then that you'd been very kind. I thought there were some very nice things about your character, and"—she hesitated for a moment—"I remembered some of the things you'd said to me at Steynehurst. I believed that you'd gone out of your way to do everything that you could—not only for Esmeralda but for me. I thought—"

I grinned at her. "I always do my best for my clients."

She said: "Do you? Do you think I can believe that now?"

"You mean after the Selby incident? Just because I didn't sit up like a little dog and say my piece when Selby wanted me to." I threw the cigarette stub in the fireplace. "The trouble with you is," I went on, "you just do things off your own bat. Then, when you've done them, you get angry because other people don't see eye to eye with you. When I was at Steynehurst on Wednesday night I said if anything happened you were to telephone me. You didn't. You had to telephone Selby. Why don't you do what I tell you?"

                                    Peter Cheyney

She said: "I don't see why I should—especially now. I don't think I trust you. Mr Selby doesn't trust you—not after his interview with you this afternoon."

"All right," I said. "So Mr. Selby doesn't trust me and you don't trust me. So what! What am I supposed to do—jump off the end of the pier?" I gave myself another cigarette. "Listen... you tell me something. What is all this Selby excitement about? What does he think he's going to do?"

She said: "Surely it should be obvious to you. Mr. Selby says that Esmeralda's story is so appalling that he's perfectly certain that if the prosecution were acquainted with the true facts of the case from the start—although they might be forced under the law to charge Esmeralda with murder—they would put their case so lightly that the charge would be certain to be reduced to one of manslaughter, and a possible nominal sentence inflicted on her."

I said: "Well, that sounds reasonable enough. What then?"

"Mr. Selby points out that story is, however, mainly dependent on you; that before he can submit a case to Counsel—and this matter should be dealt with very quickly—he must know the full implications of the statement which you propose to give to the police."

I said: "I understand that. But he's not having that statement."

She asked: "Why not?" Her eyes were hostile. I thought like that they looked as lovely as ever.

"I'm not prepared to discuss that at the moment."

She asked in a low voice: "Why not, Mr. O'Hara?"

"I'm not prepared to discuss that either."

She moved a little. She said: "One makes the most awful mistakes. When I saw you in this office on Monday night, I thought I didn't like you. I thought you were unscrupulous. But, as I told you, at the time I thought I needed someone who was unscrupulous. Afterwards, I changed my opinion of you. I began to think"—she smiled cynically—"some quite nice things about you. But now I know I was right the first time. I know that you are unscrupulous."

I smiled at her. But I was full of bad temper. I was tired out; nearly exhausted. I'd done a hell of a lot of thinking since Monday. I wasn't prepared to argue. And, in any event, I couldn't argue—not at that moment.

I said: "O.K. So now you know. And having got that off your chest, maybe you'll allow me to get on with some work I've got to do. My apologies once again that we haven't a lift here."

She went white with anger. She turned; went out of the office. I heard the outer door close behind her. I heard her high heels on the wooden corridor.

I waited a minute; then I walked down the passage-way; looked out of the window at the end. I saw her get into the car; make a "U" turn; drive away.

I thought: Well, that's that!

I went back to the office; sat down at the typewriter.

                    Peter Cheyney

3

IT was a quarter to twelve when I got to Pell's flat. I rang the bell and waited. Inside my breast pocket I could feel the envelope that contained the thick wad of folded foolscap—the typescript of my statement. I was satisfied with that statement. It was a nice piece of work. I hoped that Detective-Inspector Gale would like it as much as I did.

Pell opened the door for me. He was wearing a black velvet smoking jacket and smoking a cigar. He looked contented and pleased with himself.

He said: "Come on in," and led the way along the passage to the sitting-room at the end. He indicated a big armchair with a table set close by with the boxes of cigars and cigarettes. I felt that Pell was in good humour; that he was satisfied with life; that he was prepared to be mentally generous with me—up to a point, of course. The idea made me laugh inside.

He went to the corner cupboard, produced the whisky, glasses and siphon, mixed the drinks and put mine on the table at my elbow. Then he went and stood with his back to the fire—a burly, important, figure, looking at me with a cheerful smile.

He said: "So you're still worried? What's the trouble now? I suppose you didn't like the police getting hold of this business before you made up your mind to go to them and tell the story first. Still it doesn't make much difference. The news would have come out some time."

I said: "Yes... I knew that. Anyway, I never intended to go to them."

He raised his eyebrows. "No?"

"No," I repeated. "I knew you'd put them on to me directly I told you that the suicide theory was out; that I knew that Ricaud had been murdered."

He looked at me in surprise. "What the hell do you mean? What d'you mean by saying that I'd put them on to you?"

I smiled at him. I could afford to. The situation so far as I was concerned was funny. It was amusing to see just how he would shift and turn in his mind to try and rebut some of the stuff I was going to give him.

"Of course you did," I said. "You had to. You had to do it to protect yourself. Immediately I left you yesterday, you had a meeting with yourself. You knew that if I went to the police and told them my theory about Ricaud being murdered, they'd want an explanation from you as to why you framed that murder to look like a suicide. So you thought you'd cover yourself by going out and telephoning through to the Yard. You didn't give them a name. You just told them that it didn't matter who you were, but that you knew that Ricaud had been murdered; that he hadn't committed suicide. You suggested to them that if they liked to interview a Mr. Caryl O'Hara at the Malinson Hotel he would be able to substantiate that theory. That's what you did. And you did that so that when they asked you why you'd rigged the murder to look like a suicide you'd be able to say that you were sorry you'd done it; that you'd

                                      Peter Cheyney

made amends and put the job straight by tipping them off on the telephone anonymously."

Pell said quietly: "You must be stark, staring, raving mad. You—"

"Nuts," I said. "In a minute you'll tell me that you weren't down at 'Crossways' on Tuesday night; that you didn't find Ricaud dead on the settee; that you didn't frame that suicide. Well, don't waste your breath. I know you were down there after Esmeralda left and so does Gale—the Detective-Inspector I saw last night. I told him even if I didn't do it in so many words."

Pell finished his whisky in one gulp. He put his hands in his pockets. His eyes were hard and brilliant.

"What do you mean—you told him, even if not in so many words?"

"I told him to photograph the tyre tracks on the loose gravel drive at the back," I said. I grinned at Pell. "Those marks tell a hell of a story. There were the tracks of Ricaud's tyres going from the road to the garage—that was when he got back from London in the afternoon. Over these were the tyre marks of Ricaud's car when Esmeralda drove it out of the garage, down the drive and on to the road when she was leaving, after she'd killed Ricaud; and then there were your tyre marks arriving on top of everybody else's, over hers, after she'd gone. You can see where you stopped at the back portico and, after you came out of the house, turned the car and drove on to the road. You've got an odd diamond tread tyre on the rear near-side wheel of your car."

There was a silence. A silence charged with dynamite. It seemed to last for a long time. Pell's face changed. It lost the pleased look; it began to look just a trifle perturbed. Not too much. Just a little.

He laughed. It wasn't a very successful laugh but it was a laugh. Then he said in a frank and hearty voice: "You and I are a pair of damned fools, O'Hara. We've both been playing hide and seek with each other. You've been holding out on me and I've been doing the same thing, I suppose. It's damned funny."

I said: "Is it? It isn't going to be funny for somebody or other."

"You mean Esmeralda Ricaud," he said. He shrugged his shoulders. "She killed Ricaud," he went on, "and she'll have to pay the price. You know she killed him and so do I."

I didn't say anything. There was another long silence. Pell looked restless and uncomfortable. He wanted me to go on talking. But I wasn't playing. I just stayed put and inhaled cigarette smoke.

"Of course I went down there," he said at last. "And—well, it's no good beating about the bush— when I saw Ricaud lying there dead, I was damned sorry for Esmeralda. If ever a fellow deserved death it was Ricaud. So I did my best for her. I thought I'd make it look like suicide."

"You were pretty damn glad he was dead, weren't you?" I asked. "It suited your book. And you hadn't expected Esmeralda to do it on Tuesday night, had you? You'd hoped she'd do it on Monday night—the night when I met her and brought her back to London. But you were very pleased to see your old boy friend lying there dead with his mouth shut for ever."

He waited a bit and then he opened his mouth to speak. I stopped him.

"Cut it out, Pell," I said. "I know all about it. The whole damned works. What d'you think I've been doing these last five days?"

I stubbed my cigarette out in the ash-tray.

I went on: "Now that you know that I know, and the police know, that you were down there after Esmeralda had killed Ricaud, you'll have to come out into the open, won't you, Pell? You'll have to admit that you found the note—the top page of it—that Ricaud was writing on the writing table; that you picked it up with your handkerchief and laid it on the hearth-rug. You'll have to admit that you went outside and fired a shot out of your .32 Colt automatic—the sister gun to the one Esmeralda used—into the ground in the garden, came back, wiped your fingerprints off the butt, put Ricaud's fingers around it so as to get his prints on the gun and then let it drop out of his hand on to the rug. You'll have to admit all that. But you won't mind admitting it."

He said almost fiercely: "Why don't I mind admitting all that?"

"Because you've got a nice little story ready to explain it," I told him. "Your story is that Mrs. Ivory was an old client of yours; that she'd come to you last Monday worried sick about Esmeralda and asked you to help her; that you'd put her on to me and I'd turned the job down. So you went down there to see Ricaud and found him killed and you knew Esmeralda had done it because Mrs. Ivory had told you she'd threatened to do it."

I waited a bit, but he didn't say anything. What the hell could he say?

"So then, being a nice chivalrous man who can't bear to see a woman in trouble, you framed the killing to look like a suicide, so that poor Esmeralda who'd had such a lousy time should get off. And you did it for your client—Mrs. Ivory. It's a nice story," I said, "except that I've got one that's a damned sight better because it happens to be the truth."

Pell had got his nerve back. Now he was thinking quickly. His brain was working at top speed. Now he had to find out just what I knew.

He grinned at me. He said: "I've always thought you were a trifle nutty, O'Hara. Now I know you are. But you interest me. Tell me your story that's a damned sight better because it's the truth."

"You framed Ricaud's murder into a suicide so that you could go on blackmailing Mrs. Ivory for the rest of her life," I told him. "If I hadn't turned this so-called suicide into a murder—and I was the boyo who started this murder stuff—the police would have accepted Ricaud's death as a suicide. In a. few weeks it would have all blown over. But two people would have known that it was murder... you and Esmeralda. So that after a bit you would go to Mrs. Ivory and tell her that you knew that Esmeralda had shot Ricaud. And she'd have

                                      Peter Cheyney

paid you to keep your mouth shut. And she'd have gone on paying until you or she were dead. That's how it is and you know it."

Pell said: "You're mad. You couldn't prove that and you know it. You couldn't prove it in a million years."

"I'm not going to try," I told him. "And it doesn't matter anyway. In any event, it's going to be pretty tough for you."

I sat there smiling at him. He didn't like that. It scared him. He began to talk.

"Now look here, O'Hara... now look here..."

"Shut up," I said. "And sit down. You'd better take things easy whilst you've got the chance."

"What the hell do you mean?" he asked. He was trying to bluster; to be the old Pell; he was trying to make himself feel good and brave.

"Go and sit down in your chair behind the desk," I said. "I'm going to tell you why you're going to hang for killing Ricaud—"

He opened his mouth to speak. I put up my hand.

I said: "All right... I know you didn't kill Ricaud. But you're going to hang for it. I've fixed that. It's all nice and tidy and it all adds up. You're going to hang for killing Ricaud and the cream of the joke is you didn't do it. Now, are you going to sit down and listen, or shall I go and take the statement I've got in my pocket— the story of how you killed Ricaud—down to the Yard without even telling you why you're going to be hanged? Which would you like?"

I sat coolly smiling at him. And I didn't feel tired any more. I felt good.

He went and sat down behind the desk. He said, almost quietly: "This is some sort of blackmailing racket. You're trying to chisel money out of me. Just because you've stumbled on the fact that I framed that suicide you think you've got me where you want me. You haven't." He tried to grin cynically. "But go on. I'm curious... damned curious. I'd like to know what all this bunk amounts to."

I said: "All right. I'm going to tell you two stories. One story is what actually happened and the other is the story that I say happened. The story that's going to hang you. See? Now listen to the first story. The true one.

"In 1945 Mrs. Ivory came to you and commissioned you to go to New York and see that her divorce suit against Ricaud went through. She did this because she didn't trust him. She knew what a heel he was. You took fifteen hundred pounds from her and you went. You went to America, met Ricaud and the pair of you cooked up a neat little scheme. You were to tell Mrs. Ivory's attorneys that she wanted to stop the divorce proceedings, after which you and Ricaud—or one of you—got a Form of Decree, filled it in, got it stamped somehow and, in due course, sent it to Mrs. Ivory. That was Ricaud's idea. And a very good idea it was—for him. Then he was to marry Esmeralda who was crazy about him, and he and you were to share the money he

                                    Peter Cheyney

got from her. And you both knew he'd get the lot. He did get the lot. Well?..."

He sat silent, looking straight in front of him.

I went on: "So that was that. Everything went well for you both. He came here to England and Esmeralda married him. He gave her hell and started her on drugs to keep her tied to him. He had to do that because if she'd ever tried to get a divorce, before she could divorce him here she'd have to produce evidence of his divorced status from Mrs. Ivory. And he, and you, knew damned well that if that happened you were both sunk. So he kept her quiet by giving her dope—when she couldn't last out any longer without it. Then she took to drinking and started to go to hell generally. But what the hell did you care? You and Ricaud had her money, and if she'd had more money you'd probably be getting it now. It was when she'd come to the end of her money that the trouble began."

He reached for the whisky bottle. He poured himself out a big drink and drank it neat. I could see his fingers trembling.

"A nice pair—you and Ricaud," I said. "The most poisonous pair of bastards that ever hounded a defenceless girl to a life that's a damned sight worse than death."

I lighted a fresh cigarette. Just to cool off.

"Last Monday," I went on, "Mrs. Ivory—who thought you were straight—a man who could be trusted—came to you and told you that she was worried about Esmeralda. She told you that Esmeralda had come to the end of her money; that Ricaud was giving her hell; that she'd threatened to kill him. She asked you to go and see him and try and scare him off.

"You put her on to me. But you got Esmeralda's address from her first and, immediately she'd left your office, you went and saw Esmeralda at Montacute Place. You waited until the hall-porter went downstairs and then you slipped up to her flat. You talked to her and she gave you a drink—the hall-porter saw the extra glass on the tray afterwards—and you sympathised with her and asked how you could help her.

"She's been drinking. She was in an excited, neurotic state. She told you that she was going to a party that evening, and that afterwards she was going to have a show-down with Ricaud. She said she'd like to kill him. She probably said that she would kill him if she had something in her hand to do it with when she'd had enough liquor. She probably said that to you, because she practically said the same thing to me.

"Then you got an idea, Pell. You said your little piece and you came back to this flat and you got one of the two .32 Colt automatics you possess. One was in your office. I've seen it in your desk there. The other one was probably here in the flat and wasn't even out of its original packing. A cardboard box big enough to take the gun and three ten-shot clips of ammunition. That's how they're packed. You sat down at the typewriter and typed out a label addressed to Esmeralda at the flat. You stuck it on the parcelled gun and you took it round to

Montacute Place. You waited till the hall was clear and you slipped in and left it on the table.

"You knew that Esmeralda would be so cock-eyed when she got that parcel delivered to her before she went to 'Crossways' that she wouldn't even bother where it came from. She'd be overjoyed at getting something to fix Ricaud with.

"Well... she got it. That was the gun I took off her on Monday night. It was your gun, and you had the other one of the pair."

I stopped for a minute. Then: "How am I doing, Pell?"

He didn't answer. He was looking straight in front of him. His eyes were glassy. He looked very ill.

"On Tuesday," I went on, "I put Esmeralda into a nursing home. Before she went she asked for her gun back. I wouldn't give it to her. She said she wouldn't go into the nursing home unless I did. So I gave it back to her; but before I did so I took out the entire ammunition clip. I thought she'd be safe like that. You see, I was afraid she'd kill herself.

"On Tuesday evening," I went on, "I went to her flat while she was in the nursing home. Ricaud had left a note for her telling her to go and see him at 'Crossways' at ten o'clock. He told her that he was going to the Bahamas to some woman; that he was prepared to be reasonable if she was. That meant he wanted more money before he went away.

"He'd written that note at her flat. I could see the writing on the blotter. And he'd written another note.

The second note was to you. It had to be. In it he told you to see him at 'Crossways' at twelve o'clock—midnight. And he told you to bring some money with you otherwise it wouldn't be so good for you because, as he'd probably told you before, if he didn't get what he wanted from you he was going to write and tell Mrs. Ivory how you'd stopped her divorce; how you'd swindled her. He knew she couldn't do anything to him. First of all he would be in the Bahamas, and secondly he was still her husband, and if she wanted a divorce—a real divorce—she'd have to pay him some more for it.

"Ricaud sent that note to you on Tuesday afternoon by hand and I bet you were burned up when you got it. Weren't you, Pell?"

I waited for quite a bit but he didn't say anything. He looked like an ugly image—frozen.

"But you knew you'd have to go and square things off with him. You knew he'd got the drop on you; that if he wrote and told Mrs. Ivory the truth you'd be for the high jump, so you made up your mind to go. Probably you went prepared to pay him off.

"But Esmeralda didn't get his note. I got it. I've still got it. When it arrived she was in the nursing home. She left there about ten o'clock and went to Montacute Place. She had a shot of heroin to pull herself together, and a drink or so, and she heard from the hall-porter that Ricaud had telephoned just after ten and said he was writing to her. She tried to ring him and couldn't. So she went down there.

                                      Peter Cheyney

"But before she went she reloaded the automatic. She'd realised by now that I'd taken the ammunition clip out. She reloaded with one of the other two clips of ammunition that you'd so kindly delivered for her. She used one and left the third and the cardboard box. I've got those too, Pell... the third clip and the box.

"Then she went to 'Crossways.'"

I got up. I picked up my glass, walked over to his desk and mixed myself a drink. Now I was feeling as tired as death.

I looked at Pell. He was sitting with his chin resting on his hand looking across the room. His face was taut with fright.

I went back to my chair.

I said: "She went to 'Crossways.' When she went into the drawing-room, Ricaud was sitting at the writing-table writing the letter to her. He'd just finished the first page. He was about to start on the second page when she came into the room. Ricaud was pleased about that. So she'd come after all!

"He went over and lay down on the settee and she stood by the fireplace and they had the usual business all over again. And then Ricaud told her he'd got to have some money; that he was leaving England for the Bahamas and another woman next day; that if she didn't find some he was going to make a lot of trouble for her and for everybody.

"She said she hadn't any money and then he cut loose and told her that she wasn't even married to him; that Mrs. Ivory—her friend—was still Mrs. Ricaud;

that she'd better try and get some money from Mrs.
Ivory.

"That was too much for Esmeralda. She got out the
gun and, as Ricaud tried to get up, she pushed it against
his head and squeezed the trigger.

"And that was Ricaud... that was."

I fished out a cigarette and lit it.

"After she'd gone, you arrived," I went on. "You
came in by the side door and you found Ricaud. And
were you pleased! You'd probably got some money or
your cheque book on you—that and your automatic—
your other .32 Colt automatic to scare him with in case
he tried to knock you about—as he did me!

"You must have stood there and licked your lips. So
she'd done it at last. She'd killed him. What you hoped
she'd do on Monday night she'd done on Tuesday night.
You must have got a kick out of that. With Ricaud dead
there was no one who could give you away. You were
right on top of the job.

"You took a look around. You saw the light on the
writing-table. You went over and saw the note he had
written. You realised that the top page—all that he had
time to write before she arrived—was the perfect suicide
note!

"You just couldn't resist it. If you could frame the
job as a suicide you'd have Mrs. Ivory where you wanted
her for the rest of her life. You'd be on easy street. You
knew she was rich and she'd pay anything to protect
Esmeralda.

                                              Peter Cheyney

"You knew Esmeralda had shot him with the fellow gun to the one you had. You knew that neither of those guns had ever been fired and therefore no ballistics expert could check from which gun the bullet had come.

"You went out into the grounds and fired a shot with the barrel of the gun in the ground. You cleaned the gun, put his fingerprints on it, put the note on the rug, left the discharged cartridge case from Esmeralda's gun where it was because that was O.K.

"Then you took a last look and you made your big mistake. Just in order that no one should know exactly what time he'd killed himself—because you had been there—you pushed the settee nearer the fire. But you did that from behind and you didn't realise you'd pushed it too near to the fire.

"I saw that when I arrived and I pushed it back.

"I knew you'd been there, Pell. I knew it was you. I knew you'd wait to see if the police accepted the suicide theory. They would have too if it hadn't been for me.

"Then I came to see you and told you that I was scared; that Ricaud had been murdered, so that you'd have to do something about it. Well, you did. You had to get the police on to Esmeralda. You telephoned anonymously and told them and put them on to me. And that's as far as we've got. And how do you like that, Pell?"

He said in a peculiar, dry voice—a hoarse voice: "Even if that's true they can't hang me for that... she did it... I didn't kill him... she did it..."

"Oh, yes..." I said. "Of course she killed him. But you haven't heard my second story, Pell. You haven't heard the story that's going to hang you for killing him. Would you like to listen?"

He looked up at that. He looked at me. I could see him trying to wet his lips with his tongue.

I said: "Why don't you have a drink, you louse? You're not very brave now, are you? You're brave enough with women who are down and out and can't fight... people like Esmeralda... people who trusted you like Mrs. Ivory... you're pretty brave with them, aren't you... you and your late unlamented pal—Alexis Ricaud?"

I poured out the whisky. I gave it to him. I watched him drink it. His hand was shaking.

"Listen to this, Pell," I said. "I think it's good. This is my story, and this is how I'm going to get you hanged for killing Ricaud...

"Everything is the same until you arrive at 'Crossways.' See, Pell?... Everything is the same. Except for one or two little things afterwards. But those little things are going to put you at the end of a rope."

I looked at him. His hands were shaking so much that he'd clasped them together to keep them still.

"You arrive at 'Crossways,'" I said. "You go into the drawing-room and you see Ricaud lying on the settee. You go over to him. You think he's been shot because you can see the burn mark on the side of his head. Then you look close and you realise that he isn't dead. He's unconscious from shock.

"Then you get it. You see the whole thing. You understand what has happened. Esmeralda has put the gun up against his head and shot him with a blank cartridge. He's fallen back unconscious and she's gone off believing that she's killed him!"

I waited. I let him think that one out.

He came to life. He said: "It's a damned lie. She couldn't have done that. The gun was loaded..."

"Not in my story, Pell," I said. "In my story—in my statement to the police—I say that she couldn't have shot him, and do you know why, Pell?"

He looked at me. I gave him a big grin.

"Because I'm going to swear on oath that I took the slugs out of the cartridge cases," I said. "Not that I took out the whole ammunition clip, which I did. If I'd done that she might have reloaded—as she did actually reload. I'm swearing that I removed the lead slugs with my penknife, put the cartridge cases back in the clip, and put the clip back in the gun before I gave it back to her. She wouldn't know what had been done. My story is she shot Ricaud with a blank cartridge; that I'd taken the slug out. No one's going to find any extra ammunition at the flat because I've got that. See, Pell?...

"Listen..." I went on. "Listen to the rest of my story There you are looking at Ricaud, who is lying there unconscious—because she'd only fired a blank cartridge at him a few minutes before you arrived—and you see the note on the writing-table. You read it and you get a big idea.

"The idea is that you'll finish the job for her! You'll finish Ricaud off. If it's taken for suicide you can still blackmail the Ivory. If it's taken for murder, Esmeralda is accused. And she'll admit she killed him. Because she believed that she did kill him! Because she didn't know it was a blank cartridge. So, in any event, you thought you'd be safe."

I said soothingly: "Isn't it a lovely story, Pell?"

His voice seemed to come from a long way off. He said—I could just hear him: "How can you prove that, you—" He called me a very rude name.

I said: "I'll tell you, Pell. But first let me tell you what you did in my story.

"You made up your mind to finish Ricaud. You took your gun out of your pocket—remember it's the fellow to the one you gave Esmeralda—and you stuck it against Ricaud's head over the burn mark made by her blank cartridge, and you pulled the trigger.

"You picked up your ejected cartridge case—leaving hers on the floor, wiped the gun, put his prints on it, left it on the rug, put the suicide note on the rug and cleared off.

"Now," I went on, "you'll want to hear how I can prove these things which I say you did. Listen carefully, Pell... you're pretty good at weighing up evidence, aren't you? Well, check on this. See if you can pick a hole in it."

I waited a minute to give him a breather. Then I went on: "When I give the police my statement of how Esmeralda tried to kill Ricaud but failed because the gun

                                    Peter Cheyney

was loaded with a blank cartridge, and how you finished the job off and then framed it as a suicide—when I give them that little story (which you and I know is a fairy story) I'm going to prove it. I'll tell you how:

"If my story is true they've got to find another gun. They've got to find Esmeralda's gun. They'll find it. I've already found it. When they've found that gun, they've got to find this evidence:

"First of all they've got to find my fingerprints under Esmeralda's on the butt and the body of the gun. Because I handled it when I gave it back to her before she went into the nursing home.

"They will find them because I did handle it and they're on the gun.

"Secondly—and more importantly—they've got to take the ammunition clip out of that gun and find nine cartridges from which the leaden slugs have been extracted. They're going to find them because I took the slugs out after she'd killed Ricaud when I found the gun. But they're not going to know that, because I handled the gun by the edges with a handkerchief. So there won't be any prints of mine over hers.

"They've got to find my fingerprints on every cartridge case in the ammunition clip and on the clip itself. They'll find 'em. I put 'em there. Lots of 'em.

"Thirdly, they've got to find my fingerprints on the ejected cartridge case on the rug. They'll find them because I handled it—deliberately. They'll find lots of my fingerprints on it.

"Lastly, my dear Pell... they'll want to know that you arrived after Esmeralda—in order to kill Ricaud after she'd failed to kill him. They'll find that. They'll find your tyre marks over hers. And that's going to be the end of you, Pell. And the cream of the jest is that even if Esmeralda says she killed Ricaud, they're not going to believe her. They're going to tell her that she's wrong; that she only thinks she killed him."

I pitched my cigarette stub into the fire and lit another.

"When they've got my story," I said—"all of it. The story of what you and Ricaud plotted against the Ivory and Esmeralda, the story of the fake divorce and the fake marriage, the story of his note to you, of your going there to see him because you had to go to see him; the story of your planting your second gun on Esmeralda last Monday and all the direct evidence of the gun, the fingerprints and the blank cartridge cases—when they've got that, Pell, they're going to try you and hang you by the neck until you're dead.

"And when they do—on the morning they string you up, I'm going to have a double whisky and soda on the strength of the world being rid of one of the lousiest heels in history—John Epiton Pell."

He began to talk. His voice was strained and wheezy; he could hardly breathe. His red face was even more flushed; his fat jowls were trembling.

He said: "Listen, O'Hara... I've got a good business. There's a partnership for you in it. I've got money—and you can have some of it—"

"How much?" I asked.

His eyes lit up. He said quickly: "You can have seven—ten thousand. You can have it tomorrow...."

"Nuts," I said. "That's chicken feed. You'd have had to pay Ricaud plenty, wouldn't you? If he'd been alive. What about twenty thousand?"

"It's a lot of money," he said. "But I'll manage it. I'll manage it somehow. For God's sake, O'Hara..."

"It's not enough," I said. "It wouldn't be enough if it were a million."

I went over to the desk.

"Listen, louse..." I told him. "Maybe you haven't been very interested in the life of Esmeralda Ricaud. She was a pretty, laughing girl once. She was romantic. She was in love. She wanted to be married and have children, to lead a full decent life. What did you do to her, Pell? She's a drunk... a heroin addict... one who'll never be cured because she's too far gone. Whatever happens to her, she's finished.

"But what did you do to her—you and Ricaud? What did you make of her? You've killed her life—whatever it may be in the future it'll be no good to her. You condemned her to a living hell. You swindled Mrs. Ivory of her money. You cheated her of her divorce. How you'd have grinned—you and Ricaud—if she'd ever married again. Married someone else before she was divorced from Ricaud. You'd have been able to do a little more blackmailing!

"Even out of the death of Ricaud, your side-kicker, your fellow blackmailer, your brother ruiner of women, you had to try and make a bit. You had to frame a suicide so that you could still blackmail the Ivory.

"You've had it, Pell... You stink in my nostrils. When I was in Formosa, I thought the Japs were the lowest form of life. Well... maybe they didn't know any different. But they—even they—weren't as bad as you. You're the end."

I took the typewritten statement from my breast pocket. I showed it to him.

"There it is," I said. "A story that's half-true and half-fiction. My story of how you murdered Ricaud.

"There it is and, goddam you, Pell... I'm sticking to it!"

I picked up my hat and went out.

I drove back to the office. I sat down at the typewriter and finished off my statement. I told how I'd just read it over to Pell; that he'd practically admitted it; that he'd offered me a partnership in his business, and ten thousand pounds; then twenty thousand, to keep quiet; to support him in his lying story that after he'd found Ricaud's dead body he'd framed it to look like suicide because Mrs. Ivory was his old client.

Then I signed the statement, put it in an envelope, sealed it and addressed it to Detective-Inspector Gale at Scotland Yard.

And that was that!

4

IT was half-past one in the morning when I parked the Rover in the courtyard at Scotland Yard, went into

Peter Cheyney

the reception room and gave the big envelope to the constable on duty.

"See that Detective-Inspector Gale gets that as soon as he comes on," I said. "And don't lose it. It's dynamite."

The constable grinned. "He'll get it in two minutes, Sir. He's working late on a case. I'll send it up right away."

I said all right. I said that if Gale wanted me I'd be at the Malinson Hotel. He could telephone me any time after I got back and I'd come down if he wanted to see me.

I drove back to the hotel. I asked the night-porter to send me up some tea. While I was talking to him I put my hand in my jacket pocket and found the railway folder.

I took it out and showed it to him.

He said: "A nice place, Torquay, Mr. O'Hara. I used to work there once. You'll find that hotel's very good. It's old-fashioned and quaint, and the gardens are lovely."

"I'm going down there, Trigg," I told him, "within a day or so. I'm going to sit in that garden and listen to the band."

He said: "You know, Mr. O'Hara... I shouldn't have thought that you'd be keen on sitting in an old-world garden, listening to a band. But maybe you're bored with London. Nothing ever happens these days, does it?"

I said: "No... nothing much."

I went up to my room.

CHAPTER SIX

SATURDAY — REACTION
1

THE telephone bell began to ring at nine o'clock. I woke up and looked at the ceiling. I was so tired that it took me a few seconds to collect my wits; to remember. The telephone continued ringing. I got out of bed; walked across the room; picked up the receiver. It was Gale.

He said cheerfully: "Good morning, Mr. O'Hara. Chief-Detective-Inspector Millin has asked me to get through to you. He's read your statement. He'd be very grateful if you could come down here and see him, and he'd be glad if you could come as soon as possible."

"All right," I told him. "I'll be there in half an hour. What did you think of the statement?"

"It's one of the most concise documents I've ever read in my life, Mr. O'Hara," said Gale. "And it told me a lot."

"I'm glad about that." I smothered a yawn.

He said: "That rather short verbal statement of yours on Thursday night—I realised you'd left a lot of blanks. I wondered why, and I was curious when you said that you might amend or add to it when you made your full written statement. Now I understand." He went on:

"I'll tell the Chief-Detective-Inspector you'll be down in about half an hour."

I said: "O.K." I hung up.

I took a quick shower. The warm water made me feel better. I skipped shaving because I was too impatient to hear what Millin had to say. I dressed; went down to the garage; drove round to the Yard.

Gale met me in the entrance lobby. He took me to an upstairs office. Millin was seated at his desk, in the corner under the window. He was a thin-faced, grey-haired man. He might have been anything. Like Gale, he didn't look to me like the popular idea of a C.I.D. officer.

He said: "Sit down, Mr. O'Hara, and let's have a little talk. Will you smoke?" He pushed a box of cigarettes towards me; held out his lighter.

He went on: "I'm very grateful to you. I think you've done a good job of work and I should like to tell you here and now that we're satisfied—as near as we can be—that what you've said in your statement is correct. The whole evidence from the first indicates that your theory that Pell killed Ricaud, after Mrs. Ricaud had fired a blank cartridge at him and left him unconscious, is correct."

I said: "I'm glad you're satisfied."

He smiled. "I'm satisfied," he said. "At least I'm as satisfied as I can be at the moment." He looked at me keenly. "It seems to me that you've done a lot of work that ought to have been done by the Police. And I'm glad that you've done it so successfully. It might have been a little difficult if you hadn't." He smiled again.

I asked why.

"You can answer that question for yourself, Mr. O'Hara. The police have a very old-fashioned idea that they like to do their own murder investigations. They don't like private citizens—even if they do happen to be private investigators—doing their work for them. Professional jealousy, I suppose." He laughed. "Still, nothing succeeds like success. You've succeeded and so it's all right. If you hadn't, I suppose I should be talking sternly to you about 'obstruction,' 'withholding information from the police' and all that stuff."

I said: "I was working for a client. There's an old-fashioned rule in my business—you have the same one, I believe—that if we start something we see it through."

"All right," he said cheerfully. "Let me say officially that we forgive you."

He sat back in his chair, took a cigarette from the box and lighted it. He said: "Tell me something... this is just personal curiosity... I'd like to ask you a question, and I'd like you to know that I'm asking this unofficially. You were working from the start only for Mrs. Ivory— the lady who's tried to be such a good friend to Mrs. Ricaud?"

I nodded.

"We've talked to everybody mentioned in your statement," said Millin, "including Doctor Quinceley, of course. He says that you told him that you were working for Mrs. Ricaud's relations. I suppose you thought you wouldn't have got any co-operation from him unless you did say that?"

I said: "Yes. I knew he'd be in a difficult position. But I wanted his assistance—and I got it the best way I could. I hadn't any time to waste either."

"I can understand that," he said.

"Everything I did was leading up to my interview with Pell last night," I said. "I wanted to see him and confront him with the statement that I was going to put in your hands. I wanted to feel that I'd been right all along on every point. And the only way I could do it was that way."

"You took a chance," he said. "Of course Pell is going to deny what you say about that interview. He'll have to. If he admitted it, it's tantamount to pleading guilty right away. So he'll deny it. And he'll also deny that he offered you twenty thousand pounds to keep quiet and to support his story about having nothing to do with the murder, and that he framed the suicide set-up because he wanted to help Mrs. Ivory—who had once been his client."

"Of course he'll deny it," I said. "What else can he do—except plead guilty right away?"

He nodded. "He'll hang. He hasn't a chance whatever he says or does—not in the face of the evidence." He went on: "There's one thing that intrigues me. I've read your statement through half a dozen times and I can see how you've mapped out every move in the game. I'd like to say that I think that statement is a marvellously concise and analytical piece of writing. But there's one thing that does interest me very much. What made you suspect Pell right at the beginning? You say in your statement that late on Monday night you came to the conclusion that Pell was somehow involved in this business. I'd like to know how you worked that out."

I said: "It's simple. On the Monday afternoon I was a witness in a divorce case and we got the decree. The decree was awarded on my evidence. I'd handled that case for the Pell Agency and Pell had agreed to pay me a thousand pounds on the day that we got the decree. I wanted that money and he knew it.

"When Mrs. Ivory came to see me on Monday night, she told me that she'd seen Pell that afternoon and asked him to work for her. He'd refused to do it. He told her some story and then he suggested that she came and saw me. That's why she came to my office. When I was talking to her she said that Pell had told her that he wasn't going to pay me the thousand pounds because he thought there might be an intervention in the case. She told me I ought not to worry about that a great deal because she was prepared to pay me a like sum to work for her. You understand that?"

He nodded.

I went on: "The first thought that came into my mind was that she was talking rubbish. I couldn't understand why Pell should say such a thing. Work it out for yourself. I've done quite a lot of work for Pell—always successfully. He regarded me as a good, trustworthy operative that he could call in to help him any time he wanted one. Quite obviously, if he'd thought that

                    Peter Cheyney

something was going wrong with that decree—which was ridiculous because if the Judge hadn't liked my evidence he wouldn't have granted the decree—the first thing he would have done would have been to telephone through to me. He would have been worried about what his professional clients—the lawyers who'd employed him on the case originally—were going to say. I couldn't understand why Pell should say such a thing to a woman he didn't know. Then I thought of an explanation. Can you guess what it was?"

He said: "I might try. Perhaps I could guess. I wonder if you thought that she'd either made that story up, or perhaps talked Pell into suggesting something like that so that you'd want her money and would consent to work for her."

"Right," I said. "That's exactly what I did think. I was entitled to think that. And that made me a little angry with Mrs. Ivory. But after my interview with Ricaud, I came to the conclusion that she had told me what she thought was the truth. In other words, I now believed that Pell had told her that story about not intending to pay me the thousand pounds, and this was his reason: He had to think of a quick excuse for turning down Mrs. Ivory's business. He'd handled confidential business for her before and been well paid for it, but he didn't want to handle the Ricaud affair. How could he? But he wanted to know what was going on, and so he thought at once that the thing to do was to get me put on the job.

"But he realised just as quickly that he was up against a snag. He knew that I would only take the case if I wanted to or, if I didn't want to, only if I were hard up. So he tried to create a situation in which I would be certain of taking the case. He told Mrs. Ivory that he wasn't going to pay me the thousand. He hoped that I would take on her work and have the row with him afterwards. That way he expected to be able to get from me information about Ricaud's reactions.

"I got that idea. I got that idea after I'd seen Ricaud on Monday night. When I searched Pell's diaries and found that Mrs. Ivory had seen him last year before, I knew I was right. After that, working from that basis, everything was... well, fairly easy."

He said, with a smile: "It may have seemed fairly easy to you, O'Hara, but I think it was a damned good piece of investigation." He laughed. "It's very funny, the public always believe that private detectives never run into a case like this. I hope you've enjoyed it."

"Yes... in a way I have. It's given me quite a lot to think about."

"It must have," he said. "Tell me something else.... You say you got the idea that Pell was mixed up somehow in this business on Monday night—after you'd seen Ricaud. When you found Ricaud dead, and came to the conclusion that he'd been killed, and someone— not necessarily the murderer—had framed the thing to look like suicide, you thought of Pell again. You had some sort of proof of that because of the writing on the blotter that you saw in the Montacute Place flat—that

                                    Peter Cheyney

blotter was very interesting by the way; our experts liked it a lot—but it wasn't conclusive proof. When were you certain in your mind that Pell was the murderer?"

"A good question," I said. "I'll tell you the answer. I was certain that Pell had killed Ricaud—after Mrs. Ricaud had thought she'd killed him with the blank cartridge—when I had my talk with the hall-porter at Montacute Place. In my statement I described the conversation I had with him. You will remember that he said that someone brought a small parcel and left it on the hall table for Mrs. Ricaud to receive before she went out. That parcel obviously contained the gun that she took down to 'Crossways' on Monday night. It must have. You'll see why in a minute.

"Realise that I knew all about Mrs. Ricaud's gun. I'd handled it and examined it when I took it away from her. I knew it was a .32 Colt automatic. When I discovered Ricaud's body and concluded that someone had framed a suicide out of a murder I noted that the supposed suicide gun was a .32 Colt automatic."

He nodded. "I'm with you so far."

"I knew that Mrs. Ricaud hadn't framed the suicide act. She couldn't have moved the settee. She wasn't strong enough. Therefore someone had done it afterwards. After she had gone. I knelt down and took a close look at the gun. I knew it wasn't Mrs. Ricaud's gun."

"How did you know that?" he asked.

"The gun was lying on the floor with its left side uppermost. There was no mark on it. On the left side of

Mrs. Ricaud's gun there was a small scratch—something like a cross—I saw that when I was taking the slugs out of the clip, before I returned it to her, on the afternoon when she went into the nursing home. So I knew that the gun on the floor wasn't her gun."

He was listening intently. He said: "Go on..."

"Then I knew something for certain," I said. "I knew that when she'd gone she'd taken her gun with her. I knew that the person who came after her and framed the suicide had left another gun—knowing that it was the same make and the same calibre as Mrs. Ricaud's gun.

"And that person knew that she'd used a .32 Colt automatic when she had tried to kill Ricaud, because he was the man who had left the fellow gun for Mrs. Ricaud at Montacute Place." I smiled at Millin. "It was tough on him that he hadn't a chance to notice the scratch on the left-hand side of her gun. The scratch was probably made by the gun rubbing against her keys—or a nail file—or something like that, in her handbag."

He nodded. "I think you're pretty good, Mr. O'Hara. I promise not to commit any murders when you're about."

He knocked the ash from his cigarette. "Now, to return to the official side of this business, I think you ought to know that we've pretty well confirmed everything you've said in your statement. We find that your deductions about the tyre tracks on the loose gravel drive at the back of 'Crossways' are correct. Ricaud drove his car back there in the late afternoon.

                                    Peter Cheyney

He put it in the garage. That was the first set of tyre tracks coming in. Later, after she'd believed she'd killed Ricaud; after she'd left him unconscious on the settee, Mrs. Ricaud must have walked out of the house, the gun in her hand, in a sort of daze, down that crooked path that leads through the clearing.

"I suppose, poor woman, when she got to the clearing she only then actually realised the awful thing she'd done. She thought she'd killed her husband. Then, I imagine, she wondered what on earth she was going to do. Close to the clearing there is a rhododendron bush—where we found her pistol. And she must have dropped it there. I can picture her leaning up against the nearby tree wondering where the devil she was going to. Then she must have thought of Mrs. Ivory's house in Sussex; that there would be refuge for her there.

"So she went to the garage, started up Ricaud's car and drove it out. She hit the wing of a milk lorry in Maidenhead as she drove through. She must have had a narrow escape there. Of course she wasn't in a fit state to drive a car but luckily for her the roads were clear and she got down to Sussex.

"Then, superimposed on the tracks of her car—going out—were the tracks of Pell's car going in. The rest of the evidence matches up. Your fingerprints and hers on the butt of the pistol. Your fingerprints on the cartridge cases. Gale here, who has been working all night on the job, tells me that the ends of the cartridge cases were pinched in. I'd like to know "—he smiled at me—"and this is again just to satisfy my curiosity, why you did that. I suppose that was to stop the cordite charges from falling out?"

I said: "Yes. When I gave her back the gun, my first idea was to take the complete magazine clip out, but I thought that would be foolish. With the magazine right out she was certain to see the empty space in the butt and, sometime or other, she might have tried to get a fresh magazine. But I knew that if I merely took the lead slugs out, pinched in the tops of the cartridge cases, reloaded them into the magazine and replaced the magazine in the butt, she'd never be wise to what I'd done. At any time she tried to shoot herself or anyone else she'd give herself a nasty shock and that would be all. Incidentally, I must say that at the back of my mind there was the idea that at some time or other she might try to kill Ricaud."

He said: "I quite understand. Well, thank you very much, Mr. O'Hara. You've been of great assistance to us." He smiled again. "I've gone so far as to ask the 'P.I.' Department here to mention your name in connection with this case. I think that's only due to you. Of course I haven't been able to say very much, but it may do you some good professionally."

"Thank you very much," I said. "That's kind of you." I got up. "I'll be on my way. I was proposing to take a holiday, but I expect you'd like me to stay in town."

He shook his head. "I shouldn't worry. Just let Gale have your address in due course, so that we can get in touch with you if we want to. Of course, you'll be the principal witness at Pell's trial when we get him."

                                   Peter Cheyney

I raised my eyebrows. "You mean he's gone?..." I asked.

He nodded. "He got out of his flat some time early this morning—we think about four o'clock. And he left in a hurry. I've no doubt that we shall pick him up."

I said: "I expect you will. Tell me... things being what they are, shall you do anything about Mrs. Ricaud? Will you make some charge against her?"

He said slowly: "No... that won't be necessary."

I thought: Well, that's that.

I went to the door. I'd got it open when the telephone bell rang. Millin put the receiver to his ear. I was nearly out of the room when he looked up and said: "Just a minute, O'Hara."

I went back into the room and closed the door. He was listening at the telephone. After a minute he said: "All right, Stravens... just do the usual thing. You can identify the rear near-side tyre?... It's uninjured?... It's got a diamond tread on it, hasn't it? All right... you know what to do." He hung up the receiver.

He said to me: "Well, we shan't get Pell, O'Hara."

I asked: "Why... what's happened?"

He shrugged his shoulders. "Apparently he drove his car over the old chalk quarry near Dorking. It's a drop of two hundred and seventy feet. That must have happened about seven o'clock. The local police surgeon says he'd been drinking heavily. The car's pretty well smashed up, but I've just confirmed that the rear near-side tyre had the diamond tread on it. I suppose he couldn't face the music. He knew what he'd got coming to him and he preferred to take that way out."

He got up. He said: "I think we can regard the Ricaud murder case as closed."

We smiled at each other. We shook hands. I said goodbye and I went away.

I got into the car; drove to the Malinson; put the car in the garage. I was very tired. I went up to my room and stood in front of the dressing-table; looking at myself in the mirror.

I said to my reflection: "Well, you old So-and-So, you pulled it off! It's all right."

Then for a moment I didn't feel tired. I felt good. I'd got rid of that old "Formosa" feeling once and for all.

I looked at my wrist-watch. It was a quarter-past eleven—and a bright, sunny day.

I took one small swig of whisky, telephoned down to the girl at the desk to give me a call at six o'clock and to send up a double Martini just after six.

Then I undressed and went to bed.

2

THE girl on the telephone desk called me at six o'clock. I asked her to send up the Evening News with the Martini.

I read the report in the paper, sitting on the bed, drinking the cocktail. It said:

RICAUD SUICIDE WAS MURDER

Police investigations following the "suicide" of Alexis Ricaud, who was found shot on Wednesday last, at "Crossways" a Georgian house near Maidenhead, have established that the dead man was murdered and that the killer planned the "suicide" scene. The inquest which was to have been held today was adjourned.

Intensive enquiries by Chief-Detective-Inspector Millin of Scotland Yard, whose co-operation was requested by the Berkshire police, resulted in the discovery of another automatic pistol, of the same make and calibre as that used by the murderer.

It is believed that the killer had planned, in the event of the police discounting the suicide theory, that suspicion should fall on another person—a woman— who had visited the house on the night of the tragedy.

Automobile tyre-tracks on the loose gravel drive at the back of the house formed important clues in the investigation.

This morning, at eight-thirty, the body of John Epiton Pell, a private detective, whom the police wished to question in regard to the Ricaud murder, was found at the wheel of his wrecked car at the bottom of the chalk quarry on the Dorking-Reigate road.

Mr. Caryl O'Hara, a private detective, who had interviewed Alexis Ricaud, in the course of an investigation, on the night preceding the murder, was able to give important information to the police authorities. Acting on this information the search for Pell resulted in the discovery of the wrecked ear and his dead body.

I finished the Martini, took a warm shower, dressed and went down to the restaurant. I ate dinner and thought about Pell.

I thought that the only constructive thing he'd ever done was to kill himself. By doing that he'd saved a hell of a lot of trouble for everyone—including himself.

They were a sweet pair—Pell and Ricaud. But Ricaud had the brains. Pell only thought he had. Ricaud's best piece of work had been when he'd talked Pell into faking the decree in Mrs. Ivory's American divorce suit. That was a master stroke. Even if the whole thing came to light, Ricaud was safe. Once out of America he was out of the jurisdiction of the Court; Mrs. Ivory was still his wife and if she wanted to get free from him she'd have had to pay plenty. But she and Pell were both domiciled in England—they were both English—and she could have brought criminal charges against Pell at any time.

Pell knew that, but was certain that Ricaud would never be in a position to tell the story. He underestimated Ricaud; I thought that Ricaud had all the nerve in the world. He was a very clever, very tough egg. I thought that a lot of people—including quite a few women—would be very glad to know that he was dead.

The waitress told me I was wanted on the telephone. I took the call in the booth in the hallway. It was Selby.

He said: "Mr. O'Hara, I tried to get you before, late this afternoon, but they told me that you were asleep, so I didn't let them disturb you. I feel, having regard to what I said at our last interview, that I ought to tell you that I realise now that it was impossible for you to be quite frank with me. I realise that, situated as you were at that time, you could not possibly tell your story."

I said: "That's how it was. Do you know all the story now?"

"Yes," he answered. "Everything. Chief-Detective-Inspector Millin, of Scotland Yard, came down to Steynehurst this afternoon. He told us all about your statement; the information that you'd given the police and about your amazing interview with Pell. Mr. Millin said—humorously of course—that he hadn't been quite certain what to do about you—whether to charge you under a Section of the Police Act or give you a medal."

I grinned. I said: "He compromised by giving me a mention in the Evening News. I'll settle for that."

He went on: "Mrs. Ivory has told me that she considered you have acted with the greatest courage and integrity. She—"

I interrupted. "I don't agree. If I take money to do a job I try to earn it. Integrity oughtn't to be a virtue outside the scope of a private investigator."

"Which brings me to the point," he went on. "Mrs. Ivory tells me that you haven't been paid anything; that you and she had a misunderstanding over some small matter and that you had returned the retainer she had paid you. She has instructed me to send you a cheque for a thousand pounds. She asked me to say that she considered the payment inadequate. Would you like it to be increased? I have authority to do that."

I said: "No. A thousand pounds is right. She thought it so and so do I."

He asked: "Shall I send the cheque to you at the Malinson Hotel?"

"Thanks," I said. "You can send it at the end of next week. I'm going on a holiday. I shall be back about then. If I haven't returned, it can wait for me."

"Very well, Mr. O'Hara," he said. "And I'd like personally to thank you for your co-operation—even if I wasn't aware of it."

I hung up and went into the bar. The bar at the Malinson is a cheerful place. I like it. Just then it was deserted and George, the bar-tender, was polishing glasses, whistling to himself.

I bought a double whisky and soda; took it to the lounge seat in the corner and sat down.

So that was that. That was the end of the Ivory business. Everything nicely tied up and put away. And a thousand pounds.

I thought about the money. With what I had left of Pell's money after buying the Rover and my running expenses during the week, and the thousand to come from Selby, I would be about eleven hundred strong. Not bad. More than I'd ever had since I came back from Formosa and blued my back pay and gratuity in one long sweet jag.

With eleven hundred pounds I could create a new set-up. A good office; a secretary. Those few words in the Evening News meant a lot too. Not to the ordinary public maybe, but to lawyers and people who used private detectives. They'd read it and remember my name. Selby's firm would probably be able to use me too. And the Insurance Companies would see it. I'd always wanted to work for Insurance Companies. It's nice work. But you have to be good.

Well, I was good. Good enough for the Police to say so anyway.

But I was sorry in a way. I didn't quite know why. I wondered whether I was missing the excitement of the last five days. I'd taken a chance or two but that was in the game. I suppose I was missing the excitement and this was the reaction.

Or was it? Or was I missing Mrs. Ivory?

I played about with that question, although I knew what the answer was. I knew goddam well that I'd been in it from the first because of her; because of what she looked like; the way she talked and everything about her. That was why it was.

So what! It was all over and there wasn't going to be any more Mrs. Ivory. There were only going to be three pictures of her. One in the long pink coat with the powder blue pockets; one in the crimson house-coat; one—the last one—in the grey velvet-cord coat. The pictures had been good. They had been nice views. And they'd keep. Three pictures and a thousand pounds. But I supposed that it was the pictures that mattered most.

It was almost a shame to take the money!

I finished the drink; carried the glass to the bar.

The door opened and Quinceley came in. He came over, a smile on his face, He said: "Ah... here you are. They told me I'd find you here."

I asked him to have a drink. I ordered two more whiskies and sodas.

He said: "I only got back from Steynehurst an hour ago. Mrs. Ivory brought me back. She asked me to see you."

I asked: "How's Esmeralda?"

"Didn't you know?" he said quietly. "She's gone. Poor thing. She died late last night. And I can't say I'm awfully sorry. Mrs. Ivory telephoned me to go down yesterday. But I couldn't do anything. Nothing more than the local man had done. She was too far gone. She went easily too... quite a nice death."

He made it sound almost good. "Her mother and father were down there," he said. "They took her away this afternoon. She's going to be buried somewhere near their home. It's a sad business." He sighed. "Well," he said more cheerfully, "I shall have to go soon. I've got a baby case at any minute. Life's undefeatable, isn't it? They go and they come...."

I asked: "Did she say anything before she died?"

He shook his head. "Nothing much," he said. "She was practically unconscious all the time. She had a not very good heart and the shock and worry just finished her." He drank some whisky. "It's not a bad thing that she has gone."

I asked why.

He shrugged his shoulders. "She was a confirmed heroin addict," he said. "I doubt whether it would ever have been possible really to cure her of that. You know how it is. You get them off it and the treatment is tough,

                    Peter Cheyney

and they have a bad time and then, just when you think they're all right, they start off again. And she wasn't strong and not awfully happy, and I think she's better off. In fact I'm sure she is."

I nodded. I thought that he was probably right.

He smiled. "She said something that was interesting—to you, I mean—just before she went. She spoke very quietly, almost in a whisper, but I heard it. She said: 'I like Caryl—Christmas Caryl... I got him off a tree....' I suppose she was thinking about you."

I said: "Yes... she said that before. She said I was her favourite detective." I grinned. "Actually, I think I was."

He ordered two more drinks. He said: "Mrs. Ivory's coming to see you. She dropped me off at my place and she's going to stay up for a day or two, I believe. She wants to see you particularly, I think. I said I'd tell you."

I said: "Thanks." We drank our drinks. Then he said goodbye and went.

I ordered a small one and went back to my seat in the corner. I couldn't quite get it. I was wondering.

I was wondering why the hell a few minutes ago I'd felt as near sentimental about Mrs. Ivory as I ever get; and now when there was a chance of seeing her again, I felt that I wanted to duck?

And I did want to duck. I tried to analyse that one, and it seemed to me that my feeling was fairly logical. There wasn't any real point of contact between Mrs. Ivory and me. Nothing that really mattered—from her point of view I mean. And my point of view didn't matter a lot—not so far as she was concerned.

She was rich and beautiful and she felt pleased with me. She knew now that if I hadn't played it off the cuff and taken the chances I had taken that—if Esmeralda had lived—and Pell had got away with his scheme—she would have had him on her neck for the rest of her life. She knew that. And she was grateful.

So she'd told Selby to get through and fix about the money. She'd told him to pay me more if I wanted it. And then she was going to come and say a very nice thank-you. She was going to say that she understood why I'd been damned rude to her the last time I saw her; that she'd been silly to jump to conclusions after it had seemed that I wouldn't play ball with Selby. She was going to say that, and a lot more like that, and then she was going to shake hands and fade.

That was Mrs. Ivory... that was...

I thought: No. I thought it would better for one and all—especially me—if I faded first and kept the three pictures I had of her. Maybe when I'd got the new office going and O'Hara Investigations was something, I'd run into her one day and say... "Remember me?..." Maybe...

But no sentimental farewells.

And with Esmeralda gone, Mrs. Ivory would never know. Only one person could have given me away. Esmeralda. Not that she'd ever have done that. But she could have. She knew goddam well that she'd killed Ricaud, and I was lucky that she hadn't blurted the whole story out before she went.

So I thought that just at this time the quick fade-out was indicated. About some things I'm inclined to be an extremist—all or nothing.

And this time it had to be nothing.

I finished the drink. I went upstairs and packed a suitcase. Then I came down and went over to the Reception.

The Manager was there. I said: "I'm going on a vacation for a few days. I'm tired. But keep my room and bath for me. There's some more stuff coming from my rooms. They're sending it round. I'll be back at the end of next week."

He said: "Certainly, Mr. O'Hara. I expect you've been busy this week... This case in the evening papers... Shall we keep any correspondence or forward it?"

I said: "Keep it until I get back."

I went down to the garage, put the suitcase in the back of the Rover and drove away. I drove towards Joe's place.

I thought: Well... farewell... Mrs. Ivory...

3

IT was eleven o'clock. Joe and I sat at his table in the corner of "The Desert Room" and watched the boys and girls. Micky Fernanda—who came out of the jug about eight weeks ago—was dancing with the blonde who used to be sidekicker to Joe Spancey who was still inside. Micky had that cheerful look that meant that he'd got something on ice. He was looking so goddam full of himself that Joe and I reckoned that when he'd had about four more doubles he'd start telling the blonde what a big guy he was and what bloody fools the cops were. Right on the other side of the room, with a baby in a nice evening frock, who I was prepared to bet was a policewoman, was Detective-Sergeant Wellton of Central Office. Wellton was looking bored and uninterested. I thought that in about half an hour Micky Fernanda would start telling the blonde what a bloody fool Wellton was. And in about three or four months' time Wellton would pick up Micky one quiet evening and prove to him what a bloody fool he, Micky, was. After which Micky would have another long quiet spell in stir where he'd have a chance to plan how much more clever he'd be next time.

I thought that the only person in the set-up who'd get anything out of it, except the laugh, would be the blonde.

Joe said: "Some guy from the Yard—a Detective-Inspector—knocked us up at six o'clock this morning. Some guy called Gale. He was interested about what happened when Mrs. Ricaud went to the nursing home."

I asked: "What did he want to know?"

"It was about the gun," said Joe. "I told him that she said she wanted the gun and that you said no soap; you weren't going to let her have it. And then she said that if she didn't have it she wasn't going to the nursing home; and that you changed your mind sort of suddenly and went downstairs, and after a bit you came back and took

Peter Cheyney

her handbag off her lap and put the gun in it; and then she was O.K. and you and her and Millie went off."

"Did he like that?" I asked.

Joe said: "He asked me if I knew what had made you change your mind so suddenly. I said I didn't know, but we thought afterwards it was funny you giving her the gun, because both Millie and I had thought she might have tried to do something to herself; that she was right down on the ground——depressed to hell; and that you'd made up your mind not to let her have it. I said that we'd spoken about it between ourselves and Millie had said that she reckoned you knew what you were doing; that you were nobody's fool."

"That was nice of Millie," I said.

"Then he told us," said Joe. "He told us that while you were away you'd taken the slugs out of the cartridge cases, and then loaded the empty cases back into the gun and put the magazine clip back so she wouldn't know. He said he thought you'd been pretty smart to do that. I told him that I wasn't surprised; that I thought you were pretty smart anyway. Then he had a drink and said that he thought we'd been very nice to Esmeralda and that was that. He asked how business was and I said O.K.; that the bottle party business was all right if you could get the liquor supplies. He said he thought it was a nice business; that if he wasn't a dick he'd like to run a bottle party. So I told him that if I wasn't running a bottle party I'd like to be a dick. And then we both laughed. He was a nice guy."

I said: "Esmeralda's dead. She had a heart or something."

"I'm sorry," said Joe. "She was a nice little thing. A bit thin though. It's funny how some of those thin types go for dope. I suppose they get sort of bored."

I said maybe. I had another drink. Then I asked Joe for a telephone call; went to his office; rang through to the hotel at Torquay and booked a room. I said I'd be along some time next morning. Then I went back to Joe, said so long and faded.

I drove the Rover round to Mack's place and asked him to give it a wash, fill the tank and check the oil. I said I'd be back. Then I walked round to Griselda's place. I had one with her at the bar and then went into the dance room and watched the baby with the figure do her stuff. She did two numbers: Whatever you do—Don't and Don't Fence Me In. I saw the plump uncle who'd been giving her the high-sign the last time I was there, sitting at a ringside table. He was looking soulful and poetic.

After the second number the customers gave her a big hand. And why not? She was wearing a skin-tight midnight blue satin frock with jewelled epaulettes. The frock was slit to just above the knee, and every time she moved the plump uncle brightened up just as if somebody had stuck a four-inch nail into him.

They made her come back and she crooned a thing called 'I'm Hoping That You're Hoping.' This time she was giving the plump uncle the eye all the time, and when she was through he looked as if he was hoping so much that he might go up in flames at any moment.

Soon after that Winterton of World-Wide Investigations came in. He came over to my table and tried to pump me about Pell. They'd been doing some business with Pell and he wanted to get the Ricaud story out of me. I said I didn't know anything much.

At half-past twelve I said so long to Griselda and went back to Mack's place. The car was ready and I paid him and drove off. It was a fine night and I felt rested and refreshed. I thought life could be a lot worse.

I took my time. I ambled through Chiswick and on to the Great West Road. I was thinking, and the speedometer didn't go much above thirty.

I stopped at the roundabout at the intersection—the place where I'd stopped on Monday night. I pulled in to the side of the road and lighted a cigarette. I sat in the car, relaxed, and did a little thinking. I thought a hell of a lot could happen to a lot of people in a week.

My mind switched to Mrs. Ivory. I thought that when she arrived at the Malinson to do her thank-you act she'd be surprised to find that I wasn't there; that they didn't know where I'd gone. Maybe she'd think that I'd taken a run-out powder on her.

If she concluded that she'd be right. I had.

I let in the gear. I took the left fork to Staines. This time I was going to Devonshire—and I didn't mean maybe.

CHAPTER SEVEN

SUNDAY — FAREWELL TO IVORY

AT nine o'clock I passed the Chateau Bellevue on the Newton Abbot-Totnes road. It was a wonderful September morning, and even at that hour the road and fields were sparkling in the sun. Over the hedges I could see the steeple of Totnes church, and the houses and narrow streets clustering round it.

People had told me about Devonshire—about the beauty of its countryside, its red earth, its own particular sleepy air, its atmosphere of quiet charm. I realised that they hadn't exaggerated. I liked it. I knew it was going to be a favourite place for me. Already, London with its bustle, its busy streets and never ceasing noises, seemed even in this short space a memory that was almost distant.

I had been over seven hours on the road, but I wasn't tired. Even the Ricaud case was beginning to fade into the background of my mind. I liked that too . . .

I had breakfast at the Seven Stars Hotel in Totnes. Then I filled up with petrol at the nearby garage and drove slowly towards the coast. I went through Paignton, driving along the front on to the Torquay road. Occasionally, I stopped and took a look at the sea.

I stopped the car half-way down the long sea-front at Torquay. I got out, stretched and looked about me. Then I sat down on a seat and looked at my watch. It was a quarter past ten. For no reason at all I began to think about the people in the Ricaud case; to wonder what they'd been thinking of at this time last Sunday.

Ricaud. Ricaud had been very busy in his mind at this time last week. He'd been thinking about the lady who was waiting for him at Nassau in the Bahamas——the lady who was "restless "—the lady who was to be his next victim, who—whether she was aware of it or not—might be considered lucky to have avoided by a small margin the trouble he would have brought to her.

At this time last week Ricaud would have been considering just how he was going to raise money; was planning to write to Esmeralda to tell her the news of his proposed departure; to tell her to come and see him for their final interview. That note was to be written on the following Tuesday. It was to be his death warrant.

And Pell. Pell had been worrying about what Ricaud was going to do——afraid to move and afraid not to move; waiting for something to happen; not knowing that what was to happen the next day would give him only five more days of life.

Mrs. Ivory. This day a week ago Mrs. Ivory was worrying about Esmeralda; was fearful that Esmeralda, tried beyond endurance, would carry out her oft-repeated threat to kill Ricaud. Mrs. Ivory had made up her mind to see Pell next day; to ask Pell to scare Ricaud off before more trouble began.

Esmeralda. Esmeralda had probably awakened in her flat in Montacute Place with a hangover, an aching head and a soul full of misery. She had probably done some thinking—if she could think; and concluded that, given the chance, she would put an end to Ricaud if she felt brave enough; if she had something to do it with. She didn't know then that she'd feel nearly brave enough on the Monday night; that she'd have the weapon to do it with. Or that her unforeseen meeting with me would lead her to Joe Melander's flat, to the nursing home, back to Ricaud and her final scene at "Crossways."

And I? I smiled at the recollection. Last Sunday I'd been thinking that on the next day—Monday—I was to give evidence in the divorce case——the case that Pell had used as an excuse to put Mrs. Ivory on to me. I didn't like the idea of giving evidence. I knew that the other side were out to take me to pieces in the witness box. I had gone for a walk in the morning and slept in the afternoon. I had thought that if everything went well and our side won the case, I'd take my thousand pounds and go down to Devonshire.

Well... here I was... a week late maybe, and a hell of a lot had happened in the week.

I looked at the sunlit sea and the scene around me.

The railway folder hadn't told any lies. It was all there. From where the big hotel stood on the hill away on the left towards Babbacombe, the whole sweep of the bay was bathed in sunlight. The sea was blue and everything was quiet, except for the noise of the waves breaking and the seagulls. I looked along the front. Not

Peter Cheyney

far away I could see my hotel. It faced towards me and I could make out the garden with its low wall stretching towards the sea-front. That looked right too. For once the original of a picture I had seen and liked was the same as the picture.

I got back into the car; drove to the hotel. I parked the car in the drive and entered. After I'd gone up to my room I had a meeting with myself as to whether I should go to bed or not. I came to the conclusion that the day was too good. Besides, I was going to have a lot of time for sleep.

I took a bath: shaved; changed my clothes. I went downstairs.

I was walking across the lounge when a blonde waitress who was passing through said to me: "I've put the coffee in the garden, Mr. O'Hara."

I hadn't ordered any coffee but it was O.K. by me. I walked across the lounge, through a writing-room and through the french windows on the other side.

I stood on the top of the steps, and I suppose it was the biggest surprise I'd ever had in my life—and I'd had one or two.

Before me stretched the garden, and on the left, in the corner formed by the walls meeting, was an arbour. Sitting in front of it in a deck-chair, with a table beside her with a coffee service on it, was Mrs. Ivory.

Another picture! She was dressed in a mimosa colour frock and short coat. There were touches of lime green on the frock and the coat. Her shoes were of lime green.

She wore no hat. She was looking at me and she was smiling.

I took a pull at myself and walked over. I said casually: "Good-morning, Mrs. Ivory. It's nice to see you."

She said: "I'm glad you like seeing me. Would you also like to fetch that deck-chair? I've ordered coffee for you." She went on: "I saw you stop your car on the front, so I had time to prepare for your arrival." She smiled at me again.

I fetched the chair. I set it up; sat down. I watched her pour the coffee.

She asked softly: "Did you think you were going to get rid of me as easily as that?"

I said: "How did you know I was here?"

"It wasn't difficult," she answered. "I went to the Malinson Hotel. I'd asked Dr. Quinceley to tell you I was coming. I knew he would have done that, so I imagined "——she looked at me mischievously—"you'd run away. The reception said that they had no address; that they weren't forwarding any letters. But I thought, life having been what it has been to you during the last week, that probably the hall-porter would know more about you than anyone else. He did."

I smiled at her. "The folder... the railway folder!"

"You'd shown him a picture of this hotel. You said you'd always wanted to come here. So instead of staying in London, I telephoned through here, found that they could put me up and was driven down. I got here at nine o'clock this morning."

I didn't say anything. She handed me the coffee cup.

Then I said: "It must have been important."

She nodded. "It was—at least to me. You see, there was more to it than my merely thanking you, which perhaps you didn't want. However, I'm going to say thank you; to tell you how much I admire your courage and integrity. I had to do that."

"That's nice of you," I said. "But it's been a lot of fun—except for Esmeralda. I'm sorry about that."

Her voice changed. She said sadly: "So am I. But Dr. Quinceley said—and all things considered I'm inclined to agree with him—that perhaps it's for the best. Her father and mother asked me to say thank you to you for them."

There was a silence. I wondered what was coming next. Most of my life I've tried to prepare myself for situations that I thought might arise. But I wasn't prepared for this one.

She said: "I hope you didn't mind my coming down here. But you see, I wanted to talk to you. I wanted to talk to you about something I considered very important."

"Such as...?" I queried.

She looked at me sideways. "It's another case. I wonder whether you'd be interested——after you've had your rest—to handle it. It's very important and I think urgent. It will want skilful handling."

I said: "So I have to be skilful this time." I grinned at her.

"I don't know," she said. "Perhaps I shall have to be. My explanation of the business must be more clear than the one I gave you the last time when I asked you to handle a case."

I said: "Well, tell me about it. You think it's interesting?"

She said: "It should be very interesting. It concerns a woman named Leonora Ivory and a man, a rather odd man—a grand person—called Caryl O'Hara. I don't want to go into all the details now, but I think that during the week you and I might discuss the implications of this case to see just how it could be most successfully handled; just how it might be brought to what you would call a logical, and I a happy, conclusion. Do you think we might do that. Do you think you'd be interested?"

I thought: What the hell! I was licked and I knew it. I'd used up my last bit of moral courage to run away from her—not because I was scared of her, but because I was scared of myself. And I wasn't deluding myself about it. This was the one marvellously impossible thing to have happened at the end of this almost impossible week.

I said: "You win." I smiled at her. "I tried to duck seeing you. I was scared of your money, and it seemed to me that the easiest thing to do was to take a run-out and call it a day. But what's the use? You're a very determined woman. This time . . ."

"Yes?" she said. "I think you ought to know that I am very determined as far as you're concerned."

She reached for my cup and refilled it. She said, just as if there had never been a Ricaud or a Pell or anything

                                    Peter Cheyney

else: "I think this is going to be a rather delightful holiday, do you?"

I didn't answer the question. It didn't need an answer so far as I was concerned.

Then I said: "Life can be funny. Last Monday I was thinking about this place, wondering if the real thing would be like the picture. I thought that if it was—the sea, the sunshine, the hotel, everything—it would be very good. But I thought how wonderful it would be to have all those things and to be sitting here in this garden talking to you."

She gave me the coffee cup. She said softly: "Well... I'm here. Aren't you happy? Is something missing?"

I nodded. "Just one thing." I smiled at her. "In the picture you could just see the bandstand. You could see the conductor with his baton raised. The band was playing."

She laughed; then she looked at her wrist-watch. That made me look at mine. It was a few seconds short of eleven o'clock.

Somewhere in the vicinity a church bell began to chime.

And—goddam it—the band began to play!

THE END

A story from

Yesteryear's stories reflected today
Yabot AB
www.yabot.se

Dressed to Kill

Dressed to Kill is Peter Cheyney's best selling story of murder in London's West End
Available in print, as e-book and audiobook from Yabot